THE PALLBEARER

CHRISTA LOUGHLIN

One Printers Way
Altona, MB R0G 0B0
Canada

www.friesenpress.com

First Edition — 2022

This is a work of fiction. Names, characters, and incidents either are products of the author's imagination or are used fictitiously. Any resemblance to actual events or persons, living or dead, is entirely coincidental.

ISBN
978-1-03-912967-2 (Hardcover)
978-1-03-912966-5 (Paperback)
978-1-03-912968-9 (eBook)

1. FICTION, MYSTERY & DETECTIVE, POLICE PROCEDURAL

Distributed to the trade by The Ingram Book Company

THE PALLBEARER

For Aunt Jayne,
Who always believed
"I could..."
Even when I didn't believe it myself.

—And for Amanda's treasured gift of a gentle push—

Chapter One

NOTHING.

Her memory was blank.

How did I get here?

The dirt beneath her was so damp that Kelly's bones ached. She shivered, her knees clenched tightly to her chest as she rocked back and forth in the cold darkness. She had been here, it seemed, for days.

She moaned soundlessly—all that was left in her after endless hours of crying. The blackness was total. Maybe someone was in here with her. Maybe not. A memory flashed into her mind, but only for a split second. She had the faint recollection of a man asking for directions as she left work. But even that memory seemed fleeting, as if it had happened years ago. She couldn't remember anything after that.

Her mouth was completely parched, with cracked lips swollen and bleeding. She attempted swallowing to moisten her throat. Unsuccessful in her attempts, all she tasted was the grits of sand that had migrated into her mouth during her frantic screams in the darkness. Hoping to remove the sand, she used the torn sleeve of her shirt to wipe desperately at her tongue, but only succeeded in introducing more dirt into her already dehydrated mouth. She turned her head and tried to spit out the dirt, but her efforts were pointless. What little saliva she had left just irritated the stinging cuts she had amassed on her chapped lips, causing her to gasp in pain and press her head against the cold wall. Another pain, this one at the back of her head, sent a wave of faintness through her whole body. Her hands shaking, she felt for the cause. Her fingers discovered an opening where the blood was crusting over a substantial gash. She felt the stickiness of the tacky blood as she slowly rubbed it between her fingers and thumb. Instinctively, Kelly's hand moved back to her wound. She applied pressure, hoping to soothe the pain, but it didn't ease the pounding in her head.

As hard as Kelly tried, she couldn't remember anything that had happened to her. All she knew was that she wanted to go home.

Now.

Everything was black. Kelly, fighting the fear and nausea that threatened to consume her, squinted into the dark trying desperately to see. But as hard as she tried, there was nothing.

Not a glimmer of light coming from anywhere.

No windows. No cracks. Nothing. Only the dampness of the floor beneath her feet and bum as she sat curled in the dark corner, rocking back and forth, knees snug to her chest.

And then she felt it.

Kelly froze. *Am I hallucinating?* Was her mind just playing cruel tricks on her because she was blinded by the dark? Kelly felt something crawling across the top of her left foot. At first, she just felt one.

A spider?

Then she felt more. Lots more. She swiped blindly at her feet. First the left one, then the right. Then swatting frantically at both, her hands moved up her legs, then up each arm and back to her feet again. Now they were in her hair. There were hundreds of them, it seemed.

Or were there?

Desperately, she clawed at her itchy scalp, scratching so hard she nearly drew blood. Was it the solitary darkness and her imagination conjuring up her worst fears? *Is something really crawling all over me?* She took a deep breath, and then another, hoping the sensation would go away. Perhaps it was the uncertain darkness escalating these horrifying thoughts. Either way, her mind was reeling from the thought of being covered by hundreds, maybe thousands of bugs while alone in the dark with nobody to hear her screams. Her whole body felt itchy. She flailed about, hoping to shake them off. Screams and cries of pure terror escaped her raspy throat.

"Dear God, please help me! Somebody! Anybody! Help me! I just want to go home!"

The desperation was overwhelming, and she couldn't formulate a single thought. She peered into the darkness trying once again to see something.

Anything.

Even a hint of light. That's all she needed. Just enough to see her surroundings. She needed to know what was in there with her. *Was it filled with spiders, ants, cockroaches, or any other bugs I conjured up in my frantic mind; or am I all alone?* She had to know. She had to put her mind to rest once and for all.

Even if only for a moment.

The unexpected noise of a door scraping across the dirt floor immediately anchored Kelly in place. The ants and the spiders vanished.

She didn't move.

She didn't even breathe.

She just listened and waited. Aware only of the sound of her pounding heartbeat, she knew that somebody was out there.

And they were coming in.

Chapter Two

HANNAH AWOKE TO GREET an early morning sun creeping warily in through cracks in the blinds. *It can't be morning already,* she thought to herself. It felt as if she had just closed heavy eyes. Shifting slightly in bed, she curled both knees tightly up against her chest. This was too comfortable. She didn't want to move. Rolling onto her back, she stretched out and turned off her radio alarm before she was awakened by the cheerful voices of Craig and Lucky, her favourite 94.9 morning radio show duo.

Well, another restless and completely disappointing night over with, she thought. She had not had a truly good night's sleep since Kent left. Not because she missed him, but because he'd turned her life into a heap of undeserved chaos that she was still trying to sort out.

Kent Phillips. His name was the first reason she dreaded facing the emerging day. The second was a long overdue meeting with a way overpriced lawyer happening at two o'clock that she was incredibly anxious about. She just hoped Kent had finally decided to give in and sign the damn divorce papers. She couldn't believe the bastard's nerve. He was the one who had ended things without warning, not her. Now he was dragging this whole process out, probably just to piss her off. His reasons for their rapid, unforeseen breakup were nothing short of a joke.

"It's not you," he had promised her. "It's me. I just need a break for a while. With this new promotion at work, I have all these extra pressures. I'm working twenty-four seven and it's just not fair to you," *blah, blah, blah.*

Bullshit, she told herself. *What a crock of shit.*

In his own delusional mind, Kent seemed to have actually convinced himself that Hannah was a complete moron—blind to what was really happening. He had no inkling of the reality of the situation, but the truth was she did know. She knew all about his twenty-three-year-old co-worker. The infantile brunette at the office who said all the right things, did all the right things, and was just young enough that everything still pointed up. Hannah knew that he'd been screwing the homewrecking little tart for almost a year behind her back, had her set up in their own little love nest on the other side of town, and that he'd been showering her with the love and affection that was supposed to be meant for Hannah. He had promised Hannah in front of all their friends and family that he would love her, and only her, until the day he died.

"Bullshit," she murmured.

Hannah lay there recalling the numerous occasions she had listened to other women tell stories similar to hers. She had always been sympathetic to them, but in the back of her mind she felt nothing but security. She would think, *God, I'm the luckiest woman in the world. Kent would never do that to me. He loves me unconditionally. He would never even consider looking at another woman in a sexual way, let alone be unfaithful to me.*

He promised.

He promised.

Hannah laughed aloud this time. "Bullshit," she scoffed, pulling her down-filled pillow tightly over her face.

The obnoxiously loud ring of the telephone interrupted Hannah's morbid visual replay of Kent's betrayal.

"It's five o'clock in the morning," she moaned, as her hand blindly searched the cluttered bedside table for the phone. "For the love of God, who would be calling me at this hour on my day off?"

Propping herself up on one elbow, she tossed the pillow to the floor and spoke abruptly into the receiver. "This had better be good."

"Hey, it's me."

The deep, raspy voice on the other end of the line was that of Detective Richard Young, her colleague at the police department. Four years ago, their divisions had teamed up to work a missing persons case and they had gotten to know each other pretty well. Now, not only was he working with her out of Central East Division in Oshawa, he was also her partner of eighteen months. That meant that he knew her well enough to only call at this ungodly hour if absolutely necessary.

Hannah's stomach knotted immediately. She knew. Before he could speak the words aloud, Hannah whispered numbly into the phone. "They've found her, haven't they?"

Chapter Three

HANNAH ARRIVED TWENTY MINUTES later at the busy downtown Oshawa police station. At times, it felt like her second home. Weaving her way through the mixture of uniformed and plain-clothed officers on her way to meet Richard, she realized that for the first time in ages, the traffic on both highway 401 and Simcoe Street South had finally been in her favour. More often than not, the traffic was routinely heavy during her commute and it took a solid thirty minutes to make it from her urban Charles Street Landing condo in Whitby to the police station only ten kilometres away. This pleasant surprise allowed her the time to make a quick stop at the Tim Hortons drive thru to help jumpstart her early and unexpected launch into the day with a well-deserved coffee.

Before rushing out, she had quickly pulled her shoulder length, chestnut hair back into a tidy ponytail, a style she wore only when called out on such short notice. Her quick departure from home also meant faded blue jeans and a sage green hoodie from Old Navy.

As she approached Conference Room B, her left hand had a firm hold on her coffee, while her right hand held her car keys and a black weathered handbag. Nodding at the other officers as she entered, Hannah tossed her keys into her bag and dropped it on the ground beside one of the empty chairs.

She looked up and asked, "Okay gentlemen, what have we got?"

Detective Richard Young was the first to speak, rising from his chair and pacing the floor as the briefing began. "Here's what we know so far. A university student by the name of Mark Goslin found Carley Wilson, our missing girl, at around four a.m. on Simcoe Street North, right near the train tracks. She came out of nowhere and staggered right out in front of his car. He barely missed hitting her. He called 911 from his cell phone right away, but Hannah, he's pretty shaken up about the whole thing. Detective Connors is with him now taking his statement."

As she listened, Hannah studied the walls of the small conference room where any information gathered was displayed. This included everything they had collected during the on-going investigation of the missing teen, Carley Wilson, as well as the two other young women who were found dead, suspected to be at the hands of the same killer. As she scanned the sparse display, she frowned and shook her head. Familiar with her frustration, the other officers involved in the task force awkwardly avoided watching her exploration of the room. Hannah was facing one of the biggest challenges of her career. She had committed to helping others and to saving lives. No matter how hard she and the other officers had been working this case, they seemed to be spinning their wheels and it was tearing Hannah up inside.

Hannah had established her strong reputation as a skillful investigator and effective leader very early on in her career, landing her a promotion to Detective Sergeant by the age of thirty-seven. She recognized the fact that, along with those skills, she possessed something that many officers were often lacking—an experienced combination of intuition as well as empathy for the victims and their families. These qualities were undoubtedly a large part of her high success rate with the majority of cases she led.

On the North wall of the room, three photographs of young women were displayed systematically on a large bulletin board. Those women were Ana Stonehouse, Jessica Wright, and Carley Wilson. Descriptions and character breakdowns on each of these victims were posted beside each photo respectively. In bold black letters, the word DECEASED was written beneath the first two pictures. Thankfully, now the word MISSING could be removed from below Carley's. Hanging isolated on the West wall was a large map of Durham Region. This grouping of townships was significant in size with a combined total of 2,523 square kilometres. The focus thus far had been more central, including a twenty-kilometre perimeter around Oshawa, Raglan, and Port Perry where victims had been located. The map was dotted with a variety of coloured thumbtacks that indicated every detail they had accumulated—including the precise locations where these three victims had been found, right down to potential routes the killer may have taken to and from each dump site.

The Southwest corner of the room held a large whiteboard listing working theories assembled by the task force. Six officers, comprised of detectives and constables, were working day and night on this case, which had been completely devoid of even one useful lead until now. After ten weeks, they still didn't have any idea who was behind these abductions and murders, and it was pissing them off to no end.

Hannah moved back to the centre of the room and leaned over the large conference table. After taking a long, deep breath, she lifted her head and acknowledged Richard with an appreciative nod. "Well, thank God she's alive. Hopefully this will give us something to go on, and maybe she'll be able to shed some light."

Along with everyone else in the room, Hannah had been expecting a more devastating outcome. Although nobody wanted to admit it, the feared consensus among the officers was that nineteen-year-old Carley Wilson would be found dead like the other two women who had fallen prey to and been brutalized by the province's most recent psychopath.

"How is she? Is she able to give us a statement?" Hannah directed her question to Richard.

"Not yet," he replied. "They transported her directly to Sunnybrook Hospital in Toronto. She's in the ICU and the doctors said it will be a while before we can talk to her. She made it through surgery, which was touch and go, but it'll still be a while before she's stable enough to talk to us."

Nodding, Hannah countered, "Keep me posted, okay?"

Richard responded with a solemn nod.

Still leaning over the table, she sighed and stared down at her hands. "Let's get a security detail over to her hospital room right away. Will someone over there let us know when she's able to talk to us?"

"They'll keep us posted on her condition. This animal really did a number on her, but she seems like a real fighter. Fingers crossed she'll pull through and be able to help us." Richard responded, not taking his eyes off Hannah.

Hannah was pissed off. "Poor thing. What the hell could anyone ever do to deserve what this maniac did to her?"

Lifting her head, her emerald eyes now located the dusty fan that hung from the paint-chipped ceiling. Staring aimlessly at it, all she could think was, *this world has gone completely mad.*

Chapter Four

Charlie Gibson was the court-appointed lawyer defending Matt Davidson. The stodgy counsellor, a slight man in his late fifties had greasy salt-and-pepper hair lightly dusted with dandruff. He had a grey tint to his face and an overall weathered complexion. After looking at him, some would say he'd had a hard life. Bobby Ross didn't agree. He summed it all up to a continuous path of poor choices, which included decades of excessive booze, Craven A's, and repeatedly placing bets on the wrong horse. Couple that with a high stress job and that left the lawyer with not much more than a depleted bank account, a collection of bad suits, and a worn-out liver. As Gibson randomly shuffled the mess of papers on the desk at the front of the courtroom, he looked up to see the bail court officer lead a handcuffed Matt Davidson into the courtroom and seat him in the empty prisoner's box to his right.

The court clerk then announced in a loud voice, "All rise."

Chairs scraped loudly across the hardwood floor as the Crown Attorney, Gibson, and defendant rose simultaneously. They all watched intently as the Justice of the Peace entered the courtroom and took his seat. Silence followed until the clerk firmly ordered, "Be seated."

Matt was fidgeting, noticeably uncomfortable in his own skin. This was his third court appearance and bail hearing in as many years. *You'd think he'd be all too familiar with his surroundings by now*, Bobby thought as he watched Matt's nervous behaviour. You could tell that Matt was still quite unaccustomed to the courtroom. Bobby jotted down a few quick notes in the small book he always carried with him. He had been following Matt Davidson since his first arrest three years ago. Matt had been charged with possession with the purpose of trafficking, an unproven charge that ended up being dropped. Some people believed that "Daddy" had something to do with that, although nobody could prove it. Bobby sniffed a story there and strongly suspected that at some point in time, Matt's bad boy persona and his misfortune of being in the wrong place at the wrong time would come back to bite him. And it did—two more times—and Bobby wanted to get to the bottom of it.

Bobby Ross was an investigative reporter with one of Toronto's largest newspapers, the Toronto Star. He never intended to make his living telling other people's stories, however he'd been unsuccessful in having his own personal work published. Someday he hoped to get the recognition he deserved. Until that day arrived, he made his living digging deep and finding answers where other people had failed. It wasn't his original dream, but he was good at it.

At twenty-nine, Bobby was tall, remarkably charismatic, and single. He was often told by his friends that, with his sophistication and handsome appearance, he was an ideal catch who could attract the eyes of many appreciative women.

Most of Bobby's friends wondered why he was still single. Everyone thought he had it all. But Bobby was still searching for that perfect partner. He had come close to settling down once before, but something had been missing. He realized he wanted more. He wanted a woman who would challenge him to be the best he could be every day. Someone who would love him for who he was and who he still aspired to become. Someone he could share every aspect of his life with. He wanted a friend, a partner, a lover, a confidant. He refused to settle for anything less. Everything had to be authentic and complete for Bobby to finally take that illustrious walk down the aisle, the walk he had not committed to up to this point.

After listening to the Crown explain all the reasons that his client should not be granted bail, Charlie Gibson rose from his chair and began stating his case to the Justice of the Peace, or the JP to those frequent to the courtroom.

"Your Worship," he started. "Given the fact that my client has never had any previous convictions and is not considered to be a flight risk, we request that he be released on bail and his father, who couldn't be here today, pose as a suitable surety to post a bond in the amount of ten thousand dollars, no deposit. Given the uniqueness of my client's situation, I don't think that a jail stay would be the right course of action."

The JP didn't raise his head as he peered over the top of his bifocals. In an annoyed tone, he questioned the lawyer's request. "And what unique situation might you be referring to, Mr. Gibson?"

Charlie looked down at his papers seeming very uncomfortable with the JP's rhetorical question as His Worship carried on.

"I certainly hope you're not suggesting that I show him leniency based on the fact that his father is a well-known public figure. This is your client's third arrest on the same charges. Possession with the purpose of trafficking is a serious offence, Mr. Gibson."

"Your Worship, I appreciate the fact that my client has a history with the courts. However, I must emphasize to the court that he was never convicted. I also want to bring forth the fact that there is an on-going investigation into allegations that my client is being set—"

Charlie's sentence was cut short as Matt's chair flew back and he scrambled to his feet from the prisoner's box to lunge the ten-foot distance towards the stunned lawyer's table. The papers that once rested neatly in front of him were now falling to the floor in the confusion. Matt's handcuffed fists loudly hammered the table while Charlie's chair toppled backwards. Even the large bail court officer had trouble reaching Matt in time to prevent the unexpected outburst. The courtroom was suddenly alive with chaos and loud gasps from startled onlookers.

"You bastards," Matt bellowed. He sounded like a lunatic as he continued, "I'm not going down for this! Somebody is trying to set me up! This is the third time—don't you people get it? Don't you see what they're trying to do to me? Why doesn't anyone believe me?"

"Order!" The JP commanded, three rapid strikes from his gavel being totally ignored by everyone. "I said order!" he hollered.

As the third strike of the gavel sounded, stunned observers of the courtroom watched in awe as the six-foot four-inch bail court officer tackled Matt in a seemingly effortless display of athleticism. In ten seconds flat, Matt was on his stomach with his hands still cuffed and a small laceration over his left eye. As the bail court officer and another courtroom officer succeeded in lifting him to his feet, they efficiently removed his handcuffs, pulled both arms behind his back and re-cuffed him securely. After replacing him in his seat in the prisoner's box, both officers took position on each side of Matt as a precaution until the courtroom settled down.

The JP, his patience now dwindling, got back to the matter at hand. "After witnessing this excessive outburst, bail is now set at fifteen thousand dollars. Now please remove Mr. Davidson from the courtroom at once before I find him in contempt. Take him back to his cell until he posts bail. And Mr. Gibson, you'd better get control over your client. I will not tolerate another outburst like that in my courtroom. Do you understand me, Counsellor?" The JP asked sternly, not breaking eye contact with the agitated lawyer.

Charlie Gibson, still in a state of disarray, replied, "Yes, Your Worship. I'll handle this."

The JP continued with, "The First Appearance date will be set for five weeks from today, on November thirteenth at nine a.m." Fed up and annoyed, he sarcastically added, "Maybe by that time your client will have figured out if he'll be entering a plea of guilty or not guilty." With one last frustrated pound of the gavel, the JP immediately rose from his chair, descended the three steps, and returned to the normalcy of his chambers.

Bobby glanced around the courtroom at all the stunned faces. The room was alive with whispers amongst all that had just witnessed this crazy turn of events. Those who had been following the high-profile case could understand why Matt Davidson had been arrested again, but what they couldn't comprehend was his unlikely outburst in the middle of the courtroom. Once they got to the bottom of things, this was going to make for a great story.

And Bobby Ross was just the man to make it happen.

Chapter Five

"I still can't believe this happened," Mark said wearily, holding his head.

Mark Goslin, a twenty-one-year-old engineering student at the University of Toronto, was driving home to Port Perry for the weekend when a mysterious, bloodied girl suddenly stumbled out in front of his car and collapsed to the pavement. "God, this is so surreal—so much to process. I hope she's going to be okay. She's the girl that's been all over the news, right? The one that went missing—the one that everyone's been out looking for?" Mark was shifting in his seat, visibly shaken. His brown eyes darted nervously around the room, not quite sure what to focus on as his hands caressed one another.

As an honour student at U of T, he spent most of his time in class, completing assignments, or studying for exams. It was apparent that he was completely unfamiliar with this type of situation and seemed uneasy being any part of this scenario. He was just a small-town guy with high hopes and dreams for his future, completely blindsided by this unexpected turn of events.

"Yes," Connors replied. "Her name is Carley Wilson and she'd been missing for five days."

Detective Constable Jake Connors was an eight-year veteran with the department. He was married once, to another officer, but it was very short lived. Not only were they young at the time, but trying to maintain a marriage when promotions are involved only creates animosity. It doesn't make for a great romantic relationship. Since his divorce three years ago, the tall, blonde, self-assured detective had dated a handful of women, but last year had finally settled down with Kate. She was the attractive ER nurse who had tended to him when he was inadvertently stabbed while trying to apprehend a suspect during a home invasion robbery. From that point on, Kate had tended to more than his injuries.

Jake started with the Durham Regional Police Service as a cadet at the age of eighteen, but it wasn't long before he started making a name for himself—a real go-getter. When a call came across the radio, he was usually the first to respond. When things were quiet during his shift, he went searching for things to do. Tickets to write, bad guys to catch, and he certainly wasn't scared of a hard day's work. His drive, ambition, and initiative finally awarded him the recognition he deserved, and quickly. At the age of twenty-six, he was the youngest detective constable in the department. Not only did he now outrank most of the officers from his graduating class at the Ontario Police College in Aylmer, he had also earned the respect of his fellow colleagues and his superior officers, something which he held in the highest regards.

"Now, Mark, I just need to inform you that we will be videotaping this interview. Are you okay with that?" Detective Connors asked.

Mark, looking around the room at Jake and then up towards the video camera mounted high on the wall in the corner of the room, responded with, "Sure. That's fine."

"Okay, I want you to start from the beginning, Mark. Where were you coming from and where were you headed to?"

"I left campus around two-thirty in the morning and was heading home for the weekend. I was finishing up a paper I was writing and didn't want to lose my train of thought, so I worked late until it was finished. I figured I'd miss most of the traffic if I just left then instead of waiting until morning." With that said, he gave a confident nod.

"Okay," Jake continued. "Where's home, Mark?"

"It's actually my parents' home—30 Deacon Lane in Port Perry."

Jake nodded, taking notes while Mark was speaking. "I know where that is. Go on; what happened next?"

"Well, it was nothing out of the ordinary. Just the usual drive. Since it was the middle of the night, there was barely any traffic. I was just driving along listening to my music and thinking about the assignment I'd just finished." Mark replayed his uneventful journey towards his parents' house.

"You headed straight home? You didn't stop anywhere, take any detours, or call anyone on your cell phone? Nothing like that?" Jake asked, trying to cover every little detail.

"Nope. It was just a regular drive home, nothing unusual at all. Well, until that girl ran out in front of me."

"Carley Wilson?" Connors remarked.

"Yeah. Well, I didn't know who she was at the time. I only realized that when I got here and heard everyone talking about her."

"Where exactly were you when Carley ran out in front of your car?"

"I was headed North on Simcoe Street past Raglan. I was past the train tracks and about halfway up the big hill at the Ridges, but not as far as Coates Road."

"What happened then; what did you do next?" Connors asked.

"I slammed on my brakes and veered to the shoulder. I didn't know what to do so I grabbed my cell phone, got out of the car, and ran over to her. By the time I reached her, she'd collapsed. I thought maybe she was dead, but either way, I knew I had to call 911. As soon as the dispatcher answered I gave him my name, told him where I was, and begged him to send an ambulance right away." With pursed lips, Mark blew out a long breath from deep within his lungs, as if to cleanse away the horrific memory.

"And then what happened?"

"I told him there was a girl who might be dead or dying in the middle of the road and that I needed help right away. He told me to stay calm and reassured me that the police and an ambulance were on the way."

"Did the girl say anything?" Connors pressed on, trying to trigger anything in Mark's memory.

"No. The dispatcher asked if she had a pulse and I told him I didn't know. He told me to put my fingers on the side of her neck to see if I could feel anything. I tried, but there was just so much blood..."

"It's okay, Mark. Take your time." Jake gave Mark a reassuring pat on the back as he moved around the table.

"He told me to put my fingers on her wrist instead. When I did, I thought I could feel something. A faint pulse maybe, but I couldn't be sure. How should I know? I've never even taken a CPR class!"

Mark, now tightly clenching his fists, was getting upset and seemed repulsed. Obviously, reliving this nightmare was taking more of a toll on him than he had anticipated. Realizing that Mark needed a few moments to compose himself, Connors asked, "Hey, Mark, how about a cup of coffee? Sound good?"

This guy needed a few minutes to cool down. He was getting pretty worked up and Jake wanted to make sure he got his entire statement in case he broke down for good. Not only was he feeling overwhelmed being forced to relive this traumatic experience, he was also exhausted.

"Got anything stronger—whiskey perhaps?" Mark attempted an awkward smile, trying to compose himself.

Jake just smiled as he left the room. "I'll be back in a second." He wanted to give Mark some much-needed time to regroup and collect his thoughts. It wasn't his fault that he was in this position. It just so happened to be *his* car that Carley Wilson stumbled in front of. No matter who it was that found Carley that morning, the situation would have taken a toll on anyone. Moving towards the break room to grab coffees, Connors turned the corner to see Hannah emerging from the conference room.

"Morning, Detective Sergeant Phillips." Connors grinned, anticipating her reaction.

"Not for much longer," Hannah bit back. "God, how I miss my maiden name."

Jake smiled. He admired Hannah's strength. After all the bullshit that her soon-to-be ex-husband put her through, she was still able to laugh. Three years ago, he and Hannah had been partners briefly. It didn't last long, but they'd still acquired a mutual respect for one another and had spent quite a few hours analyzing their failed marriages over drinks at Riley's Pub. They would hang out on occasion to blow off steam while trying to solve all of life's little problems. So far, they had failed miserably with that, but had some kick ass hangovers in the books as proof of their valiant attempts.

"Listen, Jake: are you still with the guy who found Carley Wilson?"

"Yeah, I'm just grabbing us coffees—Mark needed a break. Why?"

"Mind if I sit in with you?" she asked.

Jake nodded. "Sure. It wouldn't hurt to have another pair of ears."

Hannah grabbed herself a coffee and followed Jake, now armed with two coffees himself, back down the hall and into the interview room.

"Mark, this is Detective Sergeant..." He paused. Not wanting to slight Hannah twice within the matter of minutes with the reminder of her impending divorce, Jake rephrased his introduction. "Mark, this is my colleague, Hannah. She'll be sitting in while we finish taking your statement. Is that okay with you?"

Hannah gave an empathetic smile to Mark as she extended her hand, shook his firmly, and then sat quietly in the chair closest to the door.

"No, I don't mind at all." Mark said as he took a sip of his hot coffee.

"Okay," Jake proceeded. "When we left off, you were checking for Carley's pulse? What happened next?"

"Well," Mark continued, "the 911 dispatcher said he'd stay on the line with me until the cops and ambulance arrived. He was telling me to keep her warm, hold her hand, and keep talking to her. Stuff like that. There was just so much going on; I can't remember everything he said. It all happened so fast."

"I understand." Jake nodded. "How long were you trying to talk to Carley before the police and ambulance showed up?"

Mark continued. "It couldn't have been five minutes. They were pretty fast getting there." Mark sounded impressed with the EMS unit's response time.

"Anything else you can think of that you may have forgotten? Anything you can tell us would be helpful." Jake asked, hoping to trigger Mark's memory.

"No. That's about it. I just kept talking to her, trying to reassure her that help was on the way, but she never made a sound. She didn't even move. She was hurt pretty bad and there was so much blood everywhere. I saw that her stomach was pretty messed up, so the dispatcher told me to put my hand there and keep lots of pressure on it. So, I did. And that's when I heard the sirens coming." The corners of Mark's mouth were turned down in a look of disgust. "How could anyone do that to another person, Detective Connors?"

He looked questioningly at both Jake and Hannah, searching for some type of understanding. "I mean seriously, what kind of sick twisted bastard could do that to another human being?"

Hannah and Jake watched helplessly as Mark's face paled, looking nauseated. He put his head down on the table and took a couple of deep breaths.

"You did great, Mark." Connors said, admiring this guy's courage. "I think we have everything we need for now, but if you do think of anything else, no matter how silly it may seem, please call us right away. Here's my card." Jake pulled his business card from the inside pocket of his navy suit jacket and handed it to Mark. "Call me anytime, day or night. And if you can't reach me, you can also reach my colleague, Detective Sergeant Phillips." Jake acknowledged Hannah with a nod and turned his gaze back to Mark, "Don't be afraid to call us, okay?"

Hannah nodded in agreement.

"Okay, thank you officers." Mark stood to leave the room. After shaking Mark's hand, Jake and Hannah escorted him into the hallway and watched as he walked away.

Confirming with Jake, Hannah turned to him and asked, "The Forensic Identification Unit is still on scene, right?"

Jake nodded. "MacDonald and Fisher are there with their unit."

"Good. Richard and I are heading up there now. Are you okay to wrap things up here?" Hannah asked.

"Yeah, I'll finish up this report and I'll meet you there as soon as I can." Jake turned and headed back into the interview room to collect the statement he'd just taken from the university student who would now probably be labelled a hero.

As Hannah watched Mark Goslin slowly make his way down the faded yellow hall towards the front doors of the station, she couldn't help but think to herself that unfortunately, after what Mark had witnessed earlier this morning, he probably wouldn't be getting a good night's sleep tonight. Or tomorrow either.

Chapter Six

HANNAH AND RICHARD'S GREY Dodge Charger slowly approached the crime scene, lights flashing but no siren, at approximately eight-forty in the morning. Yellow crime scene tape encompassed the immediate 500 square foot vicinity where Carley Wilson lay unconscious and bleeding not six hours earlier. The rest of the 5 acres surrounding the crime scene was ordered blocked off by the first officer on the scene and uniformed patrol officers now secured the perimeter.

The Forensic Identification Unit had been at the scene since four-thirty in the morning, so the ground was now scattered with dozens of small yellow flags penetrating the soft grass. Investigators closer to where Carley had been found were donning white hooded jumpsuits, masks, blue plastic gloves, and their shoes were covered in disposable blue booties to prevent any contamination of the crime scene. As they moved slowly throughout the area, they were meticulously photographing and documenting everything they could. More forensic markers were selectively being positioned along the blood-stained asphalt as two of the investigators crouched down to take closer pictures using a small L-shaped ruler as a reference. Their precision as they placed the varied collected specimens into the small plastic evidence bags was exact and methodical, allowing for nothing to be overlooked. The grid search would be lengthy and tedious, but the investigators didn't want to miss one solitary piece of evidence that could potentially be used to track down this monster.

Uniformed constables were being dispatched to canvas the area and knock on every door interviewing any potential witnesses who may have seen or heard anything out of the ordinary within the last twelve hours. Officers were also able to determine if any house or property had video surveillance, including doorbells with video capabilities, to secure and examine more thoroughly back at the station.

As their unmarked cruiser rolled to a stop at the bottom of the large hill known to locals as "the Ridges," Hannah and Richard emerged from their car. Scanning the area quickly, Hannah was relieved to see that the press had not managed to sneak through the perimeter. *Good,* she thought to herself. *That's one blessing.* She knew that as soon as the press caught wind of this, the place would be crawling with camera crews and reporters, which would only hinder their investigation. The longer they could be kept at bay, the better the chances of collecting all their evidence uninterrupted. She had two patrol cars blocking the stretch of Simcoe Street from Raglan Road to Coates Road, but all it would take is a local news chopper flying overhead for the shit show to begin.

As the detectives made their way towards the scene, Hannah spotted someone coming towards her, waving his arm in the air. It was Dave Fisher with the FIU.

"Hannah." Fisher called her name as he moved towards her.

Dave Fisher was as good as they come. He had twenty-three years with the department—the last thirteen working with the FIU—and his record was impeccable. He was a heavy-set man in his early fifties with rose colored cheeks, probably due to high blood pressure and lots of well-earned stress over the years. He was an exceptional man and brilliant at his job. As he approached, Hannah smiled to herself recalling a funny memory from years ago. As Dave moved toward her, she noticed that the small, thin patch of hair that was usually neatly combed over his balding head from ear to ear was now sticking straight up from the cross breeze. She remembered an occasion on which her inspector had made reference to Dave's hair being "a landing strip for flies." She struggled to dismiss that visual from her mind, but as he reached them, his hair was still standing at attention.

"Hey, Dave. What have you got for us so far?" Hannah prompted, her eyes scanning the area. She observed the rest of the team now, still busy taking photographs of the entire scene while collecting and documenting items in small, plastic evidence bags.

"Well, I think this time we may have caught a break." He said with a hopeful sigh.

"Really?" she perked up. "Did you find something useful?"

"You see that fence line right there?" he said pointing to a semi-dilapidated barbed wire fence about eight feet from the ditch.

"I do" she said cautiously. "What about it?"

"You see," he continued, "we found a piece of material stuck to one of the barbs on it."

"And…?" she inquisitively pressed on.

"And, until the lab tells us otherwise, it's a match to the material that our victim was wearing when she was found."

He stopped and awaited Hannah's response.

"How is that useful to us, Dave, if we know she was wearing clothes made of that same material?" Hannah looked very confused and somewhat disappointed. What she thought might be useful to this investigation now turned out to sound very uninspiring.

"Aha," Dave smiled deviously. "I haven't finished."

Hannah squinted and gave him a look that implied, *would you just get to the point?*

Dave continued, "While we were removing that piece of material from the fence, MacDonald noticed something stuck to a splinter on the cedar fence post about twelve feet from there. 'What was it,' you ask?"

Hannah, looking quizzically at Dave, made a rolling hand motion that signaled him to keep the explanation moving and get to the good stuff.

"What we found, D.S. Phillips, was another, much smaller piece of material."

Hannah, looking intrigued, glanced at Richard.

"Now, we can't be sure until we get the results back from the lab," he went on, "but we don't think it's a match to the material that our victim's clothing was made of. She was dressed in denim and cotton. This piece looked to be more of a polyester."

Hannah just stared blankly at Dave. It was only a few seconds before she turned to look back at Richard, but what he saw was the corner of her mouth turned up into a tiny but noticeable smile. Richard knew that she wouldn't show too much enthusiasm until the report on the material was back from the lab. Hannah had learned early on in her career to never get her hopes up too soon. The disappointment was unbearable if they were wrong.

"Are you suggesting that this piece of material could be from our suspect?" She spoke the words slowly and concisely. It sounded so good in her head, her excitement and anticipation showing in her perfect enunciation of each word.

Hannah clapped her hands together emphatically. Finally, they had a possible lead in finding this animal. She regained her composure with a long, deep breath.

"Now don't go and get too excited just yet; it could just as easily be nothing," Dave said.

Hannah disregarded Dave's downplay. Her gut told her otherwise. "Good work, Dave. Let me know the second you hear back from the lab. We'll want to get on this one right away." Hannah's eyes found Richard's smiling face. She could see the glint in his eye and the look on his face that clearly said, *we're going to nail this bastard.*

Chapter Seven

Bobby Ross returned to the sanctity of his small office. He tossed his notebook on his desk, sat back in his leather office chair, threw his feet up, and admired the shine on his polished black Dockers. With his hands folded behind his head, he stared out the window of his 22nd floor office. The view was incredible. It overlooked Lake Ontario and Toronto's downtown core, including the iconic CN Tower.

What a magnificent structure, he thought. He was amazed every time he looked at it. He'd always had difficulty comprehending how a building of that enormity and design could have even been constructed. *What a wonderful display of craftsmanship*, he admired—a talent he had only with words.

Bobby began replaying the events of this morning's courtroom spectacle over and over in his head. He was likely one of the only people who believed Matt Davidson was innocent of the allegations against him. His story had always intrigued him. Here's a young man whose father, a world-renowned plastic surgeon, spends most of his waking hours helping the rich and famous look younger and more attractive, just to ensure a longer onscreen career. Because of this notoriety, "Daddy" gets a lot of media attention, putting the Davidson family under constant scrutiny. Believe it or not, there are still a lot of people completely against any form of plastic surgery. Some traditionalists feel it's distasteful that a well-educated doctor of his stature is wasting his talent transforming vain, rich people when there is a dire need for physicians to care for those with real, life-threatening health concerns.

For Matt Davidson, his father's profession just meant growing up most of the time without a father. It also didn't help Matt's situation that as a plastic surgeon, his father was used to nothing less than perfection. This value was something that he demanded and expected from everyone in his life. Needless to say, it made the doctor pretty unpopular with his son, a rebellious young man who wanted for nothing and was continuously challenging authority. It was an ill-fated combination for Matt.

From Matt's first arrest three years ago, Bobby had a gut feeling that something was off with the story. He couldn't put his finger on it, but something didn't quite add up. He shifted his focus towards Matt's recent arrest, hoping to uncover a bigger story. Bobby enjoyed digging deeper into stories to get to the truth, so spending time in a courtroom waiting for verdicts or sentences of scandalous individuals to be handed down was very interesting and exciting for him. He also loved the underdog. So, until he was able to create his own personal lucky break, he would keep doing what he was good at.

After procrastinating long enough, Bobby decided it was time for his scenic break to conclude and for him to say goodbye to the CN Tower for now and get back to work. He had a long, busy night ahead of him, having collected so much information on Matt over the last three years. He had paper files, computer files, recorded interviews, and even videotaped interviews to sift through again. It had been a while since he last went through all of it, so he needed to review everything with fresh eyes if he wanted to get to the bottom of this attention-grabbing story.

Bobby got up from his chair and made his way over to his filing cabinet. Although not the most organized of cabinets, his system was sufficient enough to find what he was looking for. From halfway back in the second drawer down, he pulled out two thick manila file folders each bearing a large white label. Neatly printed in bold, black letters were the words DAVIDSON, MATTHEW.

CHAPTER EIGHT

"WHAT TIME IS IT?" Hannah asked Richard.

"It's eleven-thirty. Why? Got somewhere better to be?" Richard teased. There were times he would intentionally try to stir the pot to get a rise out of Hannah. When the situation and timing were appropriate, the two of them could slap the digs back and forth effortlessly. It usually proved very entertaining and passed the time quite nicely. However, if the timing was off—as it apparently was today—it might just prove to piss her off.

Looking completely unimpressed, Hannah glared at him.

Immediately rethinking his timing on this friendly banter, Richard regretfully asked, "Oh shit. What's the matter? Talk to me."

He was sincere with his offer to talk. As much as they goaded each other, it was always meant in good fun. He realized there was something more serious on her mind and he wanted to help—whatever the situation was. She was dealing with enough bullshit over the last eighteen months without his teasing inadvertently adding to her stress.

Turning back toward Richard, she said, "It's nothing. I'm just pissed off. I have an appointment this afternoon and I'd give my left arm to not have to go." The scowl on her face just accentuated her bitterness.

"Oh, that's right." This was all he had to say. He didn't have to push any further to find out what appointment she was referring to. He remembered. And he felt bad for her.

"I'm so sick of fucking lawyers!" she blurted out, squeezing both hands tightly into fists. "They're as useless as a beakless woodpecker! They do absolutely nothing to help you. They just take, take, take, and only look out for their own bank account! They don't give a shit about anyone else!" Hannah, visibly shaking now, continued her explosive rant until she was literally speechless.

With Richard's mounting concern, he cautiously proceeded. "What time's your appointment?"

"Two." She answered matter-of-factly, sarcastically adding, "And boy, I just can't wait! I can't wait for my lawyer to tell me that Kent didn't sign the damn divorce papers again or that he still didn't agree to the settlement terms." Flushed and shaking, she slammed her fist on the dashboard. "I just can't believe that asshole has the balls to screw me out of *my own money,* all the while he's screwing some tart with daddy issues who was probably still shitting her diapers during Y2K!"

Richard didn't bother trying to speak. He just let her go and watched her take a few long, deep breaths. He knew she needed to just let it out. Even if he did try, he'd never be able to get a word in edgewise. She had a lot to say about that asshole, and he didn't want to be the one stopping that freight train.

"But the best part is," Hannah continued her outburst, "I'll probably be asked to give my money-hungry divorce lawyer even more money today since he's burned through the hefty retainer that I already gave him! And why? Just to have a whole bunch more of *nothing* done! Isn't that fantastic? Isn't that just the best friggin' news ever?" Shaking her head, she concluded her rant with, "Fuck, I'm in the wrong profession. I could be a millionaire by now if I was a divorce lawyer."

Richard watched as Hannah stopped for another breath. Studying her carefully, he decided now would be a good time to try to break the palpable tension. Calmly, he smirked and whispered, "Hannah, you know it's really not good for your health to keep all that emotion bottled up inside. Please stop holding back what you're really feeling. Just let it all out and say what's really on your mind, okay?"

Appreciating the humour in Richard's sarcasm, Hannah appeared to be pulled back into the moment when she smiled at him. "Point taken." She seemed a little more at ease on their drive back to the station. Glancing at Richard, she said, "Thanks, Richard. I really needed that."

Richard returned the smile. "Glad I could help. Now get out of your mood, bitch."

Hannah reached over and playfully swatted his arm. Richard knew she appreciated that quality in him. No matter what the circumstances, he knew he was pretty much guaranteed to make her smile. He liked to see her smile. It was a great smile. Especially when it was aimed at him.

Richard watched as her eyes shifted to the passenger side window. Her gaze locked onto a dilapidated barn off in the distance. She was probably thinking the same thing he was. *How on earth could that poor excuse for a barn still safely house any livestock?* It probably didn't anymore. He was pretty sure that at one time it had been filled with scads of horses, because he vaguely recalled a memory of his parents driving by this farm when he was a young boy. The farm was not too far from his school and back then, it was always alive with excitement. Sometimes he'd actually see the horses being exercised, running at full speed in circles around the immaculately maintained track. It would only be for an instant, and then the car would be past it. It was sad to see it so run down now; such a toll the years had taken on it. He wondered how anyone could let such a beautiful piece of property fade away into nothing more than a junkyard. *What a shame,* he thought.

Richard's memories were interrupted by the ringing of Hannah's phone. He watched as she fumbled to open the crappy, outdated flip phone that the department still issued to every detective. You would think that with an annual spending budget of over 220 million dollars, an up-to-date phone wouldn't be too much to ask for. But no—they were stuck with these unreliable relics.

Raising the phone to her ear, she answered with a quick, "Phillips".

Richard glanced over as Hannah listened. After a long moment of silence, she leaned her head back against the seat, exhaled, and said, "Son of a bitch." Pausing again, her eyes closed as she listened to the voice on the other end. A few seconds later, her eyes opened, "Is it the same M.O. as the others?" This was spoken softly, as if she didn't want to hear the answer.

Richard knew what was coming next.

"We're on our way."

Hannah folded her phone closed and rested it in her lap. Flipping on the lights and siren, she looked over at Richard and said, "Make a U-turn. They've just found another body. And here's the kicker. She was found by a farmer about a kilometre from where Carley Wilson showed up."

Chapter Nine

MATT DAVIDSON SAT QUIETLY in his holding cell. Eyeballing the orange jumpsuit he was forced to wear, he was reminded of the tv show, *Orange Is the New Black*. Shaking his head, his shoulder-length brown hair brushed the back of his neck. He still couldn't accept that he was here in a cold jail cell yet again. It seemed like yesterday that he was here the last time. The past three years of his life replayed in his head continuously, his mind racing a mile a minute with no end in sight.

Why is this happening to me? he wondered, his brain trying to comprehend the absurdity of his all too familiar situation. With his stomach churning and his palms sweaty, he tried to fathom what he ever could have done to deserve this. His mind was blank. Sure, maybe he was a bit of a rebel and many times he did things without thinking about the consequences, but in the grand scheme of things, he could have been a lot worse. He certainly had no control over who his father was or the impeccable reputation he had earned, although that didn't seem to matter to anyone.

His faultless, hypercritical father.

His co-creator.

Daddy.

Now there was a force to be reckoned with. His father, the prominent, world-renowned Plastic Surgeon, Dr. William Davidson, didn't even have the audacity to show his face at his own son's bail hearing. How's that for support? Being photographed once again emerging from the Oshawa courthouse would obviously be bad for Daddy's business and reputation.

Oh well, he'll have to live with that, Matt thought.

Many emotions continued to race through Matt's mind as he gently stroked the bandage over his left eye. Not only the betrayal and rejection he experienced from his father during the years, but also the humiliation and embarrassment of being in this situation. Again. Huddled on a hard bench in a dingy jail cell that offered nothing but a lumpy mattress and a faucet that dripped incessantly.

After a while, the persistent dripping lulled Matt into a calm, almost tranquil state. Leaning with his back and head against the wall, his left leg outstretched, and his right knee bent to support his right forearm, his mind started to drift. He started thinking about the hot blonde he'd recently hooked up with from the strip club he frequented. He smiled as he replayed the great night he'd had with her. He started thinking about the exact moment that the blonde smitten kitten nonchalantly strolled up to the table he was sitting at. He vividly remembered the sexy red dress she was wearing as she made her final approach. One hand carried a Coors Light and the other playfully twisted a lock of hair around her index finger. He remembered smiling at her and being aroused by the unexpected situation when she had stopped right in front of him. He recalled watching as her seductive eyes very indiscreetly explored every inch of his athletic physique. He loved every second of it. It gave him the confidence and green light to reciprocate without feeling judged or sleazy. He remembered distinctly giving a quick scan of the playful young woman before his eyes came to rest on her flawless breasts. That—well those—he definitely remembered. Although she was just a patron, she would have fit in quite nicely up on stage. He also remembered her name. Sydney…something. Oh well, close enough. He couldn't remember her last name at the moment, but he did remember that they ended up back at his apartment, and he wouldn't soon forget the steamy few hours that had followed. When he'd woken up the next morning, she was already gone. She'd slipped away before he even had a chance to get her phone number. That sucked. He did want to see her again, but how would he find her? He thought about it again, over and over, trying hard to remember. *Sydney—Sydney what?* he wondered.

A loud commotion from down the hall abruptly ended Matt's steamy memory and brought him back into the present. In a nearby room, he could hear the muffled voices of police officers going about their business and the nonstop ringing of phones that went unanswered.

Doesn't anyone ever answer the phones around here? Matt thought.

Occasional profanity, muffled slurring, and the odd grunts were emerging from a cell across from Matt's. A homeless man, obviously known to the police, was being held for "disturbing the peace." It was quite clear to Matt and the other officers that he was sloshed. Matt was the unfortunate soul that got to listen to him blather on all night, totally gin-soaked and unable to form a cohesive sentence. This poor guy didn't have the foggiest idea what was actually going on. Earlier, as two patrol officers basically carried him into his cell, Matt figured that he had most likely been living in "tent city" on Quebec Street. It was a greenspace, popular for housing the homeless, only about a twenty-minute walk due south of the police station. It was just a guess though and he'd probably never really know for sure. Tonight, this guy was going to feel like he was a guest at the five-star Fairmont Royal York Hotel compared to his usual accommodations. In his lifetime, this man had probably held out many coffee cups begging passersby for spare change to support whatever addiction he may have had. Matt had heard stories of addicts so desperate for a fix that they resorted to drinking aftershave for the buzz. Maybe this guy was an Aqua Velva man, maybe not. He paused on that thought for a moment. Aqua Velva. He hoped that his own life would never look so bleak.

What a shame, he thought. Wondering if he had any family, any friends, anyone that would come and bail this poor drunk out of jail, Matt was saddened. *Would anyone even notice that he was gone? Did anyone in this world care about this poor man at all?*

That dismal thought left Matt with an overwhelming sense of loneliness and sorrow. Matt Davidson had family and he had friends. He had people in his life who he assumed cared about him. And he had a father. Nevertheless, did any of them care enough to rush out and post his bail? Apparently not. Not even Daddy.

Chapter Ten

Kelly sat trembling on the cold, damp floor, both knees pulled tightly up to her chest. She didn't dare move—or even blink. Stunned, she just listened intently as a door scraped across the dirt floor. What seemed like hours had in reality only been seconds since the door to this room had begun to open. *Who's coming in?* She panicked, her mind racing and quickly filling with frantic, horrible images. *What's going to happen to me?*

The fear that swept through her body carried her mind back to an early time in her childhood. It took her back to an instance when she was terrified of the dark, afraid of nighttime, afraid of the scary monsters that lay hidden under her bed and in her closet. Such an innocent time. A time when she truly believed that if she just closed her eyes as tight as she could, she wouldn't be able to see any of those scary monsters. And in return, no monsters would be able to see her. Such innocence. But here in this darkness at this very moment, Kelly had never hoped for something so silly to be truer. Still clutching her knees tightly while silently rocking back and forth, she prayed. Even though her family had never practiced any formal religion, she still prayed. Prayed for her life. She didn't want to see what or who was coming into that room with her. She didn't want to know. All she knew was that it was almost certainly going to be awful.

The fear and desperation that totally consumed her was now beginning to overpower her senses. She was losing control of her body. Her heart started thumping so fast and hard that she was convinced whoever was coming in could hear it pounding like a drum. She was gasping for air now, her eyes filling with tears. She tried to scream—tried to call out. But nothing happened. Only air escaped her dry, parted lips. Fear had stolen all her words, just as quickly as this monster had stolen her happy life. In her head, her screams were deafening. So loud that she thought her mother might actually be able to hear them. But in her heart, she knew that nobody could hear her cries. Not her mother, not the person coming into the room with her—not anyone. Now more than ever, all she could think about was home. She wanted to go home. But she couldn't. She was all alone. Alone in the dark with her greatest childhood fear now unfolding right before her eyes, and she was terrified.

Kelly listened now, completely aware of her increased heartbeat and clammy palms. She waited for any sign of movement, any glimmer of light.

There were no footsteps.

There was no light.

There was nothing but the darkness she had come to know only too well over the horrific time she'd been held captive. Kelly was searching the darkness now, desperately squinting with every ounce of will she had, trying to make out the doorway and whoever it was that stood in the way of her freedom. As hard as she tried though, she could see nothing.

Then his voice.

"Kelly," he whispered in a soft, eerie voice. "It's okay, I'm here."

His voice was throaty and cold, revealing no hint of emotion at all, his words lingering in the air like the stench of an overpowering cologne.

Kelly, her eyes now filled with tears, felt the panic flood her body. In that moment, everything suddenly became extraordinarily real. All she could think of was to run. She didn't know where, but she had to run. Right now. She couldn't just sit there and wait for the unknown.

She had to fight.

She had to try.

Without a second thought, she propelled her body off the floor and lunged in the direction of his chilling voice. Not even knowing where she was going, her eyes still damp with tears and her legs burning with pain from the awkward position she had held for so many hours, she hurled her arms forward as she sprang towards his voice. In her heart she felt certain that she could make it to the door, to her freedom. The element of surprise was in her favour. He certainly wouldn't be expecting this.

No. Not at all.

This would throw him off for sure.

Her head was bent down, fists clenched tightly in her sudden full-blown charge. Four frantic steps were all she could manage before she felt his strong clutch around her forearm. With an unexpected gasp, Kelly flung her body around and desperately started swinging at her captor with her free arm. She made contact with him once, and only once. With nothing but a muffled scoff, her captor struck her in the face with a force that knocked her backwards to the familiar dirt beneath her. Dazed, but still fighting, she tried anxiously to get back to her feet. She made it onto her hands and knees, blood dripping from her mouth, but a sudden dizziness overwhelmed her, shattering her dreams of escape. Her head was spinning now and the realization of what she had done overcame her. With her head hanging between her arms, supported only by her unstable knees as they prepared to buckle beneath her, she anticipated what might happen next—and she puked.

Chapter Eleven

Hannah was finishing up her telephone conversation with Detective Connors just as she and Richard pulled up to the second crime scene just off Ritson Road North. She had called Jake to let him know about the most recent development in the case.

Another body, another crime scene, another victim.

Jake already heard the news from Dave Fisher when he had called to see if the labs were back on the two pieces of material recovered from the fence post. They both knew that even though this case was top priority, the lab probably wouldn't have been able to process the evidence that quickly. But it didn't hurt to ask.

It was during that conversation that Dave informed Jake of the most recent development in the investigation: the discovery of another young woman's body. This one not quite as lucky as Carley Wilson. A different forensics unit was at the new scene since Dave's team was still working the original one.

As Hannah continued her conversation, Jake replied, "Shit. What the hell is this asshole trying to pull? Is he toying with us? You'd almost think he was trying to taunt us, wouldn't you? I mean, dumping her so close, with all those cops around, all that commotion? What the hell, Hannah?"

Hannah quickly interjected with, "What's to say she wasn't already dumped before we found Carley? Don't rule that out."

Hannah could sense the uneasiness rising in Jake. She knew this was all too familiar for him. Yeah, most cops were used to dealing with these types of cases from time to time. But for Jake, this case was hitting way too close to home and Hannah knew why.

"The coroner is already here," she continued. "She'll give us a better idea of the cause and time of death and I'll let you know."

Hannah was just as annoyed as Jake. She also believed that this jerk was taunting them. Toying with them like a game of cat and mouse—pushing the limits to see just what he could get away with. It wasn't the kind of game any of these cops liked to play.

From the other end of the line, she heard a loud thud, making it apparent that Jake had slammed his fist onto his desk. "Relax, Jake. I know it's hard, but I want you to take a deep breath and just take a minute to cool down. You know we're going to get this bastard. And when we do, he'll regret the day he was ever born."

Jake sighed and followed with, "Yeah, well, let's just hope it's sooner rather than later."

With that, Hannah closed her phone. She knew that even though they'd ended their call, Jake would still be frustrated and had most likely slammed the phone down on his end. She also knew that he'd eventually regroup, but for now was probably back at the office desperately trying to compose himself.

Hannah and Richard slowly made their way towards Shane Kimball, who was heading this secondary forensic unit. Maneuvering carefully through the crime scene so as not to disturb anything, Richard turned to Hannah and asked, "Why the abrupt finish?"

"What? With Jake?" Hannah attempted to play dumb—a hat she didn't wear well.

"Yeah. The phone call just now. Did you get cut off?"

Hannah, now replaying the call in her head as if on fast-forward, followed with, "That?" She gestured towards her phone. "No, not at all. He's just really heated right now. Dave had just told him about our latest victim and then I called—it was just a lot all at once."

"So?" Richard pushed.

Hannah, scanning the area, continued with, "He's just having a really hard time with this case, as we all are. He was finished talking about it, so he just hung up." She was trying to justify Jake's behavior as best she could, but it was useless. She didn't need to protect him. Not now.

Stopping dead in his tracks and gently grabbing Hannah's arm until she followed suit, Richard asked, "Is there something you're not telling me?" He was holding her gaze now, his head cocked slightly to one side like a puppy under the dinner table just waiting for scraps to fall.

She knew that this was going to resurface sooner or later, and she should have known her partner would figure it out. But even after anticipating this moment, all words escaped her. After a long, slow sigh, Hannah finally made eye contact with Richard and held his gaze. She watched his eyes grow wide with disbelief as she proceeded to bring things into light for him.

"Jake Connors' younger sister, Stephanie, was abducted three years ago." With that, she waited while Richard absorbed her words. His expression was like stone, as if uncertain of what he'd just heard. With her eyes still on his, she continued. "Her body was found in the trunk of an abandoned car in a wrecking yard less than a kilometre from his own house. She was beaten and partially disemboweled, similar to these recent victims. They never caught the bastard. The case is still technically classified as unsolved and that is killing Jake, but there was absolutely nothing to go on. No DNA evidence, no fibres or hair at the scene—nothing. With everything that's happened over the last couple of months, and now the games our killer seems to be playing with us, Jake is convinced it's the same guy."

Richard didn't say a word.

Hannah gave him some well-deserved time to let it all sink in. It was a lot to swallow all at once and she knew he needed time to digest it. Silently, they ducked under the crime scene tape and made their way through the heavily treed conservation area towards Shane Kimball and the rest of the investigators. Before Shane had a chance to talk to them, they were waved over by the coroner on scene, Dr. Nicky Lucas. Taking precautions to not contaminate any evidence, the two officers moved meticulously towards Dr. Lucas, deliberately stepping to avoid the many yellow numbered markers. As they reached her, she was squatting down beside the latest victim's body, a white sheet draped over it.

Hannah and Richard positioned themselves carefully on either side of the body as the coroner prepared to pull the sheet back to give her preliminary findings.

"I'm not going to lie to you, detectives. This isn't pretty." Her preemptive warning proved useless. As she pulled the sheet back, both officers gasped. Hannah watched as Richard's eyes immediately reverted to tracking the investigators' movements around the crime scene. It was obvious to her that he needed a second for things to register before he looked back down at the gruesome sight laying in front of him. After following the movements of the forensic photographer for a few moments, he spoke.

"Jesus." Richard mumbled, now squatting motionless beside the poor young woman. Hannah knew that Richard had an ironclad stomach when it came to things like this, but she was beginning to wonder if today was different. The colour appeared to be quickly draining from his contorted face. His eyes drifted towards hers and he was clearly trying hard to focus on her face. Realizing that she was also scowling in disgust, she pursed her lips and began breathing slowly and rhythmically to keep her focus on the victim and to hopefully ward off the lightheadedness that suddenly overwhelmed her. Composing herself moments later, she made eye contact with Richard, and then looked up towards Dr. Lucas. After a final deep breath, she said, "Okay, Doc. Talk to me."

Dr. Nicky Lucas was a forty-eight-year-old General Practitioner who owned her own private practice in Oshawa. In addition to that, she had hospital privileges at Lakeridge Health and had been pulling double duty as a coroner for about nine years. She was highly qualified in her specialty and very well respected by the DRPS.

Solemnly, she began walking them through what she'd found. "As you can see, we have a young female, probably early twenties, badly beaten. There are obvious broken bones with multiple lacerations covering her face and body. Based on the liver temp and degree of rigor that's set in, preliminary speculation for time of death would be within the last twelve to sixteen hours. There are multiple obvious injuries that could have been the cause of death, but we'll have to wait for the autopsy to confirm. You would think the wounds sustained to the abdomen alone would be enough to kill her, but have a look at this." Nicky pointed to dark ligature marks around her neck. "She may have been strangled."

Hannah continued examining the victim as the doctor commented, "One could only hope she was strangled first. Only a monster could hack a person open like this while they were still alive."

There was silence as they all contemplated that morbid thought. Hannah's eyes continued to inspect the body of their fourth victim, and she couldn't help but think about Carley Wilson. This would almost certainly have been her fate had she not escaped.

The silence was interrupted as Nicky continued to explain her findings. "The most obvious and disturbing of the injuries is this mess." She directed their attention to what was left of her abdomen. Shaking her head in disgust, she followed with, "Whoever did this was trying to disembowel her. Why? I have no idea."

Richard and Hannah stood in silence as the doctor noted, "There was no ID or clothing found with the victim and her fingertips have been burnt so Shane's team will try their best to get prints off her but in reality, they'll most likely have to run dental impressions and hopefully get lucky."

Not wanting to even let her head go there, Hannah directed her next tough question right at Nicky. "Any signs of sexual assault?"

"Thankfully, there are no obvious signs, but again, I'll have them run a rape kit to make sure."

"Thanks, Dr. Lucas. I'll reach out to the pathologist at the Centre of Forensic Sciences and make sure we are in that room when they do the autopsy. We need to catch a damn break right now."

Nodding at the doctor as they turned back towards their cruiser, Hannah was thinking about the pathologist who would be performing the autopsy. They were going to have a hell of a hard time with this one. From the mess of that scene, it was hard to tell if all her intestines were even there, or if parts were missing. Only the pathologist would be able to answer that question. But where would they even start?

Chapter Twelve

MATT DAVIDSON FINALLY MADE bail. Although he wasn't sure who he had to thank for his release, he was pretty sure it wasn't his father. Not this time. It was quite apparent that Daddy not showing up to his bail hearing was enough proof of the disappointment he had for him. *No,* he thought. *It wasn't him. It couldn't be. But who then?* Matt thought about who else he knew that would have that kind of money at their disposal. The kind of money they wouldn't miss should he decide to jump bail.

As Matt speculated, an officer led him down the grey corridor towards the Bail and Parole office. Once there, it took about forty minutes for the officer to complete all the remaining forms and paperwork required before Matt could be officially released. When the paperwork was finished, a second officer at the desk produced a large brown envelope from the shelf behind him. As he tipped the envelope up, Matt watched his personal effects spill onto the counter. The uniformed officer, who reminded him a little of Kiefer Sutherland, went through these items while Matt and his not-so-friendly officer escort stood witness. Although he could hear what the bail officer was saying, it sounded as though the words were muffled and distant, as if he had his hands cupped over each ear. His body was flooded with that sensation of being on Novocain while having a tooth pulled at the dentist. It felt surreal, almost difficult to distinguish between illusion and reality.

"...silver watch...silver chain...wallet...keys...gum...pack of matches..."

Matt, now realizing that the officer was reciting his personal effects held in that large envelope, nodded in agreement as he listened. He didn't care if they forgot something. It wasn't important to him. All he could focus on was the one nagging thought still puzzling him. *Who had finally come to bail me out?*

With Matt's release finalized, he emerged through the front doors of the police station panning the street looking for some hint of familiarity. *Who is this mystery person I have to thank for my release?* His eyes first searched left towards the downtown sector. He glimpsed City Hall and the public library, both magnificent in their architecture and ivy-covered stone structure. The large red maple trees that lined the busy street were brilliant with colour, while an assortment of annual flowers encompassed their bases. Those gorgeous trees with their full, mature limbs had probably been there longer than he had been alive.

Beautiful, he thought.

As his gaze shifted to his right, he spotted an old woman pushing a shopping cart, presumably removed from the grocery store a few blocks away. The cart was overflowing with empty cans, newspapers, ragged articles of clothing, and tattered green garbage bags filled with God only knows what.

Are those all of her worldly possessions? he wondered. Or just random items she had collected during her many travels up and down the lonely city streets and alleys? He studied her as she attempted to bend forward to recover a half-smoked cigarette a passerby had recently discarded. The mere thought of how disgusting her actions were didn't even seem to faze her. Matt watched as—ironically—she meticulously wiped the filter with her dirty fingers before raising it to her lips. Her shoulders rose and her chest expanded as she inhaled the deadly combination of tar and nicotine. He then watched her shoulders fall as she exhaled the second-hand smoke from her lungs. It was an obvious treat for the woman, as a huge smile of satisfaction crossed her aging, filthy face. Matt couldn't help but notice that the sparsely-toothed woman was in dire need of dental repairs; something he was almost certain she would never have the luxury of getting. Matt cringed, a small shudder running through his body. *Maybe this woman is a friend of the drunk I was forced to listen to ramble on all night long?* It was just a thought.

Matt's attention returned once again to the street in front of the police station. He watched in utter amazement as an immaculately maintained black stretch limousine pulled up to the steps in front of the building he had been a reluctant guest in for the past thirty hours. The car sat idling for what seemed like minutes before the tinted window on the driver's side automatically lowered halfway. Emerging from the driver's seat and staring with disapproving eyes right through Matt, as if he were invisible, was his father's chauffeur.

"Get in."

Chapter Thirteen

HANNAH ARRIVED AT THE law offices of Brawley, Holden, and McAllister at one-fifty-eight p.m. Even after slipping home for a quick shower and a change of clothes, she still made it to her appointment with two minutes to spare. The wardrobe change made her feel more in her element. She knew she had been underdressed all day wearing jeans and a hoodie, but it was all she could muster at five o'clock in the morning while running on little sleep and even less energy. After a quick shower that left her feeling wide awake and refreshed, she now donned a conservative pant suit. The perfectly fitted navy outfit enhanced her emerald eyes as well as her shoulder-length chestnut hair that was now pulled up into a chic messy bun. At thirty-seven years old, the fearless, self-reliant woman still possessed all the qualities needed to turn more than a few heads.

Hannah's eyes slowly panned the quaint waiting area in the busy law office. From the looks of some of the detailing, she guessed that the building itself was at least a hundred years old. The furnishings and fixtures inside were a complementary reflection of the outside. Antique bookshelves lining the entire South wall held hundreds of thick law books. There were ten-foot ceilings containing transom windows above the doors—totally useless to see out of but great to let the warm sunlight in. The reception area was filled with two antique mahogany desks, turn of the century fixtures, and four Victorian wing-backed chairs. The wainscoting on the walls looked like the original wood and very well maintained. All in all, the office was an exceptional display of history and craftsmanship.

Hannah felt a pang of envy. She had always dreamed of buying a large piece of property in the country with an old century home that she could renovate herself. She loved the warm feeling she got when she entered an old building. The history alone amazed her. *If these walls could talk,* she thought, *such fascinating stories they would have to tell.* Hannah shifted in her seat, her fingers drumming nervously on the May issue of House and Garden magazine that rested in her lap. She had absolutely no intention of reading it when she picked it up. She just thought it could be something to fidget with while she waited anxiously for her appointment.

"Mrs. Phillips?" The secretary, who had been typing like a demon the whole time Hannah waited, was now standing in front of her large desk and looking directly at her. Hannah looked up, almost startled, to see the soft smile of the secretary who didn't look a day over twenty.

Hannah nodded.

The friendly young lady continued, "If you'd like to follow me, Mr. Holden will see you now."

Rising from the surprisingly uncomfortable chair, Hannah placed her Michael Kors knock-off over her right shoulder, adjusted her jacket, and followed the secretary down the long corridor to her lawyer's office. Passing by the young woman's desk, Hannah glanced briefly at the name plate neatly situated beside a framed picture of a handsome young man, establishing that her name was Jayne. As Jayne opened the door leading into the office, Mark Holden was making his way out from behind a stunning walnut desk. It was a beautiful period piece presumably acquired at a hefty cost from a local auction house. Walking towards Hannah, he extended his hand out to meet hers. Shaking it firmly, he glanced back at the young woman saying, "Thank you, Jayne. Will you please hold my calls?"

With a nod, Jayne quickly exited the room, quietly pulling the door closed behind her.

"Can I offer you some coffee, Hannah? Maybe a glass of water?" Mark Holden's smile was charming and friendly, but Hannah still couldn't get past the feeling that this guy was robbing her blind. She had been on the defensive even before she set foot in the building, so she was finding Mark's charm and charisma very unnerving. She knew she had to stay strong and stand her ground.

How is it, she wondered, *that I'm tough as nails when it comes to policing and my day-to-day life, but when it comes to dealing with this lawyer, I feel like my typically sturdy backbone is crumbling beneath me?*

Not today, she thought.

No more.

It ends now.

She straightened her shoulders, her chin held high and replied, "No thank you, I'm fine."

As Mr. Holden made his way back to his oversized chair behind the desk, Hannah situated herself in the visitor's chair directly across from him. After adjusting his chair, the lawyer opened the file folder that was laying on the desk in front of him. Scanning it quickly and then closing it again, he leaned over his desk to rest his forearms on the blotter and interlaced his fingers.

Oh great. Here it comes, she thought. Hannah felt her face starting to flush.

"Hannah, I spoke with Kent's lawyer again this morning." After a brief pause, he followed with, "I hate to be the bearer of bad news, but..."

Mark didn't finish his sentence. Instead, he watched Hannah's facial expression transform and knew that she was going to have a huge reaction to his unfinished remark.

Hannah felt the hairs on the back of her neck stand up as her heart rate quickened. Feeling her face grow flushed and warm, she also realized her jaw hurt from clenching her teeth so tightly. Her heart was still pounding angrily in her chest when she recognized the need to pause for a moment before inadvertently reacting in a way she may end up regretting.

Hannah knew that Mr. Holden could see the look of frustration and anger on her face. Her eyes glassed over and the furrow above her nose was now creased into an angered expression of loathing and betrayal—a feeling to which Hannah had unfortunately become way too accustomed.

Mr. Holden decided it was time to continue explaining the point he had started to make moments earlier. "Listen, Hannah, let me explain."

He didn't get far before Hannah interrupted him in an emotional outburst. Her emerald eyes, now squinting and peering directly into his own, could have pierced him with her rage. "Are you going to tell me that Kent still didn't sign the goddamned divorce papers? You've got to be kidding me! This is a joke, right?" The volume of her voice was rising quickly, but still not to the point of yelling. She was heated, and judging by the understanding look on Mark's face, he knew it.

The lawyer proceeded with caution. "Now listen, Hannah. You didn't let me finish. What I was about to say was that Kent's lawyer informed me he has agreed to sign the papers, but there's a contingency. He wants the financial terms amended."

Hannah was pissed.

Mark ended with, "If you do that, he'll sign them today. If you don't, he's prepared to keep things the way they are right now." Mr. Holden slowly sat back in his chair, stretched his arms up behind his head, and interlocked his fingers. "What do you think?" With that question posed, he awaited Hannah's response.

You overconfident son of a bitch, Hannah thought. *I would love to reach over that desk and smack that smug look right off your face.* Hannah was not impressed and was seriously doubting the reason for even paying this guy. So far, he hadn't helped her one bit, other than squandering her bank account.

With the feeling of disbelief still lingering in the air, Hannah bluntly asked, "What the hell are you talking about? Why would I amend the financial terms? It's simple—he owes me a lot of money. Period." Hannah watched as Mark shifted uneasily in his chair. "Mr. Holden, when I walked in here that first day, you were the one who told me that my case was cut and dry. What I want to know now is how a cut and dry case can be dragged out for eighteen months with absolutely nothing at all getting accomplished? You said it was simple. So why is it that now, thousands of dollars and eighteen months later, you are still telling me that we've gotten absolutely nowhere? That he won't sign the papers because he simply doesn't want to pay back all the money that he rightfully owes me? What in Christ's name is that all about? He's acting like a spoiled goddamned toddler."

Hannah's decibel had now climbed nicely into a yell. Although she was proud of herself for finally speaking her mind about her soon to be ex-husband, she was having a hard time completing her outburst. *Oh, to hell with it,* she thought. *I'm paying this guy big bucks, so he can listen to me for a change.*

Holding his hand up to interrupt Hannah, he interjected with, "Mrs. Phillips, I hear what you're saying, and I totally understand your frustration. In the grand scheme of things, your case should be open and shut. The only problem is, we can't drag him in here by the nose and make him sign the papers. It doesn't work that way. Yes, you're absolutely right. He owes you a lot of money and he damn well should be paying you, but we both also realize that you can't get blood out of a stone." Mark sounded empathetic now, but she still wasn't wavering on her attitude towards him, and he was about to find out exactly how she felt about the situation.

"Don't give me that bullshit, Mr. Holden! My lying husband was living two different lives! While I was working my ass off to support us both, he was actually out playing house with his girlfriend. He deliberately faked a promotion that would involve working longer hours just to keep up his charade. Who does that? It's diabolical! So now he's rewarded for lying, cheating, and racking up thousands of dollars of debt with *her*, and I'm expected to pay for all this? This is absolute horseshit! He's been shacked up with her since we split up, living the high life, while I'm forced to pinch pennies because I'm left responsible for all of *his* debt! What's wrong with that picture, Mr. Holden? No—better yet. Explain to me what's right with it!"

Hannah paused for a moment. With her eyes starting to tear, she closed them for a second, took a deep breath in, and then slowly exhaled. After opening them again, she looked across at her lawyer and saw that he was staring compassionately at her just as a single tear trickled down her cheek in defeat.

She could tell he felt bad. She could also sense that he may have just finally realized there was nothing right about this situation. Nothing at all.

Chapter Fourteen

As Hannah stepped out onto the busy sidewalk in front of her lawyer's office, she welcomed the cool, autumn breeze on her flushed face. She felt drained and, at that particular moment, completely devoid of any emotion at all. She just felt defeated. The meeting, as brief as it was, played out just as she had suspected. Hannah was confident of three things prior to her unproductive meeting with Mark Holden.

Kent would not have signed the divorce papers.

Kent would still have no intention of paying back all the money owed to her.

Kent would still be an asshole.

Hannah just rolled her eyes as the last thought ran through her mind. Why in the world would she ever think otherwise? Kent was, and always would be, a self-serving asshole. As she rounded the corner onto University Avenue in Toronto, her phone rang, interrupting her depressing thoughts. She kept an even pace, weaving in and out through the oncoming rush of people targeting their own individual destinations as she opened her phone and held it to her ear.

"Phillips." As she awaited the response on the other end, Hannah quickly dodged an oncoming scooter accompanied by two leashed poodles who looked to be on a serious hunt for a fire hydrant.

"Great news, Hannah." Her partner sounded enthusiastic in her ear.

Abruptly, she came back with, "Well, it'd better be after that dismal meeting. What's up?"

Without hesitation he announced, "The hospital just called—Carley Wilson is awake."

"You're shitting me, right?" Hannah was skeptical. It seemed pretty sudden considering everything the poor girl had been through. "Is she well enough to talk to us?"

"The doctor said she woke up mumbling some pretty cryptic things. I think the sooner we talk to her, the better. If she can remember anything at all, we should get it while it's fresh in her mind."

"Agreed. I'm just heading into the parking garage now. I'll meet you at the hospital in twenty." With that, Hannah closed her phone and placed it back in her handbag. Entering the parking garage, she hit the button on her keyless remote to signal her horn and then swiftly headed in the direction of her car. She eyeballed her navy Nissan Rogue as she approached and realized it was in desperate need of a wash. In the dirt, somebody had written the words WASH ME on the rear driver's side window. *Duly noted*, she thought.

Passing behind a black SUV parked opposite her car, she noticed the vague outline of a figure in the back seat. It was hard to tell for sure through the dark, tinted windows but she was almost certain that someone was there. It seemed strange to her since there didn't seem to be anyone else in the vehicle. The driver and passenger sides appeared empty as she approached the truck, but there definitely was a silhouette in the back seat, however subtle. Opening her car door to get in, Hannah had the distinct impression that whoever was in that truck was watching her. Feeling the tiny hairs on the back of her neck come to life, she momentarily thought about investigating further, but decided to shake it off and just get to the hospital. One of the pitfalls of being a cop for so many years was the tendency to overthink everything.

Reversing out of her parking space, her thoughts returned to Carley Wilson. She hoped that the young woman might be able to shed some light. At this point, Hannah would welcome any information Carley could give them. They really needed to catch a break—and soon. Thinking about that reminded her that she needed to touch base with Dave Fisher to see if the labs had come back on the material recovered from the fence post. Hannah knew it was doubtful, but it would be a distraction on her drive over to Sunnybrook Hospital. As she grabbed her phone out of her handbag and dialed Dave's number, Hannah was completely unaware of the black SUV that now followed her.

Chapter Fifteen

MATT DAVIDSON WAITED ANXIOUSLY in the unwelcoming study of his father's 6,700 square foot mansion situated right in the heart of the lushest part of the city. It boasted fourteen rooms, a heated swimming pool, four car garage, extravagant perennial gardens, and was expertly maintained by five long-time staff members. Matt felt nervous just being in this house again. His memories growing up in this grandiose environment were not fond ones at all. They were very difficult times. Matt learned at an early age that no matter what he did or how hard he tried, he could never please his father with anything. His grades were never high enough, his room was never clean enough, his trophies were never big enough. The doctor had his bar set so high that, even with a ladder, Matt was never going to reach it.

Matt recognized that there was never a strong father-son bond—especially after his mother died. He just figured that the reason his father was so demanding and critical of him was because he was lonely and missed his wife. There was never a conversation that wasn't challenged. If Matt said black, his father said white. If Matt said dog, his father said cat. Matt spent most of his lonely youth doing backflips just trying to please him. He just wanted some acknowledgment. Some recognition. Some acceptance. No matter how hard Matt tried, it didn't make any difference at all. His efforts always went one of three ways: unnoticed, disparaged, or criticized in his father's contemptible eyes.

Now he found himself back in this familiar study, those same agonizing feelings of inadequacy and shame now bubbling to the surface like a sabered champagne bottle. His eyes investigated the dimly lit room while he waited for his father. Displayed meticulously on one wall, he noted a wide variety of diplomas and certificates showcasing his father's many achievements, while directly behind his father's desk, he spotted the pride and joy wall. His father actually named it that, *the pride and joy wall.* That always irritated the hell out of Matt because there wasn't one single picture of his own son or late wife on this wall. Not one.

Instead, it flaunted the doctor's own trophies, keepsakes, and mementos from his younger years. "The glory days," as his father liked to call them. The time in his life where all he did was go fishing for sport and hang out at the lake with his buddies. Looking at these pictures and keepsakes only managed to amplify Matt's feelings of inadequacy, seeing as not one of his own accomplishments earned a spot on the pride and joy wall.

Matt began fidgeting when he heard the heavy footsteps coming down the hall towards the study. He knew there was going to be yelling. He knew there was going to be a lecture. He knew there were going to be harsh, disparaging remarks made by his father. He knew it all too well because he'd been in this situation before—many times. As he leaned uneasily back in his chair, his hand fiddled with his earlobe and he wondered, *how do I keep getting myself into these situations?*

The large double doors to the study opened abruptly, a loud thud echoing in the room as one door smashed into the wall behind it. Matt's father charged through the doors, walked around behind his walnut executive desk, and adjusted himself comfortably in his chair. Not once since making his grand entrance had his eyes broken contact with Matt's. Dr. Davidson leaned into his desk and rested his arms on the perfectly organized papers laying in front of him. Still not having broken eye contact with his son, he finally spoke.

"What the hell is the matter with you, Matthew?" His father's tone was harsh, his words direct and to the point. Dr. Davidson was a statuesque man in his late fifties. His salt and pepper hair was styled neatly into a pompadour. His green eyes pierced Matt's as they held his gaze. His six-foot four-inch frame was covered by a grey Brook Brothers suit that intensified the brightness of his eyes considerably.

Matt felt himself sink into his chair, as if trying to completely disappear from this demoralizing situation. His fidgeting came to a sudden halt when he realized he had not taken a single breath since his father had entered the room. *Here it comes*, he thought.

His father, still sounding infuriated, continued. "Why is it that every time I turn around, I seem to be bailing you out of some new shit you've gotten yourself into? Haven't you learned by now? Can't you get it through your thick, senseless skull to quit pulling this crap? What the hell is it this time? Whose fault is it? Who are you going to blame this time?"

Matt watched and listened as his father kept firing off questions while glaring at him, daring him to respond.

"Really, Matt, I'm waiting. Who are you going to blame now? Because I already know that you're going to try to convince me that it wasn't your fault again."

Matt shifted uncomfortably in his seat. He knew his father wouldn't believe him. He didn't believe him the last two times so why would it be any different now? He figured he shouldn't even bother trying to explain. What was the point? All Matt really wanted to do was get up and walk away from his father and all of his unwarranted judgements. It just seemed futile to state his case and then have his father ridicule him for telling the truth. He decided that regardless of which route he chose, his father's skepticism and disbelief was inevitable. Even though he couldn't wrap his own head around the situation, Matt knew that he was innocent—even if his father didn't agree. Deciding that he had absolutely nothing to lose, he proceeded to state his case.

"Dad, I don't know who I'm going to blame. I don't have the faintest clue why this keeps happening to me. All I do know is that I didn't do anything wrong."

"You didn't do anything wrong?" The cynicism in his father's voice was obvious.

"No. I didn't do anything wrong. Why do you find it so hard to believe me?" Matt was sincere in his efforts to make his father understand, however useless it was. He was tired of feeling like he was on trial whenever he spoke to him. All he ever wanted was his father's love, trust, and approval. Not the constant doubt, disbelief, and put downs.

"Matt, this is your third arrest in three years. That's why I find it so hard to believe what you're telling me."

Matt watched as his father shuffled a couple file folders on his desk, obviously contemplating his next remarks. Concluding his selfish lecture, he ended by saying, "I've helped you out many times in the past, but this is getting ridiculous. I'm not willing to repeatedly put my own neck on the line for a worthless, two-bit criminal. Do you realize how this affects my life? My reputation? I'm sick of it—we're done. Consider this the last time you're getting any help from me. From now on, you get yourself into this shit, you can damn well get yourself out of it. You're on your own."

Matt watched his father sit back in his chair, his cheeks growing flushed as he glared at him. No words were spoken as the two men now sat in silence, neither one of them breaking eye contact. Matt wondered what to do next. *Should I push the situation, or just sit here?* Feeling too intimidated to force the matter any further, he took his father's final angry remarks as the end of the conversation. Rising from his chair, he turned towards the doorway. As he cautiously opened the door to leave, he stopped in his tracks. Glancing back over his shoulder, all he said to his unsupportive father was, "Somebody is trying to set me up. I don't know who, or why, but I'm going to find out."

With that, he left the silent room.

Chapter Sixteen

RICHARD ANXIOUSLY AWAITED HANNAH'S arrival at the hospital. He decided to wait for her near the 5th floor nurse's station rather than disturb Carley Wilson. He paced the floor uneasily, up and down the busy corridor, retracing his steps numerous times before a nurse finally asked if he needed assistance. As he began to explain his intentions to the heavy-set woman, a doctor in green scrubs and matching cap approached him, his arm extended.

"Detective Young?" he questioned, firmly shaking Richard's hand.

"That's right." Richard looked curiously at the anonymous doctor, awaiting an introduction.

Smiling, the doctor continued. "I'm Dr. vanKessel. Carley Wilson is my patient. I've been expecting you." The doctor motioned towards the wealth of black chairs in the nearby waiting area and the two men moved towards them. Positioning themselves directly across from one another, the doctor continued. "Listen, Detective, I know you're just here to do your job and I empathize with your situation, but I'm afraid I have some discouraging news."

Watching the doctor's facial expression closely, Richard didn't feel very confident about what might be coming next.

The young doctor continued reluctantly. "Not long after we contacted you, Carley slipped into a coma. We didn't anticipate this, but it happened. We don't know why. She had regained consciousness, her vitals were good, and considering all she'd been through, we were hopeful that she'd remain stable."

Richard was speechless. His eyes were staring blankly, almost helplessly, at the dismal beige paint that covered the waiting area's walls.

"To be honest," the doctor continued, "we aren't exactly sure why this happened. We're running tests as we speak. However, it doesn't look like you're going to get your interview today after all."

Richard felt completely discouraged. Speaking with Carley would have been a chance at their first strong lead, and now having taken a turn for the worst, it totally knocked the wind out of his sail.

Dr. vanKessel rose from his chair and gave Richard a compassionate squeeze on the shoulder. "We can't anticipate how long she'll remain in this condition, or if she'll wake up again at all. This girl has been to hell and back these past few days and, quite frankly, we were surprised she was speaking at all so quickly after surgery."

"So, what now, Doc?" Richard anxiously ran his fingers through his hair and scratched determinedly at the back of his head.

"Pray," The kind doctor advised. "That's all you can do for her now." With a solemn nod, he headed towards the nurse's station and paused briefly to pick up a chart before looking back over his shoulder. "Sorry you came all the way down here for nothing, Detective. I'll be in touch if there's any change, okay?"

Richard nodded in appreciation and then leaned back in his chair. Wondering how Hannah was going to take the news, he pulled out his cell phone and made the call. When he heard her voice on the other end, all he said was, "Fuck."

Chapter Seventeen

MATT DAVIDSON DEPARTED HIS father's house, slamming the solid door behind him. After descending the steps leading to the cobblestone driveway, he climbed into his Bolero Red 1967 Chevy Camaro Z/28 while replaying the awkward situation he'd just been in. He was miserable and really just needed to shake it off. As he pulled onto the busy street, he accelerated right towards his favourite watering hole. After that fiasco, he needed a night out to blow off some steam, and he knew just the place to forget all his troubles. Temporarily at least.

Ten minutes later, Matt turned into the parking lot of the strip club he frequented and found an empty parking spot near the employee entrance. He climbed out of his car and made his way around the side of the graffiti-covered building while passing what was undeniably a drug deal in progress. Across the street, his eyes landed on a man and woman going at it on the hood of a black Mustang convertible. *Whatever would my father think*? Matt chuckled.

As Matt approached the front door of the seedy club, a bald, mammoth-sized bouncer with a tarantula tattooed on the top of his shaved head nodded at him and opened the opaque door.

"They cut you loose again, Matty? I heard you got busted for good this time?" The arrogant bouncer laughed as Matt playfully cuffed him on the side of the head. Winking, he crossed the threshold into the dimly lit bar where his only objective was to consume copious amounts of alcohol and, if he was lucky enough, find himself a fine-looking companion for the night. He milled through the crowd on his way to the bar, scoping out any potential companions. As he passed the bar, Matt reached over a bar stool to pick up the bottle of Corona that the experienced bartender had waiting for him. Holding it up in the air with a smile and quick wink, he signaled a thank you to the sexy bartender he knew only as Lexy.

The music was really loud. *Too much bass,* he thought, but it was a great tune. His eyes found the stage to his right and explored the movements of a gorgeous brunette with legs up to her armpits. She was confidently swinging herself around the brass pole, wearing only a G-string, a pilot's hat, and a black necktie. After her final spin on the pole, Matt watched her drop face down and begin slowly grinding her hips on the stage as if it were her lover.

Now that's hot, Matt thought.

The cheers and loud cat calls that erupted from the horny men was deafening as she provocatively removed her G-string. Turning his attention back to the crowd, Matt continued wandering through the busy club. The persistent flicker of the strobe lights throughout the sexy pilot girl's performance finally stopped. As he moved towards his favourite table, someone—hopefully a woman—unexpectedly grabbed his ass. Matt glanced over his shoulder to see a cute blonde with low-rise jeans and a pink cropped football jersey smiling back at him.

This one may even be of age, he thought, his dampened spirits now lifting. As he approached the small, round table in the corner of the bar where he normally sat, he noticed a man sitting by himself staring directly back at him.

Who's this tool? Matt wondered. He was way too clean cut to be in a place like this. The pressed shirt and khaki pants were tolerable, but the hair cut—this pretty boy looked like he had just stepped out of an issue of GQ. Matt realized that the weird expression on his face must have been obvious to the man as he noticed the stranger beginning to smile. He immediately got up from the table and moved towards Matt.

"Mr. Davidson?" The stranger questioned.

"Who's asking?" The skepticism in Matt's voice was loud and clear.

The stranger, now extending his hand out to shake Matt's, responded. "My name is Bobby Ross, and if you'd let me, I am here to help."

Matt looked stunned, still staring at the GQ geek standing in front of him with his hand outstretched. Reluctantly, Matt returned the handshake with one hand, while pulling a chair out from the table with his other. He swung the chair around and straddled it backwards, resting his arms on the back of it and facing the stranger. With both men noticing the awkward silence, Bobby cleared his throat and was the first to speak.

"Matt, as I mentioned, my name is Bobby Ross. I'm an investigative reporter with the Toronto Star."

Matt jumped in defensively. "Ah, shit, you've got to be kidding me? Another vulture just looking to get the dirt on me." Matt was pissed off and it showed.

Bobby didn't speak, knowing full well that Matt wasn't finished.

"I can't get a moment's peace with you guys always on my back." He continued his speech as Bobby just sat there and listened. "So, you think I fucked up, too? Well get in line. So does everyone else. If you were that interested in my story, you would have been at my bail hearing the other day, not wasting my time here now. I haven't done anything. I'm just here to blow off some steam. There's no crime in that, is there?"

Matt watched Bobby shake his head and then shift positions in his seat. "Look, Matt. I'm not here to exploit you. Actually, it's quite the opposite. And just for the record, I was at the courthouse the other day and witnessed the entire shit show."

Matt's eyes narrowed as his head tilted a little to the left. Looking straight into Bobby's eyes, he saw sincerity, but he was still skeptical. These assholes were always in his face, trying to dig up dirt where there wasn't any. He figured that since he was a nobody, people were trying to aim the fallout at his father—taint the good doctor's reputation with scandalous gossip about his wayward son. Well, he wasn't concerned about his father's reputation. He never really cared too much for his father, not after the way he treated Matt growing up. What bothered Matt was the constant interruptions in his personal life. How many times could they keep arresting him with only circumstantial evidence? He was fed up with all of it.

"So," Matt continued, "Why are you here and what the hell do you want from me? Are you following me?" His voice was still hesitant but a small part of him wanted to believe this stranger.

Choosing his words carefully, Bobby's response was truthful and direct. "Yes, as a matter of fact, I was waiting for you, Matt. I've been following your situation from the time you were first arrested three years ago. It was a big story, and everyone wanted a piece of it. However, most of these 'vultures,' to paraphrase you, only have one thing on their mind—themselves. They just want the big scoop and the money and notoriety that go with it. The difference is, I'm not like the rest of them. I'm not only in it to further my career. I'm in it for the truth and I find your story very curious."

Matt was confused. "What do you mean, 'curious?' You like following the fucked-up son of the famous doctor around to see what kind of trouble he'll get himself into next? Maybe get some dirt on him to smear his father's exceptional character—knock his pompous ass down a few notches, is that it?"

Matt took a long swig of his beer as his eyes found their way through the smoky haze generated by a fog machine and on to the sensual body of an Asian-American beauty now on stage. She was swinging a lasso wearing nothing but a cowboy hat and red G-string. He wondered if her voluptuous double Ds were the result of his father's handiwork. No way—who was he kidding? She'd never be able to afford the outrageous cost of his services.

Bobby continued talking, recapturing Matt's attention. "I thought this would be a good place to look for you. You mentioned this bar in an interview you gave two years ago, and you seemed to like it." Glancing around the room, Bobby finished with, "I can see why. There certainly are some very pretty ladies in here."

Bobby took a quick swig of his beer and said, "I guess you're wondering why I'm here."

Matt didn't respond right away, so Bobby continued. "I want to help you, Matt. I don't believe the charges against you. I think something really stinks here. I'm not sure what, but like I said earlier, I've been following your case from the start, and something just doesn't quite add up."

Matt's curiosity was piqued.

"During your little outburst in court the other day, you seemed thoroughly convinced that someone was setting you up. I guess what I'm trying to say is that I'd like to help you figure that out. That is, if you want me to?"

Matt was still trying to read this guy and decide for himself whether he was on the up and up. Ultimately, it boiled down to one simple fact: nobody believed he was innocent. So, if this guy was offering his help to prove this, Matt certainly wasn't going to be the one to stand in the way of him doing that.

Chapter Eighteen

KELLY SQUINTED AS HER eyes adjusted to the intense light suspended from the ceiling above her. Her head pounded and she felt strangely foggy. Her tongue slowly explored her split, swollen lips while her bloodied mouth was raw with cuts and crusted with the unmistakable taste of iron. She wasn't sure how much blood she'd swallowed, but she could certainly taste it. As she rolled her head from side to side, desperately trying to get her bearings, she suddenly became very aware of the fact that both of her wrists were restrained by leather straps, keeping her securely anchored to the cold table on which she lay. She struggled suddenly against the leather restraints—panic engulfing her mind and overcoming her body—but to no avail. The restraints didn't budge. Her ankles were also fastened securely in place, leaving her totally incapacitated, completely helpless, and at the mercy of her captor. As her body began to tremble and her head pounded even harder, the images of what she had done came rushing back to her.

What did I do? What in the name of God was I thinking? What would possess me to believe I could have escaped? Is this my punishment?

So many thoughts swarmed her frantic mind. Squinting, Kelly tried to see her surroundings, but the brilliance of the round light above her was so intense to her sensitive eyes, making it impossible. As her eyes fixated on the light itself, they started to tear from the sheer intensity. Blinking repeatedly, trying to familiarize them with the brilliance wasn't working; they just reflexively closed against the intensity. Kelly didn't want them closed. She'd just fought a fearful battle against the darkness and now she was forced to battle against the brightness. *This isn't fair,* she thought. *I just want to be able to see something. Anything!*

It was only then that she heard the muffled noises coming from somewhere to the right of her. It sounded like water running. Her eyes were still shut tight as she listened more closely to her surroundings. This time, not only did she hear water running, she heard the distinctive sound of someone washing something. Water was splashing and things were banging around what sounded like a sink. *Who's with me and what are they doing?* Her head spun quickly to the right when she suddenly heard whistling. Her captor was softly—yet sadistically—whistling the always annoying tune, "Don't Worry Be Happy."

Sick bastard, she thought, slowly trying to squirm her wrists free from their restraints. The running water stopped abruptly, but his constant movements continued to torment her. He was still out of her sight, banging things around haphazardly in the corner of the room. It sounded chaotic and disorganized, almost like he was searching for something. A loud clang echoed through the room when metal objects of some sort crashed together. Without warning, her body reflexively jerked with the sudden scare. It sounded like he dropped a stainless-steel bowl full of utensils, but in spite of that, the sick bastard never missed a beat from his whistling. She heard him fumbling as he retrieved whatever it was that he'd dropped and then slammed it down onto what sounded like a metal shelf of some kind.

Kelly's heart leapt, the fear inside of her growing with each passing second. That familiar sound instantly brought back the distant memory of the time she was rushed to the hospital to have her appendix removed. That's exactly what this reminded her of.

Surgery!

Oh my God!

Panic and adrenaline now surged lightning fast through her body as she felt a single tear trickle down her cheek and land in her ear. It hit her like a ton of bricks as she realized what was actually happening.

Bright lights, metal instruments, cold metal table. What's this sick bastard going to do to me? Driven by sheer terror and panic that now seized total control over her body, Kelly struggled frantically, desperate to free herself. It didn't matter though. No matter how hard she tried, her attempts were useless.

The whistling stopped.

She listened as the heavy footsteps came closer, her helpless body still strapped to the cold table. The light that was initially too bright for her eyes was now looking softer, more subdued—as if somebody was dimming them. Deep down, she knew that they were still as intense as they had been all along. It was her own eyes that were failing her. As the footsteps now reached the side of the table, she blinked three more times, the lights fading completely, then passed out.

Chapter Nineteen

After the disappointing trip to see Carley yielded nothing, Richard met up with Hannah at the station and they headed back over to the second crime scene to have another look. They had hoped Shane Kimball from the FIU would have something new to share with them, but he didn't. After another walk through the same gruesome scene, they headed back towards their squad car, both feeling disgusted as if it were their first time seeing it. No words were spoken until they were steadily seated in the cruiser. Even then, it was a few moments before Richard finally spoke.

"Are you okay?" he asked her warily.

Hannah took a deep breath before responding. "No, I am not okay, Richard. This is so messed up—and I can't shake the visual of what he did to that poor girl." Her hands came up to caress her temples with slow, circular motions, trying to massage away the horrendous images now embedded in her mind.

Richard sat in silence. Hannah knew he sensed her frustration and was giving her a moment to regroup. She never purposely meant to take her anger out on him, but sometimes it just happened. She watched as he gazed out the window, closely watching the investigators still cautiously working their way around the crime scene hoping to find evidence that would help catch this freak.

The moment was interrupted when Richard's cell phone rang loudly through the silent vehicle. Hannah watched as he raised the phone to his ear.

"Detective Young." He said softly into the phone, sounding rather deflated.

Hannah watched as he listened intently to the anonymous person on the other end. Quietly observing him, she noticed the small lines around the corners of his eyes and mouth. Some people referred to them as laugh lines. She could see how they could get that name. Richard did have a great smile, and a rather infectious laugh. She never really noticed how handsome he actually was. He was her partner—she never really looked at him that way before. But now that she had, she felt an unexpected smile emerging within her. She quickly dismissed that thought, bringing herself back to the reality of the situation just as Richard ended his conversation.

"Thanks, Jake. See you in a bit." Richard folded his phone closed and turned towards Hannah. "The labs are back on the material they found on the fence post at the first scene."

"And?" Hannah stared intently at him.

"They're not a match. One was from Carley's clothing and the other is an *unknown*."

Hannah smiled. "Did they run it for DNA?"

"Yeah, still waiting on that."

They were both silent as Richard put the car in reverse and backed out onto Ritson Road. As they made their way out towards the main road, Hannah was totally lost in thought. Up to this point, the killer had been extremely careful not to leave so much as a hair on any of his victims. Now, with this piece of material, they might finally get lucky. She just hoped that he had left something else behind at the scene.

As Richard slowed down, approaching the stop sign at Raglan Road, Hannah gasped as if she'd seen a ghost. Rounding the corner directly in front of them was her worst nightmare realized.

"What in the actual fuck is he doing here?" She cursed as her head turned, slowly tracking the direction of the police cruiser that had just made a left turn right in front of them. Hannah was pissed beyond words. She watched as Richard's hands tightened on the steering wheel and knew why her partner didn't say a damn word about what he had clearly just seen. "And why the hell is he headed towards my crime scene?"

Taking a deep breath, Richard finally spoke. "Well, there's only one way to find out." With that said, he glanced in his rearview mirror, then quickly over his left shoulder and made an abrupt U-turn. His acceleration was noticeable, gravel shooting out from beneath his tires, as he headed back towards the crime scene they had just left.

"That rotten son of a bitch," Hannah muttered. "Who the hell does he think he is anyway?"

The gravel crunched and spit loudly under the tires as Richard skidded to a stop in almost the exact same spot he had left only moments earlier. The car had barely come to a full stop before Hannah was out of the Charger and moving quickly towards the other police cruiser. As she came up behind the car that was now parked beside the coroner's wagon, she watched both the passenger and driver's side doors swing open.

A tall, attractive man slowly climbed out of the driver's side. As he rose to his feet, he slowly and dramatically adjusted his tan trench coat and straightened his paisley printed silk tie. Eyeing up the crime scene and ignoring Hannah as if she wasn't even there, he slammed the car door shut and started to walk in the opposite direction. As the second officer emerged from the passenger seat, he saw Hannah coming towards them and shook his head, announcing, "Now listen Hannah. We're just doing our jobs. Let's not make an issue of this, okay?"

Hannah erupted. "You stay out of this, Murphy. This doesn't concern you."

Detective Murphy raised both hands in the air as if conceding her point and leaned back against the cruiser, folding his arms across his chest. By this point, Richard had positioned himself right behind Hannah, ready to back his partner up if needed. Hannah turned and held her hand up, signaling him to stay out of it. She could tell he knew she just needed a couple minutes with this moron by herself.

"Just what the hell do you think you're doing here?" she called out to the driver of the car as he walked away from her.

He stopped in his tracks and slowly turned back towards her—a cocky smile now quite apparent on his lips. "Hannah, it's been a while. How have you been?"

"Don't you start with me, asshole," she angrily bit back. "This is my crime scene and you have no business being here."

The driver just smirked, sarcastically responding with, "*Your* crime scene? Oh, that's right. I forgot you're the only cop on the force." He moved towards her only to be immediately shot down again.

"This is *not* your jurisdiction and you damn well know it. Now this is the last time I'm going to ask you to leave, and then I'm going to make you." Hannah felt her blood pressure rising as she tried to grasp the nerve of this arrogant asshole.

"Newsflash, Hannah. This *is* my jurisdiction—almost two weeks now. I took a transfer from 41-Division, so from one detective to another, I guess that makes this *our* crime scene." Still wearing that smug smile, he added, "Did you miss me, Hannah?"

Hannah felt nauseous. She stared blankly at him for what seemed like an eternity before turning towards Richard, her eyes pleading as if to say, *make him take that back*.

Richard, standing there helpless, could do absolutely nothing about what had just happened. She knew he was just as shocked as she was.

The self-righteous detective continued. "Now, if you don't mind, I'd like to get back to work."

Hannah watched as the two detectives made their way through the brush towards Shane Kimball. Hannah and Richard were still standing motionless on the gravel as the detective stopped, turned back towards her and called out, "By the way, Hannah. You look fantastic."

Searching her flustered thoughts for the right response, the only words Hannah could come up with at that moment were, "Fuck you, Kent!"

Chapter Twenty

"slow down, mrs. griggs. Let's take this one step at a time." Detective Constable Jake Connors was trying his best to calm the distraught woman who, moments earlier, had stormed through the front doors of the station demanding to speak with someone immediately.

The woman was hysterical and yelling to anyone who would listen. When the Staff Sergeant at the front desk saw Jake passing by, he waved the detective over to see if he could help with the uncertain situation. Approaching the woman, Jake wondered whether she was a nutjob or sincere in her quest.

Pensively, Jake introduced himself, then asked, "Mrs. Griggs. What's wrong? What exactly is it that you need from us?" She finally made eye contact with Jake as he added, "You need to calm down and talk to me or else I won't be able to help you. Will you please let me help you?"

Nodding, Mrs. Griggs took a couple of long, deep breaths while wiping at her swollen eyes with a crumpled fistful of tissues. She stared intently at the clean-cut officer as he led her down the hall and into the detective's office. As she positioned herself in one of the visitors' chairs, Jake perched himself on the corner of his desk and didn't even blink when Mrs. Griggs continued right where she'd left off with the Staff Sergeant.

In a calmer, more monotone voice laden with disbelief, she numbly reported, "It's my daughter. She's missing."

Detective Connors' facial expression altered slightly. Maybe this woman wasn't crazy after all; maybe her concerns were valid.

"How long has it been since you've seen your daughter, Mrs. Griggs?" Jake was hesitant with his line of questioning, so as not to alarm her.

"She left for school on Tuesday and I haven't seen or heard from her since." She bowed her head now as the tears reemerged.

Jake's stomach tightened and he immediately had a bad feeling in his gut. He moved from his half-seated position on his desk around to the far side and sat in his chair. As he rolled the chair closer to his desk, he reached for his notebook and began taking a detailed statement from the worried mother. With everything needed to proceed within reach, he began to question her. There were definitely important things that needed to be asked.

"Mrs. Griggs. What is your daughter's name?" He was speaking softly now, hoping that his tone would help calm the distraught woman.

"Kelly. Her name is Kelly Lynn Griggs."

Writing this down, he continued. "And how old is Kelly?"

"She's twenty. She'll be twenty-one in May."

"Do you happen to have a recent photograph of your daughter with you?" Jake suspected that, as a mother, she most likely carried one in her purse. It just seemed to him the natural thing a mother would do.

Jake watched as her trembling hands rummaged through her purse until she succeeded in pulling out a picture of her only child. Quivering, she reached over and handed it to him, pausing briefly to glance at it one more time before surrendering it to him. He looked at the picture of Kelly and then at her mother. He could see the similarities in their features. Both were attractive women with dark hair and wide, almost helpless-looking brown eyes.

"Mrs. Griggs, did you and Kelly have a fight or disagreement of any kind the last time you saw her?"

She looked surprised at his question. "Absolutely not. Kelly and I never fought. That's exactly the reason her father isn't in the picture anymore—all the constant yelling and fighting. We just couldn't take it anymore. It was no life for either one of us, so I finally built up the courage to kick him out. He was a big drinker, you know."

Jake, understanding her implication, gave a sympathetic nod.

"Anyway," she continued, "because of that, we made a pact that with Leonard gone, we'd never have a good enough reason to fight again. And we don't. We get along famously."

Jake continued making notes in his book. "Was Kelly dating anyone, Mrs. Griggs?"

The woman shook her head. "No, not anyone serious. I mean, she'd go out on dates once in a while, but she didn't have a steady beau. The last time she went on a date was about two months ago. A young man named Matthew something. I can't remember his last name. Anyway, she was too focused on her schoolwork to get serious with anyone."

Jake looked up from his notes. "Schoolwork? Where does she go to school? What is she studying?"

"Kelly is getting her MScN—that's her Master of Science and Nursing at UOIT here in Oshawa. She's been studying and working so hard; her marks have been great and she's really excited because this is her final year."

Jake noted the proud maternal tone in her voice. "And you're sure that Kelly wasn't dating or maybe even regularly hanging around with anyone from school? Could there possibly have been someone that you might not have known about?" Jake stepped cautiously around this question. He didn't want to worry her in any way.

Firmly shaking her head, she said, "No. I'm positive. Kelly shared everything with me. If there was a boy in her life, I would know about him."

"Mrs. Griggs, you said the last time you saw your daughter was on Tuesday before she left for school?"

"That's right," she agreed.

"Well, it's Thursday now. Why didn't you report this sooner?"

Explaining in detail, she responded, "Well I tried to. I called the police yesterday morning when I found that her bed hadn't been slept in, but the officer said that Kelly is an adult and that adults don't always come home when they said they would. He told me to call her friends and any acquaintances she might have and to call back if she still didn't show up."

Jake shook his head. "Well, there is a protocol that we have to follow, however the officer should have taken your information and followed up with you."

Mrs. Griggs continued. "Well, I couldn't wait any more. I know my daughter and this is not like her. She doesn't stay away for days at a time, and no matter what the situation is she always calls to let me know where she is. She knows how much I worry about her. Something is wrong. Something is very, very wrong."

Jake continued with his questions, detailing everything, all the while his stomach continued to grow tighter and tighter. This was the fourth mother to file a missing person's report in the last two weeks and he couldn't help but glance across the hall through the window of Conference Room B. Looking back at him from those walls were the faces of four young women. Three had been identified, while the fourth—the Jane Doe from today that hadn't been reported missing yet—lay unclaimed in the morgue. Shuddering, Jake recognized that all four women had many similarities to Kelly Griggs, and all suffered from a grim outcome.

Chapter Twenty-One

HANNAH TURNED ON THE floor lamp in her living room as she entered her quaint condo, the soft amber light making the room feel cozy and inviting. The smokey grey walls and white accents soothed her. She remembered how she fought with Kent over the colour. He wanted baby blue. Hannah had just laughed. *Yeah, like that's ever going to happen*, she had enlightened him. For a brief moment her mind wandered back to her marriage, a time when she and Kent were actually happy and when coming home to this place meant being greeted at the door with a warm hug and gentle kiss. For an instant, Hannah felt sad. Making her way to the kitchen, she popped a frozen dinner into the microwave while her mind drifted back to that happier time. She recalled the night she arrived home after being promoted to Detective Sergeant.

"Kent," Hannah called out. "I'm home. Are you here?"

As Hannah switched on the living room lamp her heart leapt. Her eyes surveyed the room, but her brain couldn't comprehend what she saw. Hundreds of tiny red rose petals covered the hardwood floor, the furniture, and even disappeared down the hallway towards their bedroom. Soft music was coming from the stereo in the corner of the room and a delicious aroma was permeating from the kitchen off to the right. As she stepped tentatively into the kitchen her eyes landed on Kent, a smile on his lips that radiated the happiness he obviously felt for her and the wonderful news of her promotion.

"I made you a celebratory dinner, Detective Sergeant. Poached salmon a la Kent. Your favourite." Hannah smiled at the man she had given her heart to. The man she knew she would be spending the rest of her life with.

The beeping of the timer on the microwave brought Hannah abruptly back to the present.

"Asshole," she muttered as she made her way down the hall towards her bedroom.

A shower was just what the doctor ordered to wash away her grueling day. Hannah undressed slowly, still preoccupied with the memory that had just popped to mind. She pulled on her bathrobe and made her way to the bathroom. She turned on the shower, then quickly changed her mind. Instead, she reached for the rubber stopper and plugged the tub.

"Bubble bath," she whispered. "Even better."

Hannah adjusted the temperature of the bath water and made her way back to the kitchen. Even though her dinner was ready, she opted for the bath first. Opening the fridge door, she scanned the contents quickly before her eyes landed on it. Smiling, she reached in and pulled out the partly finished bottle of Sauvignon Blanc. Opening the cupboard above the sink, she picked out a pinwheel-decorated crystal wine glass and returned to the bathroom. Setting the bottle and glass beside the tub, she proceeded to light three candles that sat along the bottom edge of the tub. Perching on the edge, her hand slowly and rhythmically moved the water around in a figure eight motion. As it continued to fill, her mind wandered back to that memory from almost two years ago.

"Kent, dinner was wonderful. Thank you. You really didn't have to do this." Hannah was grateful for dinner. And for Kent.

"I know I didn't have to; I wanted to. You deserve it, Hannah. You've worked really hard for this and I'm so proud of you."

With that said, Kent leaned in and kissed her. It was a nice kiss, a tender kiss. They were so connected at that very moment, the world felt like it had stopped just for them. Brushing a lock of hair back behind her ear, Kent's lips moved across her cheek until they found her earlobe. After gently kissing her ear, his lips hovered there for a moment as he softly whispered three words. "I love you."

Hannah felt her heart jump as he slowly rose from his chair and scooped her into his strong arms to carry her over the rose petals, down the hall, and into their bedroom. They made love until the early morning hours and fell asleep in each other's arms. The last thing Hannah remembered before drifting off to sleep was Kent whispering into her ear, "I love you, Kitten."

Hannah turned off the faucet. She couldn't help but remember that pivotal night. In one respect, it was a night that was unsurpassed by any other. However, in retrospect, it was probably the worst night of her life. The man she had fallen in love with, the man she trusted like no other person on earth, the man who promised never to break her heart like so many others had in the past, had just cast a shadow of doubt over everything she believed to be so perfect. It was not in his actions. It was his words; words that would haunt Hannah until her dying day.

"I love you, Kitten."

Four simple words. Words that, to most people, would be considered a term of endearment. But to Hannah it was a bright red flag. The more she replayed those words in her head, the more uneasy she felt and the more her stomach knotted. Kent always said she over analyzed things. Maybe he was right. But that was her job. Whether he liked it or not, that was the way her mind worked. That's what made her so good at her job: the ability to smell bullshit.

Hannah carefully stepped into the hot bath water, steam filling the small room that was tastefully decorated. The soft creamy colour on three of the walls made her feel like she'd stepped into a thick, vanilla milkshake, while the accent wall was a rich navy tone displaying a framed picture of white birch trees. She lowered herself cautiously into the hot water and poured a glass of wine. After taking a sip from her wine glass and replacing it carefully on the edge of the tub, she lay back in the water and slowly, almost rhythmically, pulled the hot water up over her body with her hands. Sinking even lower in the tub until only her face was above the surface, she closed her eyes and drifted back to her earlier thoughts.

"What the hell is that supposed to mean, Hannah?" Kent snapped defensively.

"It's exactly what it sounds like, Kent. It's not a trick question. I asked if you are having an affair. A simple yes or no will do."

Hannah was quite calm, even though she felt like she was ready to explode. She had to confront him. It had been eating away at her since the night of her promotion. In her mind, things just weren't adding up. Late meetings, mystery phone calls, secret texts. These were all things that she usually disregarded and thought nothing of. But since that night she was overly aware of all of Kent's actions.

"What the hell would make you think I'm having an affair?" Kent was extremely hostile and defensive, which didn't bode well for him considering the circumstances.

"I'll tell you why, Kent." Hannah took a deep breath before she proceeded. "'I love you, Kitten.'"

"What?" Kent looked baffled.

"'I love you, Kitten.' That's what you said to me the other night."

"So?" His face was contorted now, looking at her as if he'd just eaten something bad.

"Kent, we've been together for six years and never once in all that time have you called me Kitten." Hannah studied Kent's face as he stood there, seemingly frozen in place.

"So?" Hannah pressed. "Who the hell is Kitten?"

Hannah's stomach tightened as she watched Kent begin to stammer, not quite sure how to respond.

"So just because I…you think that just because I called you Kitten…you really think that means that I'm screwing around on you or something?"

His nervousness and discomfort were blatantly obvious now. The reality of his body language was filling Hannah's stomach with a nauseating feeling of betrayal. Suspecting Kent was up to something was one thing, but now, being faced with the stark reality of it, it felt like she was unexpectedly hit by a cement truck.

"I don't get you, Hannah." Kent was irate. "You always do this. You analyze every goddamned thing I say. I'm sick of your bullshit, Hannah! Jesus Christ. 'Kitten.' I say one lousy thing and all of a sudden I'm having an affair? That's typical."

Kent was pacing around the living room, not really sure what to do next. Hannah was starting to regret bringing this up, but she needed to ask the question. Even if she didn't like the answer.

And she didn't.

Kent was in a rage of denial now, acting like a cornered animal with no escape. She knew it—she knew it for sure now. Kent could deny it as much as he wanted to, but Hannah now realized the truth. He was having an affair and it was only a matter of time until he admitted it.

Hannah sat up in the tub and reached for her glass of wine. Swallowing a large gulp, she wiped a tear from her cheek. She hated the fact that she sometimes still cried over Kent, but the truth of the matter was: she still hadn't gotten over how badly he betrayed her. As she continued to soak in the tub, she topped up the hot water again. *Why did he do that to me?* She thought they were happy. She trusted him to be the man who would never hurt her, never lie to her, and never stray from their marriage. They shared everything. Every dream, every goal, and every aspiration. They had no secrets from each other. They were best friends who still shared laughter and romance. Their marriage hadn't lost its spice. Whenever Hannah looked at Kent, she was drawn to him so wholly and completely. He was like a drug that she couldn't get enough of. When she looked into his deep green eyes, she got lost in them. It was like she could see his soul—see his every thought. What she saw was a wonderful man who made her believe again. He made her believe that not all men were liars, that not all men were cheaters. That he was different. He was the exception to the rule. He was the one man who would never do any of those things to her.

Laughing cynically, she wiped another tear from her cheek. *What a crock of shit,* she thought. *All men are the same. They lie, they cheat, and they only ever think of themselves.*

Hannah's thoughts were interrupted by the distinct ring of her landline. She couldn't be bothered getting out of the tub and she certainly didn't feel like talking to anyone right now, so she let her out-of-date—but completely reliable—answering machine pick it up. She let her eyes drift shut as she welcomed the sound of the soothing voice escaping through the machine in her living room.

It was the voice of Richard Young.

Chapter Twenty-Two

HANNAH PLACED HER DINNER on the coffee table and reached for the phone. As she dialed Richard's number, she took a quick bite of her potatoes and was still chewing when he answered.

"Hey, it's me." She said, swallowing quickly. "What's up?"

"I just got a call from Mark Goslin." Richard remarked.

"Who?" Hannah questioned, the name sounding familiar but feeling too mentally exhausted to place it.

"Mark Goslin. The U of T kid who found Carley Wilson."

Hannah nodded as she wiped her mouth with her napkin. "Really? What did he want?"

"He asked if he could meet with us. It seems he's remembered something else about that night and he thought it might be important."

"Interesting. When does he want to meet?"

"He's coming in first thing in the morning. Thought I'd give you a heads up."

"Thanks, Richard, but you really didn't have to do that." Hannah paused before finishing. She got the feeling there was more he had to say. "What's really on your mind, Richard?"

"What do you mean? I just wanted to fill you in, that's all." Richard sounded a little defensive.

"Richard?" Hannah pushed, sounding a little skeptical. "I find it hard to believe that you had nothing better to do at eleven-thirty at night than to call and tell me something that could easily have waited until morning. You know I'm always in the office by seven."

There was a lull on the other end of the phone. After a few seconds he finally broke the silence. "Well, I guess I just wanted to see how you were doing. You had a pretty rotten day, and I was concerned about you, that's all." Richard's tone was sincere.

"Thanks, Richard. I'm doing okay, and I appreciate your concern. I just took a nice hot bath and I'm about to enjoy a gourmet feast of Salisbury steak with mashed potatoes, courtesy of Lean Cuisine."

Richard chuckled. "Um, sounds…pathetic."

"Yeah, well, to be honest, it is." Hannah replied, looking down at her pitiful plastic tray of food. "I'd give anything for a nice sit-down restaurant at this point. I'm sick of frozen entrees."

Richard laughed again. "Well, it sure as hell beats the bowl of Ramen noodles I just devoured."

Hannah laughed, picturing the confirmed bachelor eating his noodles, most likely right from the pot.

"We're a couple of pathetic singletons, Richard. You know that? How sad are we?"

Richard paused again before speaking.

"Maybe we should fix that. Why don't you and I make a pact to have a real meal in a nice restaurant one day soon?"

Hannah thought about it for a moment before responding.

"You know what, Richard? That sounds like a fabulous idea. Deal."

"Anyway," he continued, "I just wanted to make sure you were alright. I'll see you in the morning—with coffee."

"Thanks, Richard. Have a good night."

"Goodnight, Hannah. Sleep well."

As she replaced the phone on the charger, Hannah couldn't help but think about Richard. He was such a decent man—the total opposite of Kent. She wondered if he was actually serious about having dinner together sometime. The longer she thought about it, the more the doubt crept into her mind.

Nah, he couldn't be serious, she thought. *But wouldn't it be nice if he were?*

Chapter Twenty-Three

HANNAH ARRIVED AT THE station just before seven in the morning. She wanted to go over some things before she and Richard met with Mark Goslin. Hopefully Mark would have something helpful for them, but she wasn't holding her breath. As she leafed through the papers on her desk, she couldn't help but glance up at the wall, which displayed a gruesome array of photographs of the five victims—three identified, one Jane Doe and now one missing. She stood up from her chair and moved towards them, cautiously scanning from one photo to the next. She paused in front of one picture from yesterday's second crime scene. Looking at the Jane Doe, her stomach tightened and she felt completely helpless, a feeling she wasn't totally used to. Looking back over her shoulder towards her desk, her eyes landed on a stack of phone messages that, until now, had gone unreturned. Turning her attention away from the pictures, she moved back to her desk and started flipping through the messages. Most could wait, however there were two that stood out like a sore thumb. One from her lawyer, the other from Bobby Ross.

Bobby Ross, she thought. *Why does that name sound so familiar?* She picked up the phone to return his call when a sudden movement interrupted her. She looked up to see Kent approaching her desk, an arrogant smile on his face.

"What the hell do you want, Kent?" Hannah fidgeted with the papers on her desk. If she didn't keep her hands busy, she'd be tempted to punch that smug look off his face.

"I just thought I'd bring you a coffee, Hannah. I figured you'd be here early working on the case." He leaned over and placed the hot cup on the desk directly in front of her.

Searching her head for a quick comeback—and apparently not finding one—all she said was, "Thanks, but I'm not thirsty."

"Aw, come on, Hannah. It's seven in the morning. You know you usually have at least three cups of coffee before eight a.m. I'm just trying to be cordial, seeing as we're going to be working together now."

Hannah closed her eyes and paused before speaking. She wanted to be mature about the situation and not let their personal life intrude on what was now going to be their professional relationship. This meant choosing her words carefully so as not to anger the beast.

"Kent, yes, you're a detective working here now, but let's get something straight right here, right now. You are not my partner, you do not bring me coffee, and you don't even think about talking to me unless it has something to do with this case. We are not friends, we are not buddies, and we are not even acquaintances. We are nothing. You got that?"

With that blunt point made perfectly clear, she solidified it by dropping her untouched coffee into the wastebasket and returning her focus to the mound of paperwork on her desk.

"Have it your way, Hannah." With that, Kent turned and walked slowly out of her office.

After he left, Hannah started second-guessing her bold actions. *Am I being irrational?* she wondered. *After all, he was only trying to be civil. Nope*! She shook that thought away almost as quickly as it'd entered her mind—just as the images of Kent and his lover vividly exploded right to the top of her memory bank. *You idiot,* she thought. *What the hell were you thinking wasting a perfectly good coffee like that? You should have done something more useful with it, like throwing it on his crotch.* A smile quickly emerged as she joyfully imagined that scenario. It would have her grinning for hours. Hannah shook her head to regain focus as she picked up the phone for the second time.

Bobby Ross? The only way to remember who this person was would be to call him back. She punched the numbers on the phone and waited for someone to answer. Two rings, three rings, voicemail.

"Great." She said aloud. "I guess we're still playing phone tag."

As she prepared to leave a detailed message, as prompted by the polite voice on the recording, she heard Richard's husky voice as he came into her office.

"Are you talking to yourself again? You know, they say that's the first sign of senility." Richard's smile was bright as he carried a tray of coffee towards her desk. Losing her train of thought, Hannah decided to hang up and try this Bobby guy later. Richard handed her one of the cups and she was elated. She'd hoped he would remember to bring coffee this morning, especially after having trashed a perfectly good one only moments earlier out of mere spite. She leaned back in her chair and inhaled the fresh aroma before taking her first sip. She loved the smell of coffee first thing in the morning.

"Well, did you get any sleep last night?" Richard asked curiously.

"No, not really. My mind was on other things." What she really wanted to say was that since they'd spoken on the phone last night, her mind had only been on him. Instead, she kept that little tidbit to herself.

"Is Mark Goslin here yet?" She asked, rising from her chair.

"Yeah, they're all set up down the hall. Ready to go find out what he has to say?"

Hannah smiled. "Ready as I'll ever be."

With that, they carried their coffees down the hall, opened the door leading into the interview room, and Richard closed the door behind them.

"Hi Mark." Hannah smiled, extending her hand to shake his. "It's nice to see you again. How are you doing with all of this?"

"I'm okay." Mark nodded as he shook her hand and then Richard's.

"So, Mark. Detective Young here tells me you may have remembered something else from the other night."

Mark's eyes wandered to Richard and then back to her. "Yeah, I don't know if it's going to mean anything to you guys or not, but I thought I should mention it just in case. I don't know why I didn't think of it when I was here before. It just kind of came back to me last night."

Hannah's caring eyes found Mark's and, while trying to reassure him, she pulled out one of the chairs and sat down beside him. "Sometimes," she said, "when people endure a traumatic experience, their mind will block things out. It's a kind of protective mechanism that's built into our bodies. It's a way of protecting us when we're in shock or experience a trauma."

She watched as Mark nodded, his hands fidgeting with the pull string on his U of T hoodie, then continued. "For some reason, sometimes we just need a little time for those memories to come back to us. Anything you have to tell us may be useful. Why don't you tell us what else you've remembered and let us decide if it's relevant?" Hannah took that time to pause, wait, and just listen to what he had to share.

"Well, it suddenly hit me that when I was on the road with Carley, talking to the 911 dispatcher, a car came by; kind of out of nowhere."

"A car? I thought you said nobody was around?" Richard questioned, looking at Hannah.

"I know—I have no idea how I forgot that," Mark said, shaking his head. "I guess I was a little shaken up. Well…" he said truthfully, "a lot shaken up."

Hannah cut in politely with her next questions. "Do you know what make, model, or colour it was? Did you get a look at the driver or the license plate? Was there anything about this car that stood out to you?" Hannah paused for a moment, awaiting his response.

"I don't know exactly. I guess when I was replaying it in my head, something just didn't quite add up. And no, I didn't get a good look at his face or the license plate." He looked back and forth between the two detectives, trying to decide which one looked more confused.

Disappointed that he was unable to give a description of either the driver or car, Hannah asked, "What do you mean, something didn't add up?"

"Well, for starters, it seemed to come out of nowhere. I don't remember seeing any headlights approaching or hearing any motor coming my way. It just seems a little weird now that I look back on it, that's all."

Hannah made some notes in her book while Richard moved around the table, clearly trying to make sense of what Mark had just shared. Hannah knew they would have to make another trip out to the crime scene to have another look around the area.

"Is there anything else you remember about that night, Mark?" Hannah's tone was empathetic.

"Well, like I said, I don't remember the make or colour of the car, but what I do remember is yelling to him for help as he got closer, and he just stared at me."

"He didn't offer any assistance at all?" Hannah leaned forward in her chair and tucked a stray lock of hair behind one ear, her chin coming to rest on her hand.

"Nope," Mark said. "He didn't even flinch. He just stared at me and then kept driving. I'm pretty sure he was mumbling something as he drove away, but I couldn't make it out. I was too focused on what the 911 dispatcher was telling me to do, but as he drove away, I'm pretty sure I called him an asshole."

Hannah stood up rubbing the back of her neck and headed over towards Richard. Very quietly, with her back to Mark, she whispered, "Are you thinking what I'm thinking?"

Richard smiled. "I believe I am. I'll take care of it."

Mark watched as Richard quickly left the room, leaving Hannah still positioned with her back to him. Turning around slowly, she smiled at Mark.

Looking a little confused himself now, he smiled and asked, "Was it something I said?"

Hannah smiled back and said, "Yes, I believe it was."

Chapter Twenty-Four

HANNAH STAYED WITH MARK in the interrogation room while Richard made his way promptly down the corridor towards the elevators. While he was pushing the elevator call button with his left hand, his right hand was reaching into his suit pocket for his phone. Glancing down as he quickly punched in some numbers, he continued through the open doors of the elevator and pushed the button marked L2. The doors closed in front of him as he spoke.

"Hey Warren, it's Richard Young. I need you to do me a favor. I'm on my way down."

Placing the phone back in his pocket, he stared up at the descending numbers above the elevator doors and prayed that Warren would be the man to help him. He hoped that while he was following up on this lead, Hannah was going to be able to further jog Mark's memory.

Upstairs in the interview room, Hannah continued her line of questions with Mark.

"Mark, do you remember anything at all about the man you saw in that car? Anything at all?" Hannah was hoping that if he remembered the car, he might remember a description.

Mark shook his head. "I don't think so. It was dark and it happened pretty fast."

"Okay, then. Let's go back to the car. What do you remember about the car?"

Mark paused, visibly searching his memory.

Hannah could tell he desperately wanted to help, but it was clear that his memory was still a little foggy. She continued, trying to trigger the mental images trapped somewhere deep in the recesses of his subconscious brain. "Was it a big car? A little car? Van or SUV?"

"It was a big car." Mark sparked to life. "Yeah, I remember now. It was a big car—old—like a Cutlass or something. One of those clunky V8 gas-guzzlers," he announced, seeming proud of himself for suddenly remembering this.

"Okay, great. Do you remember what colour it was?"

"It was a dark colour. Maybe blue or black. And I remember there was a lot of nasty exhaust coming out of the tail pipe. It was strong; almost made me choke." Mark seemed pleased with his sudden recollection of details, and it showed in his face. He was shifting anxiously in his seat, obviously proud that he was able to help.

Hannah, still taking notes, looked up at Mark and saw that his movements had suddenly stopped. She stopped writing and stared at the expression on his face. "Are you okay, Mark?"

"There was something else about the car," he said.

"What is it? What else do you remember?"

"I know this sounds bizarre and almost impossible to believe, but I remember seeing a bumper sticker on the car. After I called him an asshole and he was driving away, I distinctly remember staring at the back of the car—at that bumper sticker."

With hope apparent in her voice, Hannah asked, "Mark, if you were looking at the back of the car, are you sure you didn't get a glimpse of the license plate?"

"No, I didn't. I was focused on the bumper sticker because it was so unique."

Feeling a little disheartened that he wasn't able to recall the license plate, she asked, "What was it that made the bumper sticker so unique?"

"It was simple. All it said was BLONDES ARE NOT DUMB."

Hannah looked quizzically at Mark. "Why is that so unique?"

Mark's expression turned into a small grin before he answered. "Because it was stuck on upside down."

Hannah slowly smiled, too. *Cute,* she thought, but how many of those stickers were in circulation? Thousands, probably. At any rate, it was something to follow up on. Hannah's mind momentarily shifted to Richard and wondered how he was making out with Warren.

Downstairs, the elevator doors opened and Richard stepped out onto the second floor. He turned to his right and headed towards the 911 Call Centre. As he entered what he considered to be the heartbeat of the police station, his eyes scanned the many call stations and dedicated switchboard operators, in search of one particular person. Nodding at the civilian contractors as he made his way through the complicated maze of cubicles and computer systems, he spotted Warren in the back corner.

Warren was smiling while waving him towards his desk. Approaching his dispatcher friend, Richard extended his right arm and shook his hand with a strength and confidence acquired over many years of meet and greets.

Warren was the first to speak. "What can I do for you, Richard? You sounded urgent on the phone."

"Well, I don't know if you can help me or not," Richard said, "but I'd sure as hell like you to give it a shot."

"I'll do my best," he said. "Shoot."

"I've got a witness upstairs with D.S. Phillips who has indicated that one of your dispatchers may have inadvertently caught something important on tape."

Warren looked perplexed. "What do you mean exactly?"

"I've got a young man up there who called 911 from a crime scene two days ago and, if my hunch is right, more than just his conversation with the dispatcher was actually recorded."

"Like what?" Warren asked.

"Like someone else at the scene who was talking in the background. Is there any way we could cue up the recording and have a listen?"

"Sure we can, Richard, but you know it's a crap shoot, right?"

"I know it is, but right now, I'm willing to roll the dice."

Chapter Twenty-Five

HANNAH SMILED AS SHE ran into Jake coming back from the break room, coffee in hand.

"Hey Jake, I've got something that I'd like you to follow up on for me."

"Sure, what is it?" He asked after swallowing a gulp of his long overdue caffeine fix.

"I just had another sit-down with Mark Goslin," Hannah said, reminding Jake of who he was, "and he seems to remember a lot more about the other night than he initially did."

"That's great," Jake nodded. "Anything solid?"

"Not yet, but certainly some good places to start. Richard is following up on one of the leads," Hannah continued, "but right now, I was hoping you could follow up on the other one. I've got something else that I have to take care of."

"Sure, what do you need me to do?" Jake seemed eager to help and had an abundance of energy when it came to this case—even more so than usual. Hannah was certain it was because he strongly believed there was some connection with his sister's death.

Hannah proceeded to fill Jake in on the details. "Mark said he remembered a car pulling up out of nowhere when he was with Carley. He thinks it was a dark blue or black car, older model, similar to a Cutlass. He didn't get the license plate number, but it was old enough to be burning a lot of oil—lots of thick emissions—and it had a distinctive sticker on the driver's side bumper."

"What did it say?" he asked, taking another sip of his coffee.

"It said BLONDES ARE NOT DUMB—but it was stuck on upside down."

Jake smiled. "Cute. I actually remember seeing that one before, but it was years ago. If there aren't too many left in circulation, we may just get lucky."

"You never know," she said. "Anyway, if you don't mind running a search on the vehicle and bumper sticker. Any hits we get, we can run through Service Ontario and start pulling names. Who knows, we may just catch a break yet."

Jake had already turned and was headed back to his desk when Hannah's phone rang.

"Phillips," she answered. Hannah was originally on her way down to the second floor to see how Richard was making out with Warren and the 911 recording. Instead, she stopped dead in her tracks as she listened intently to the voice on the other end of the phone. She quickly started moving towards the elevators again as she said, "Thanks, we're on our way."

Keeping her phone in hand as she entered the open elevator doors, she pushed the button marked P and immediately called Richard.

When he answered, all she said was, "Hey, it's me. Meet me in the parking garage, we've got a lead."

Hannah waited for Richard beside the unmarked cruiser in the damp garage. As her eyes scanned the underground lot, she saw lots of white police cars, nicely washed and waxed, impeccably maintained. There were some civilian vehicles as well—officers' personal vehicles, and those of the civilian contractors, secretaries, and maintenance staff that all converged in this building on a full-time basis. She saw the drive through car wash made available to the officers to help maintain the appearance of their patrol cars. She had to laugh remembering the time that her car got stuck in the unpredictable wash. What a sight that was. With no maintenance staff around to help her at the time, she was left with no choice but to climb out of the vehicle while the wash was still running at full tilt. She was soaked from head to toe. It was absolutely nothing she'd soon forget. Still smiling at the memory, she glimpsed a black SUV parked at the far end of the underground. Before she even had a chance to speculate on who got the new ride, Richard came flying out of the elevator like a bat out of hell. "Alright," he announced. "Let's get this show on the road."

Richard and Hannah both climbed into their grey Charger and headed towards the exit ramp. Even though they were not going fast, loud screeching emanated from the garage as the tires rounded the turns on their way out, up the steep incline towards the exit, and under the arm of the parking barricade. They turned onto Centre Street and headed downtown towards the 401. It would take the better part of an hour to get to the pathologist's office at the Centre of Forensic Sciences, so Hannah started to recap her phone call with Dr. Lucas. Both thoroughly engrossed in their conversation during the commute to the lab in Toronto, neither of them was aware of the black SUV now following them.

Chapter Twenty-Six

RICHARD LOOKED SURPRISED AND impressed when Hannah passed on the update from Nicky. "That's incredible—dental records already. That was fast."

Hannah was equally impressed. Dr. Lucas must have pulled some serious strings to get those results so quickly. "When she called," Hannah continued, "she said that she'd spoken with the pathologist who'd performed the autopsy and that he'd found something interesting and wanted to meet asap to go over his findings."

"She didn't tell you anything else on the phone?"

"No, she said the pathologist wanted to show us in person. Must be something big." Hannah was beyond anxious to find out the identity of this young woman. Since Carley remained in a coma, unable to speak, this was the only approach available at the moment to hopefully find any leads that might help unmask this predator. Maybe now they'd be able to link them in some way.

Hannah's hands reflexively grabbed the dashboard as Richard squealed to a sudden stop. The driver of the Lexus in front of them had slammed suddenly on her breaks to avoid hitting a German Shepherd that had come bounding into traffic from a nearby driveway. The dog's owner stood looking mortified at the end of the hedge-bordered driveway. She was trying desperately to leash the animal and looked remorseful for almost causing an accident. She did the polite, almost embarrassed, nod as both vehicles started to accelerate.

"That's it, lady. Control your wild beast." Richard laughed as he watched the owner getting farther away through his rear-view mirror. "You gotta love that. The dog weighs twice as much as the owner. Good luck with the obedience training, lady." They both snickered.

Roughly fifty minutes later, they pulled into the packed parking lot at the CFS building. Richard parked the cruiser, then they made their way across the parking lot and through the revolving front door into the lobby. Holding their badges up for security to see as they passed by, they promptly continued on their way to the bank of elevators to the right of the front entrance. This wasn't their first rodeo. They knew exactly where to go and what the procedures were.

Once in the elevator, they pushed B1 and headed to the basement, where the pathologist's office was located. It always felt so ominous down there and Hannah never seemed to get used to her visits, but unfortunately it was all part of the job. Exiting the elevator, Hannah and Richard's footsteps on the hard cement floor echoed loudly against the grey cinder block walls as they descended the sloping hallway towards the morgue's autopsy rooms. Security lights were anchored to the ceiling intermittently, casting a soft amber hue amidst the occasional fluorescent light fixture. Hannah got a sudden chill and adjusted her jacket accordingly. She didn't like being here at all. It usually meant that someone had met with an unfortunate demise and it was her job to help put all the pieces together.

As they rounded the corner into the cold, uninviting room, they were greeted by the pathologist who had performed the autopsy, Dr. Paul Wilchuck. He was wearing a baby blue gown, matching cap, and white latex gloves. He was adjusting his glasses and discussing an X-ray with his lab assistant. Both Richard and Hannah had worked with Paul over the years on many different cases. As the Chief Medical Examiner, he was absolutely brilliant and incredibly thorough. Hannah was confident that if there was anything unusual, he'd be the man to find it.

Richard spoke first. "Paul, it's great to see you again. Not always the best circumstances, but regardless, a pleasure." Richard nodded, signifying the conclusion of his greeting.

Hannah's eyes scoped out the draped outline of a body lying on the stainless-steel exam table. Almost everything in the room was stainless steel. She couldn't help but notice the strong odour of iron that lingered in the air. It was a cloying remnant after draining the blood from the body before the internal autopsy began. The overpowering smell still made her queasy, even after all these years.

Hannah's gaze finally left the autopsy table, in search of Dr. Wilchuck instead. With a smile and a quick nod, Hannah jumped right down to business. "So, what have you got for us, doctor? Who's our victim?" she asked.

"Well, I pulled a few strings and we got lucky. Turns out, your vic here had a very unique dental abnormality that narrowed down the search tremendously. You see this?" he said, pointing to the dental X-ray displayed in the view box. "Your victim suffered from a condition called Hyperdontia."

Recognizing the confused looks on the detectives' faces, Dr. Wilchuck proceeded to explain further. "Hyperdontia is the presence of one or more extra teeth in the maxilla—or upper jawbone. It simply means that your victim had an extra fourth molar on the upper right side of her mouth. Given the uniqueness of the dental impressions, that made narrowing down the field a little less challenging."

"That's unusual, alright," Hannah remarked. "Wouldn't you think that she would have had that removed or repaired over the years?" Hannah shrugged, glancing over at Paul.

"Nah, removing it would have only caused her unnecessary pain. As unusual as it is, it probably never even bothered her. It would have been there from the time her molars came in. It probably just seemed normal to her—her body would have just naturally compensated over the years, so she wouldn't have even known the difference."

Richard looked at Dr. Wilchuck, who was now leaning next to the X-ray box that contained their victim's dental films. "Well, I guess it's a good thing for us that she never had it repaired. At least now she won't be a Jane Doe anymore."

Hannah was nodding in agreement as she directed the million-dollar question to the pathologist. "So, Paul, tell me. Who's our victim?"

The doctor reached for a manila file folder on the stainless-steel counter, opened it, and lifted the top page to reveal the name written on the page beneath it.

"As I informed Detective Connors when he called, her name is Sydney Anne Ashton. She's nineteen years old, blonde hair, blue eyes, 5'4", and petite, weighing 110 pounds. In speaking with the detective just before you got here, he said that she'd last been seen by her mother leaving for school five days ago." The doctor proceeded to pass the file folder to Hannah so that she and Richard could look through it as he spoke.

"Five days ago? Why wasn't she reported missing?" Hannah was confused. *What kind of mother doesn't notice her daughter is missing?* she wondered.

At that point, the doctor jumped in with some solid advice. "Well, that's where it gets a little confusing," he said. "I think this is the point where you call and speak to Detective Connors. He can fill you in more—that's his job and way out of my scope."

Hannah was punching Jake's digits into her phone even before Paul finished his sentence. Jake answered on the second ring.

"Connors."

As Hannah paced the concrete floor in the dank basement, she put Jake on speakerphone so Richard could hear their conversation. "Hey Jake, we're still down at the CFS with Dr. Wilchuck. He mentioned you had an update for us."

Jake proceeded to inform them of the whirlwind of things that had transpired over the last hour since he'd seen Hannah. This included his phone call with the pathologist, as well as notifying the victim's next of kin. In this case, it was Sydney's mother, Nancy Ashton.

"Hannah, I just left her and she was absolutely devastated—completely distraught, but also immediately confused. She demanded to know why there hadn't been more done to help find her daughter."

Hannah was baffled by this comment. Shrugging her shoulders, she asked, "What the hell does she mean, '*more done*?' How could we *do* anything if she hadn't reported Sydney missing in the first place?"

Jake attempted to clarify. "Mrs. Ashton claims she *did* report this to the police—several times. She told the officer on the phone that she had special circumstances, making it difficult for her to file the missing person's report in person, but was clearly under the impression that the police had been out looking for her the entire time."

Still totally confused, Hannah sighed, wanting to clear up the obvious. Doubtingly, she reiterated, "Special circumstances? What special circumstances would she be referring to?"

As Jake began to answer the crucial question, his sentences became choppy and garbled. All that they could make out was bits and pieces of random words, leaving Jake's sentences totally unintelligible. Hannah was sure being in the basement had a lot to do with the interrupted cell service, but it didn't make it any less frustrating. Especially when they were on the verge of learning the special circumstances Jake was referring to. They'd have to wait until they were back upstairs and had a signal again to find out the rest of the story. Tucking her phone back into her jacket pocket, she turned her attention back to Paul.

"So, what did you find as the official cause of death?"

Before he responded, the pathologist carefully pulled the sheet back to reveal the remains of Sydney Ashton. With gloved hands, and using a sterile instrument as a mock pointer, he proceeded to present and describe his findings.

"Well, as you can see, the injuries are numerous and quite varied. She has multiple lacerations over her entire body, most likely inflicted during violent and repeated confrontations with her captor. There are ligature marks with moderate bruising around her neck, wrists, and ankles. There are two fractures in the occipital skull bone, a compound fracture of her right radius and ulna in the forearm—most likely defensive wounds—and three of her ribs are fractured in two different places. Not to mention the contusions and swelling on her face and back. Unfortunately, these are the most minor of her injuries. This poor young woman took one hell of a beating, that's for sure. Most of her internal organs were bruised and her spleen was ruptured."

As the pathologist continued, Hannah was slowly making her way around the steel table, eyeing every possible angle of this young woman's battered and broken body—every cut, every bruise.

Paul held the attention of the room as he started to talk through his working theory. "Here's what I think. From what I can make out from the impressions taken from the back of the skull, your guy hit her from behind with something heavy, but thin. From the shape of it, and from my many years of experience, my money would be on a tire iron, or something similar. This knocks her out cold. Some while later, she wakes up. She's feisty, our Sydney, and he doesn't like that. She's fighting back with everything she's got so he puts the boots to her, desperate to subdue her. The cuts and lacerations on her face and body were probably inflicted during this struggle, which by the way, could have gone on for hours. It was during this brutal confrontation that the defensive wounds to the right forearm were incurred. Our killer was most likely about to hit her with something and she instinctively brought her arms up to block her head. Bam, broken arm in two places. The ligature marks around her wrists and ankles were obviously another attempt to keep her restrained and under his control. There is also evidence that the oxygen to her brain was interrupted at least three times in the final hours before her death. What this means is that she was asphyxiated to the point of losing consciousness, but then our killer released his hold. Incidentally, the fibres recovered from around her neck have already been sent over to trace. We should have the analysis back shortly."

Paul paused to take a drink from his water bottle and then continued with his theory. As he did, Hannah used the moment to ask the question that was probably on everyone's mind.

"So, what's your take on this?" she asked, pointing directly to her abdomen. "Please tell me she was already dead when he did *this* to her."

"There was a large, jagged incision made across her abdomen, most likely while she was unconscious, but at some point she woke up. It's clear from the interruption in the cut." Paul was now pointing to the spot in the incision where the killer's concentration and contact with the skin was evidently interrupted.

"I think this monster was trying to disembowel her while she was still alive but got interrupted when she regained consciousness. Most of her small intestine and some of her large intestine was pulled out of the abdominal cavity but were still attached when he dumped her. Why? Well, that's your job to figure out. Maybe something, or someone, interrupted him. Maybe the sick bastard just didn't have time to finish what he started. Who knows what was going on inside this psycho's warped mind?"

Paul stopped and let everyone absorb the theory he'd just put forth. Richard and Hannah remained silent, trying to digest the gore he'd just described.

"Finally," Paul continued, "I think the guy panicked. I think he had planned to remove her organs while she was awake, but her screams and struggling got the best of him. At that point, he strangled her unconscious again."

"Sick bastard," Hannah muttered. "What in the world would ever possess someone to do something like that? What purpose would it serve? Why take any of her organs?"

Richard looked over at Hannah and could tell immediately from the contorted look on her face that she was equally disgusted and outraged.

She looked up at Paul and asked, "Was there any evidence of sexual assault?" Even though sexual assault could mean the potential for finding some solid DNA evidence, a small part of Hannah hoped Paul would say no. This young woman had been through enough without adding that to the list of injuries.

"I did a rape kit, vaginal and rectal swabs, scraped under the fingernails, all the usual steps. There were no obvious signs of tearing, but the ultraviolet light did show the presence of semen in and around the vagina and upper thigh. If this monster didn't rape her, then she'd recently had intercourse with someone else—at least within the last five days. Otherwise, the sperm would have died off. I've sent everything down to the lab and put a rush on it. We'll know something as soon as they do."

"So? In your professional opinion, the official cause of death would be…?"

"Heart failure due to hypovolemic shock," he responded. "When a person loses more than twenty percent of their blood supply, it's impossible for the heart to pump a sufficient amount of blood to the rest of the body, which in turn causes multi-organ failure—including the heart." Shaking his head as he looked down at Sydney's body, he followed with, "It would have been quick."

Hannah took a moment to let that sink in and then thanked the doctor for his time and expertise. "I think Richard and I are going to head over and introduce ourselves to Mrs. Ashton. I'm anxious to meet the woman whose daughter's laying on a slab in the morgue because she didn't think it was imperative enough to tell anyone that she was missing for five days." Hannah's fury was apparent, and the men were experiencing it firsthand.

As they reached the door to leave, Dr. Wilchuck gently reminded her, "Don't forget what Jake said, Hannah. Mrs. Ashton says she did report it. She was told by police that they were taking care of it, remember?"

Shaking her head as she moved out into the hall, she said, "Yeah, well I'd like to get my hands on the moron that told her that."

Chapter Twenty-Seven

When Kelly regained consciousness, her head was throbbing like she had a toothache, and her face was planted solidly on the cold, damp floor. She remembered this place—this dank ground beneath her—all too well. Her parched mouth tasted like a combination of sand and dried blood that had crusted over her tongue and lined the inside of her mouth. The dirt that had accumulated in the corners of her mouth aggravated the large split in her swollen bottom lip. She clenched her teeth to fight the biting pain. She had no idea how long she had been like that or how she even got back to this room. Her memory was blank again. The last thing she remembered was laying on that cold table beneath the bright light and not being able to break free of her restraints.

Kelly tried to roll onto her back, but searing pains shot through her body from head to toe, stealing her breath away with every attempt. Trying again to move, an unintentional yelp escaped her raspy vocal cords. She paused for a moment before realizing that, if she wanted to survive, she must endure the agony. Slowly and carefully, using very small movements, she painfully squirmed and shifted slowly onto her back. Her arms and legs weren't cooperating with her brain. At this point she realized she most likely had some broken bones. Very slowly, using her palms and what upper body strength she had left, she shimmied onto her hands and knees.

What Kelly wanted was to perch against the wall in the corner, however it was impossible to see where that was without any light to guide her. With her teeth gritted, she slowly and painfully dragged herself across the sandy floor, reaching out blindly until she finally felt the cool dampness of the stone wall against the palm of her hand. Having touched the wall, a tiny hint of security flooded her body and soothed her mind. The touch of that wall reassured Kelly that nobody was lurking behind her—and when you are alone, injured, and blinded by darkness, with someone trying to kill you, that tiny feeling of security is the only thing you have left to hold on to.

Once securely tucked up against the wall, Kelly's right hand slowly made its way over her battered body. She was using her nursing skills to assess her injuries, and to find out if there were broken bones or if she was just badly bruised. After a quick examination, Kelly came to the conclusion that she was just badly beaten and no bones were broken. She could feel definite swelling in her face, and she determined that her left eye was swollen partially shut. That didn't concern her at this moment. It's not like she could see anything anyways. The bleeding from the back of her head had finally stopped but she was certain she had a concussion. But that was the least of her worries. Right now, she had to focus. What she had endured earlier—laying on that cold table, the psychological tormenting—was consuming her thoughts. She knew her captor had bigger plans for her, and she was certain his ultimate intention was to kill her. She didn't know why she was still alive—why he'd returned her to this room, but she knew one thing for sure. There was no way in Hell she was going to let herself be in that situation again. She would fight her captor to the death before she would ever let herself be strapped to that table again. She had to focus. She was talking to herself out loud now.

"Think, Kelly, think." As much as her frightened mind did not want to go back to that place again, she was trying to replay everything that had happened while she was lying strapped to that table. She remembered the bright lights, she remembered hearing the sound of water running, she remembered the whistling. She'd never forget the whistling.

"Sick bastard," she muttered.

With her eyes now closed, she reluctantly let her mind drift back to when she was lying on that table, fighting to free herself. She could hear him moving around but she couldn't see him. The lights were bright. So bright they were blinding. She was looking off to the right trying to make out the person in the room with her.

She couldn't see him.

Or could I?

She was squinting her eyes, trying to focus on something. And there they were.

Boots, she thought. She remembered he was far enough away that she could just see the bottom part of his legs in the shadow. *He was wearing green rubber boots!*

Kelly felt a surge of excitement course through her body. If she continued to focus, maybe she could remember other things as well. Closing her eyes again, she tried to calm her racing heart as she recalled what she'd seen. Her eyes had followed his feet back and forth across the dirt floor. Seeming very orderly in his actions, he was definitely on a mission to accomplish something. As he passed by her line of sight the third time, Kelly remembered seeing the bottom portion of a doorway, and the door was open. Her heart racing once again, she tried to picture that doorway more clearly. The door was open. It opened to a hallway with a dirt floor, the same as the room she was in now. There was a faint light coming in from the hall. She continued to try and pluck the images from the recesses of her memory.

Oh my God! Her excitement was uncontrollable now.

There's a hatchet!

Hanging right by the door!

She couldn't see the head of it, but she could tell by the handle that it was definitely a hatchet, and it was hanging on the wall by the door.

Her eyes sprung open with this realization. If nothing else, this gave Kelly hope that, just maybe, there was a way out of here. If she could just get out of this room, she knew she could find her way out. She believed it in her heart. She also knew that, somewhere, there was a hatchet. If she could ever find that room. She knew it was a long shot, but it was more hope than she'd had before.

Kelly leaned back against the damp wall, comforting herself with thoughts of burying that hatchet deep in the skull of her captor. The images in her mind consoled her.

Everything was so quiet.

She was almost getting used to the silence now, although it didn't change the fact that the only place she wanted to be right now was home. Home safe with her mom. Even through the deafening silence, she listened for his footsteps, listened for any hint of movement at all. And she craved water. Water and food. She was growing weak, and her mouth was so dreadfully parched and sore that she was now fantasizing about water. She'd give anything for a big, cold glass of ice water right now. She could almost taste it. She envisioned the cool liquid lining the inside of her mouth, then slowly rolling down her dry throat and landing in her empty stomach as she swallowed.

She could feel it.

She could taste it.

She wanted it.

Suddenly, with no warning at all, Kelly screamed out into the darkness. Something just touched her face.

Or had it?

Am I hallucinating again?

Am I sleeping?

Am I just dreaming about drinking water?

Her heart was pounding like a drum inside her chest as all her original fears starting flooding back. Scrambling to get to her feet and wincing with each movement, she cursed the darkness and the fact that she still couldn't see a goddamned thing. As she slid her back along the wall, cautiously sidestepping her way around the room, her eyes filled with tears.

What's going on?

Is something in here with me?

Is someone in here with me?

Then she felt it again. A soft brush against her cheek. She wiped frantically at her face, the dirt from her hands only angering the open sores. She was sidestepping faster now, moving quickly around the room. Her heart was pumping so fast it felt like it was beating out of her chest. Suddenly, she bumped into something.

NO!

She bumped into someone.

Someone was in here with her!

She started screaming hysterically, moving abruptly in the opposite direction. When she reached the opposite corner, she stopped and crouched down in silence hoping her heavy breathing wouldn't give her away.

Something touched her leg.

Sprawling out across the floor on her belly, she frantically started dragging herself across the dirt in the other direction. She reached another wall. Still screaming, she fumbled her way along until she finally felt the door. She stopped. Grabbing the handle, she began pulling with all her strength, but the door wouldn't budge. She was helpless and still blinded by the dark. The salt from her tears hurt like hell as they passed over her open sores, but she didn't care. She had to get out of that room. She was screaming as loudly as she could, her voice getting hoarser with each plea.

"HELP! SOMEBODY HELP ME! PLEASE, GOD, SOMEBODY HELP ME!"

At that moment, she heard soft, tormenting laughter coming from somewhere inside the room. Kelly, completely hysterical now, whirled around to follow the eerie voice.

"Kelly." The whisper cut through the darkness like a sharp blade.

Her heart leapt and she felt her nauseated stomach rising into her throat.

"My dear, sweet Kelly. You're not getting out of this room." The taunting whispers were more than she could handle. Her knees suddenly buckled, dropping her to the damp dirt below. The next thing she heard was his evil, sadistic laugh moving closer.

Then she felt his warm breath on her cheek as he knelt beside her.

After that, she felt nothing.

Chapter Twenty-Eight

Richard and Hannah travelled in silence for the first few minutes of their drive to Nancy Ashton's home in North Oshawa. Hannah was thinking about what their colleague had shared with them.

Could it be true? she wondered.

Had Mrs. Ashton in fact reported her daughter missing, and if so, who was the idiot that let it slip through the cracks? Things like that just don't happen. Or at least they shouldn't. She was extremely uneasy about what they might learn after talking to Mrs. Ashton.

Rounding the corner into the quaint subdivision, they found Nancy Ashton's house without difficulty. Making their way up the front walk, they both mentally noted the wheelchair ramp leading to the side door of the house. Looking at each other, they wondered if this ramp was for Mrs. Ashton, or was it merely a remnant of the previous owner? Just as they were about to knock, their question was answered. The door opened and they were greeted by Mrs. Ashton—from the confines of a wheelchair.

Holding their badges out simultaneously, Hannah inquired, "Mrs. Ashton?"

Her sad blue eyes, bloodshot from crying, made contact with Hannah's. "Yes, I'm Nancy Ashton," the woman replied softly.

"Mrs. Ashton, I'm Detective Sergeant Phillips, and this is my partner, Detective Young. We were wondering if we could speak with you about your daughter, Sydney."

As Mrs. Ashton nodded and maneuvered her wheelchair backwards out of the doorway, Richard and Hannah stepped inside. The quaint house had a cozy feel and was neatly kept. Even though the furniture was minimal, there was a very warm vibe to it and the aroma of freshly brewed coffee lingered in the air.

Mrs. Ashton led the officers down the hall towards the living room as she remarked, "I've just put on a fresh pot of coffee. Can I offer you some?"

Each of them taking a seat in tufted armchairs, they responded simultaneously, "That sounds great, thank you."

Surveying the soft yellow walls of the living room, Hannah noticed a lot of pictures of Sydney with her mother. There were no signs of a husband in the pictures, or siblings for that matter. Nothing seemed out of the ordinary. It seemed like a clean, everyday, run-of-the-mill, loving home—not the home of a mother who didn't care about her daughter's well-being.

They could hear Nancy Ashton fumbling around in the kitchen, and it was at that point Hannah called out to her, "Mrs. Ashton, can I give you a hand with that?"

After a slight pause, Mrs. Ashton emerged from the kitchen with a tray containing coffee and all the fixings placed strategically across her lap. As she carefully and skillfully wheeled her way back into the living room, she remarked, "It's quite the talent I've acquired over the years. I've gotten used to this by now but thank you for the offer just the same."

Richard stood up, lifted the tray from Mrs. Ashton's lap and placed it on the long wooden coffee table. After handing each of the women their cups, he returned to the chair by the large bay window and nodded to Hannah.

Hannah, after taking a sip, looked genuinely into the woman's eyes and softly said, "Mrs. Ashton, we are so very sorry for your loss. This must be devastating for you." Hannah watched as Mrs. Ashton's trembling hands attempted to steady the cup and saucer in her lap. A single tear trickled from the woman's eye and her head fell to her chest.

In between gentle sobs, she said, "I just can't believe she's gone. Sydney was all I had left, she was my life, and now..."

She didn't need to finish her sentence. Both Hannah and Richard knew and obliged her a few moments to compose herself before continuing.

"Mrs. Ashton, we'd like to ask you some questions about Sydney if you're feeling up to it. Would that be okay?" Hannah watched as Mrs. Ashton wiped the tears from her eyes with a tissue, which she then efficiently tucked inside the sleeve of her blouse. Hannah couldn't help but feel endeared. Her own mother used to do the same thing. You never knew when there would be a tissue emergency, but she'd be right there, fully equipped to help out if the need arose.

Mrs. Ashton was confused, and it showed in her expression. "Why would someone want to kill my baby girl? Who would want to hurt her that way? She was such a good girl. Always was."

Hannah had no response to her valid question, so instead of answering, she interjected with another question. "Mrs. Ashton…"

Hannah was interrupted with a polite, "Nancy—please call me Nancy."

Smiling, Hannah continued. "Nancy, when you were speaking with Detective Connors earlier, you told him that you had reported your daughter missing. Is this true?" Hannah waited.

"Of course it's true. I love my daughter very much and it just wasn't like her to not come home. So, I called the police right away."

Hannah looked nervously at Richard before proceeding. "Nancy, I'm sorry but we're a little confused here because the department doesn't seem to have any record at all of reports filed with respect to your daughter, and this is a huge concern for us."

Nancy looked beaten. Her shoulders dropped as if in defeat and she let out a long, tired sigh before continuing. "The thing is, Sydney was a teenager—only nineteen. She grew up without a steady father figure in her life to discipline her, and I've been in this wheelchair for most of her life. You see, when you're confined to one of these things, as hard as you try, disciplining your child can be a challenge. It's not like I could get up and chase her."

Richard and Hannah listened as Nancy went on. "Don't get me wrong. As a child, she always listened to me. But as she got older, her hormones started raging and I think she started to feel like a prisoner. If we had an argument, it became quite easy to walk away from me because of this thing." Her hands slammed down hard on the armrests of her wheelchair. "I lost a lot of my control as the parent, and over the years I grew to depend on her for so much. Running errands, cleaning, cooking. That kind of stuff. I think it finally took its toll on her. So much responsibility for a young girl, forced to grow up so quickly. It really wasn't fair on my part, but we only had each other to rely on. There was no one else."

Richard and Hannah listened attentively as Nancy shared her story.

Richard asked, "Nancy, are you saying that you hadn't seen Sydney in five days because you had a fight?"

She nodded, obviously over the top with guilt that her last words with her daughter were spoken in anger. "She did this once before. Run away, I mean. It wasn't for long though. Just long enough to cool her head—have a bit of a break. But I knew she'd come back. She couldn't stay away for long because she loved me. We needed each other."

Hannah asked, "Where was Sydney's father through all of this?"

Nancy's eyes immediately moved to a picture resting on the mantle above the fireplace—one that obviously hadn't been ignited in years. It was immaculately clean, holding no ashes, just three strategically placed logs that had probably been in that same position from the time she moved into the house. Nancy wheeled herself over to the mantle and extended her arm up towards a picture tucked in near the back. Hannah jumped up from her chair to assist Mrs. Ashton in retrieving it safely. It seemed just a little too far out of reach for Hannah's comfort. She passed it to Nancy and watched her smile lovingly at it before she returned it to Hannah's grasp. Hannah took the picture with her as she sat back down in her chair, observing this attractive young man about Hannah's height, with blonde hair, hazel eyes, and a strapping build. He looked to be about eighteen years old, standing next to a small cabin overlooking a picturesque lake. He was proudly holding a fishing pole that displayed a large fish dangling from the end. *What kind of fish?* Hannah was uncertain. In the picture he was wearing green rubber hip waders with suspenders, a fishing cap with a chin cord, and a pair of matching rubber boots.

"That's my Paul," Nancy said, an endearing smile now crossing her face.

Hannah smiled as she passed the picture to Richard. "Where's Paul now?"

Nancy paused before speaking. "He's with Sydney. He's watching over our baby girl now."

Richard's eyes widened as they made contact with Hannah's.

"I'm sorry, Nancy. We didn't know," Hannah said apologetically.

"No need to apologize. You had no way of knowing. Paul died when Sydney was just a baby. She never had the chance to know him and that's not fair. He was a good man, my Paul. A good man. Everyone loved him." Nancy was obviously recalling some wonderful memories, judging by the smile that unexpectedly emerged.

"If you don't mind me asking, how did your husband die?"

"He was killed in the line of duty."

"Line of duty?" Hannah questioned. "What did your husband do for a living?"

Nancy smiled proudly. "The same thing you both do—he was a police officer. And one night he chased an armed suspect into an abandoned warehouse without waiting for backup. By the time the other officers arrived, it was too late."

"Your husband was shot?"

"No," Nancy continued. "He was killed in an explosion. Apparently, there was a meth lab inside, and he went charging in like some hero."

Although Nancy was enormously proud of her husband, Hannah could detect a tone of resentment in her voice. And why wouldn't there be? She was now a widow because of his error in judgement.

"Anyway," she continued, "I still feel guilty about it."

"Why? You had nothing to do with it." Hannah looked perplexed. "Why would you feel guilty?"

"Because it's my fault he was there," she said, her eyes now staring down at her lap as she continued. "One night, I was home alone with Sydney. Paul was working the night shift. I heard someone trying to break into the house, so I grabbed Sydney and locked us in the bathroom. It didn't take long before he had kicked in the door and all I could think of was protecting my baby girl. The last thing I remember was someone dressed in black charging straight at us…then nothing."

The large wall clock chimed four o'clock as Mrs. Ashton wheeled herself over and refilled Hannah and Richard's coffee. After replacing the coffee pot on the tray, she continued with her story. "The next thing I remember is waking up in the hospital. Paul was at my side with Sydney safe in his arms, and I was paralyzed from the waist down. I was told that when they found me, I was laying in the bathtub and that was most likely how I broke my back."

Hannah, still listening intently, leaned back in her chair.

After taking a sip of her coffee, Nancy finished. "It was only a week later that Paul was killed."

Silence filled the air. The only thing heard was the rhythmic ticking of the wall clock above Richard's head.

"I was told later that Paul had learned the suspect he was chasing that night was the man who had broken into our home. So, you see, he was there because of me—because of us and I can't help but feel guilty for that. It's my fault Paul is gone."

Hannah's voice was soothing as she reassured her. "Nancy, this is not your fault. It was an accident. Paul was doing his job and he was trying to protect his wife and daughter."

She was empathetic to Nancy's story, and hearing it only made Hannah's drive to find her daughter's killer that much stronger. This poor woman needed some peace for once. She deserved closure.

The silence that had fallen over the room was interrupted by Richard's cell phone ringing. After opening it and raising it to his ear, he said, "Detective Young."

Hannah and Nancy watched the intense look on his face as his eyes shot over to Hannah's. "Thanks, Jake, we're on our way." Richard glanced first at Hannah, and then at Nancy, "Mrs. Ashton, I'm sorry, but we'll have to cut this short. Can we finish this a little later?"

Nancy nodded.

As they departed, Hannah shook Nancy's hand and promised they'd be in touch. Moments later, they climbed back into their Charger as Richard said, "Warren's got something on the 911 tape he wants us to hear."

"That sounds promising," she said.

"Oh, and Carley Wilson is awake. Jake's on his way over to the hospital now. We'll meet him there when we're done."

Hannah was shocked but felt hopeful. Things seemed to be going their way. At least for the moment. As they drove back to the police station deep in discussion about Nancy Ashton, both were unaware of the black SUV that still followed them from four cars behind.

Chapter Twenty-Nine

WARREN GREETED HANNAH AND Richard in his office, wearing a big smile that clearly implied, *you owe me one*. Richard propped himself up on the corner of Warren's desk as Hannah found a seat in an empty chair to the left of his cluttered desk.

"You guys are gonna love me," Warren said proudly.

"What do you have for us, big guy?" Hannah asked, smirking.

"Well, I pulled up the recorded call from the other night and had another listen, but I still didn't hear anything out of the ordinary. So, I determined the hiss frequency band and added some notch filters to eliminate the hiss. Then I played around with and tweaked some of the vocal presets, worked a little bit of my magic, and had another listen. This time, there was definitely something in the background."

Hannah looked curiously at him as he continued.

"After that, I used a cool new program we had installed last month, cleaned up the frequencies even more, and then ran it through this little computer system here." Warren was playfully tapping a large machine as he talked, finishing up with, "And thanks to all the recent technology upgrades, I was able to narrow down the sound occurrences that were caught on tape. This allowed me to drop all the conversation between our dispatcher and your kid, leaving only the background noise—vocals to be exact—once it was filtered."

Hannah and Richard seemed equally impressed and intrigued. After scanning the bank of computers, gadgets, and flashing lights, Richard looked back at Warren and said, "So, let's hear what you've got for us."

"There wasn't anything important at the beginning of the recording, so I've got it cued up to the part where your kid is yelling to our mystery man for help."

Richard nodded as Warren fired up the recording. The three of them listened intently to what had been captured in the background. What they heard was the distinct voice of an unknown male. It didn't last long, and he didn't say much, but the way he said it was chilling. Softly, almost gutturally, he murmured, "*I'm not helping that slut. She's supposed to be dead.*"

Hannah and Richard's eyes travelled from the computer to Warren's smiling face.

Quite proudly, he announced, "Detective Sergeant Phillips, Detective Young. I'd like you to meet your killer."

Hannah jumped out of her chair and slammed her fist on Warren's desk. "That rotten son of a bitch! He was there! He was right fucking there under our noses! He probably drove right by the ambulance, right by our police cars, right by everyone!"

Hannah knew Richard was pissed off as she watched him jump up, grab his phone, and angrily punch in a phone number. Pacing the floor anxiously, he waited for the unlucky bastard on the other end to pick up. From the look on Warren's face, she sensed he was relieved not to be that person.

"Dave, it's Richard Young. Listen, I'm gonna need the names of every officer and EMS attendant that was on the scene the night they found Carley Wilson. Every name—on the scene and in the vicinity. Everything. This is top priority right now." There was only a moment of silence before Richard ended the conversation with Dave Fisher. "Let me know as soon as you have the list, Dave. We're headed over to the hospital now to speak with Carley. I'll fill Jake in when we get there."

Richard snapped his phone closed as he made his way to the door. Hannah followed not two steps behind, ready to punch the first person that pissed her off. From the hallway, Hannah called back to Warren, "We owe you one."

They were both furious that they had been so close to the killer and didn't even know it. Stepping out of the elevator and rounding the corner, they were met face to face with the opportunity Hannah was wishing for—to punch the first person that pissed her off.

Kent Phillips.

Seeing Hannah approach, he stopped dead in his tracks with a smug smile on his face.

"Christ, Kent," she groaned. "Not now. You know your timing really sucks?"

Richard stepped in between Hannah and Kent asking, "Don't you have some work to do, asshole?"

Richard's reaction was not a surprise to Hannah. He had told her many times that he could stand Kent Phillips about as much as he could stand a pus-filled boil on his ass. She knew he despised the man, not only because of what he had done to her, but because he seemed to have no morals, no conscience, and still walked around like he was the cat's ass.

Kent ignored Richard's words, but obviously couldn't stop himself from commenting on her partner's defensive body language. "Would you look at that, Hannah?" he said pompously. "Your boyfriend is protecting you. That's so chivalrous. He thinks I'm going to hurt you."

Richard's rage was explosive when he yelled, "Listen up, asshole. Let's get a few things straight. Number one, Hannah is my partner, not my girlfriend—my partner. And yes, I will always have her back, as she would for me. Secondly, you fucking moron, I'm not standing here to protect her from you. It's the other way around, jerk off. I am standing here, God only knows why, to protect you from her."

Kent looked humiliated while Richard continued his rant.

"I know how much Hannah wants to throat punch you right now, but I also know that I don't want to be stuck here for the next thirty minutes filling out paperwork and writing up incident reports when she does haul off and pound on your face. We have work to do. So, if you don't mind, would you please fuck off and get out of our way?"

Hannah and Richard stormed past Kent, most likely leaving him feeling a little humiliated and a lot emasculated. As they pushed through the heavy fire door leading into the garage, Hannah glanced back over her shoulder only to see Kent looking sheepishly around the hall for any witnesses to his verbal slaughter. As the door slammed shut behind them, Hannah reached over and punched Richard in the arm.

Catching him a little off guard, he laughed and asked, "What the hell was that for?"

Hannah just smiled and said, "Well, since I didn't get to punch Kent, I had to get it out of my system somehow."

Richard laughed. "Glad I could be of assistance."

Chapter Thirty

When they reached the hospital thirty minutes later, Richard knew exactly where to go from his previous visit. They rode the elevator uninterrupted to the fifth floor and found Carley's room effortlessly. As they approached, both detectives acknowledged the uniformed officer that had been posted to guard Carley's room. The door was slightly ajar, and as Hannah and Richard entered, they were greeted by her physician, Dr. vanKessel. Jake was also in the room, standing on the opposite side next to a very groggy, but conscious, Carley Wilson. Alternately shaking hands with the doctor, they immediately inquired about an update of her condition.

"Well, it was touch and go for a while," the doctor explained, "but as you can see, she seems to be doing much better now. Slipping into that coma was definitely an unexpected complication, so we were all thrilled when she came out of it." The doctor playfully patted Carley's foot and gave her a quick wink. "You certainly had us all scared, young lady."

Carley attempted a smile, but it was obvious how painful even that was for her.

Before leaving the room, the doctor addressed Hannah. "Go ahead and talk to her, but she needs her rest. I don't want her overdoing it or getting worked up, okay?"

Hannah nodded. "Thank you, doctor. We'll be brief."

Once the doctor had left the room, Hannah approached Carley's bedside. "Carley, I'm Detective Sergeant Phillips, but you can call me Hannah. And this," she said, gesturing towards Richard, "is Detective Young, but you can call him Richard."

A half smile was all Carley could muster as Hannah directed her attention towards Jake. "And I'm pretty sure you know this guy, right?"

Jake gave her a quick smile and said, "We were just getting acquainted."

They all wanted Carley to feel safe, secure, and not threatened in any way. The poor girl had already been through Hell, so the last thing any of them wanted was to add more stress.

"Carley, how are you feeling?" Hannah's compassion was genuine, and it showed whenever she interacted with victims. Something she'd learned over many years of dealing with people was to always make sure all parties were on the same page. If the victim felt like you didn't care, you'd have no way of gaining their trust. And without their trust, they would never fully open up to you. Trust was a win-win situation for everyone.

"I'm sore," Carley responded, her voice raspy, "and a little thirsty."

Jake took the hint and poured water from a blue jug into the Styrofoam cup sitting on the bedside table. He helped hold the straw up to Carley's dry lips as she slowly sipped at the liquid. Her lips were chapped and blistered so the cool water almost certainly soothed them.

"Carley," Hannah started, "the other officers and I are trying very hard to find the man who did this to you, but we need your help."

Carley looked pensive. She had been through more than any person should ever have to endure, and this scared Hannah. She needed Carley to talk to them, so she couldn't push too hard.

Carley slowly and deliberately ran her tongue across her dry lips and begged, "Hannah, I'm terrified. That man…that horrible place… please don't let him take me. Please." Her body was trembling as tears trickled from her sad blue eyes and ran down her cheeks. Without hesitation, Jake reached out and took hold of her cold hand and patted it in gentle reassurance.

Hannah held her breath while Carley finished speaking. "I never want to go back to that place…but I want you to find that monster even more."

Hannah exhaled slowly, grateful for Carley's willingness to help. While she reached for her notebook and pen, Richard positioned his phone to record Carley's statement.

Hannah jumped right in with the obvious first question. "Carley, do you know who did this to you?"

Shaking her head, she confidently responded with, "No, but I'll never forget the sound of his voice—it was so deep and creepy. I'm pretty sure he was trying to disguise it and make it sound that way just to freak me out more. And I'm not sure of his real name, but he kept referring to himself in the third person, calling himself *The Pallbearer*."

Hannah cringed at the sadistic nickname he'd given himself. "Did you see his face?" she asked.

"No, it was always dark, except..." Her words trailed off.

"Except what, Carley?" Hannah gently rubbed her arm. "It's okay, sweetie, he can't hurt you now."

After a pause to lick her sore lips again, she said, "Except when I was in *that* room."

"What room?" Hannah coaxed.

"Well, most of the time he kept me locked in some sort of a basement or cellar. I'm not sure exactly because I couldn't see anything—it was pitch black. But a couple of times I woke up in a different room. That room was so bright I could barely see anything there either because it was blinding me."

"What was happening in that room, Carley, the one with the bright lights?"

Carley struggled to swallow against her dry throat. Jake raised the straw back to her lips. After taking another sip, she revealed, "That's where he was cutting me."

Jake, Richard, and Hannah all froze as she continued.

"It was like…it was like an operating room. I tried as hard as I could to break free, but I couldn't. He had my arms and legs strapped to the table."

As more tears ran down Carley's cheeks, Hannah gently wiped them away with her thumb. She hated making her relive this nightmare in detail, but it was necessary if they were going to catch this monster.

"The guy was deranged," she snapped. "When I was alone in the dark, he would sometimes sit outside the door whispering horrible things to torment me until I screamed." Carley shuddered at the memory before continuing. "There were times he was actually sitting in the room with me and I had no clue. Out of nowhere, he'd suddenly touch my arm or my face and totally scare the shit out of me. It was pitch black. I couldn't see a thing and when I'd start screaming and crying, he'd just sit in there and laugh at me. The guy is psycho." She was trembling now—most likely from nerves—but regardless, Richard took the initiative to cover her with an extra blanket.

In a calm, soothing tone, Hannah asked, "Carley, did this man ever say anything to you that might help us figure out who he is?"

She searched her memory for a few moments, then shook her head. "I don't think so. It was mostly stuff to scare me. Things to mess with my head and make me freak out and start screaming again. It seemed like the more I screamed, the more he got off on it."

"What kind of things would he say?" Hannah asked.

"He would mumble things like, '*Don't worry, this incision won't hurt*,' or, '*You won't feel a thing until I start pulling your guts out*.' Everything he said freaked me out because it usually meant he was about to do it."

Hannah saw that Richard was totally disgusted as she reiterated Carley's last words. "He actually said that to you? '*You won't feel a thing until I start pulling your guts out*'?"

Carley nodded, her strength and courage mentally applauded by all three officers.

"Sick, twisted bastard," Richard muttered under his breath. "Don't worry, Carley. We're gonna find this guy and you'll never have to worry about him again." His angry face looked like he wanted to kill him—but not before beating him to a pulp and making him suffer like all of his victims.

"Did he say anything else, Carley?" Hannah questioned. "Anything that might be familiar to you at all? Sometimes people who do these things are actually people we know or have met before." Hannah could see the wheels turning as Carley thought long and hard about what she had just been asked. She watched as Carley's brow furrowed as if questioning something in her memory.

"Come to think of it" she commented, "he did say something that suggested he knew me in some way. It was weird and didn't make much sense to me, but maybe it'll mean something to you."

They watched intently as she continued, waiting to hear what this psycho had said to her.

"When he had me strapped to the table in the bright room, he said, '*it all stops here—no more bad seeds*'." She paused, thinking about what he'd said to her. "What do you think he meant by that, Hannah? Did he think I was a bad person? Is that why he wanted to kill me? Because he thought I was a *bad seed*, whatever that meant?"

All three were confused by what she had just told them, and all had the same questions running through their minds. What the hell did he mean by that? Did he know her? Was he just some creep who thought she was a bad person and wanted her to die? What did he mean by "bad seed?"

"Carley, do you remember how you ended up escaping? How you got to where we found you?"

Shaking her head, she said, "The last thing I remember is him taking me off that table, putting me in the trunk of a car, and then driving for quite a long time. I'm not sure how long it was, but when we stopped and he opened the trunk and pulled me out, he stumbled backwards and fell. Without thinking at all, I just started running as fast as I could through the forest. I could hear him chasing me and calling my name, but somehow, I was able to get away from him. That's all I remember. The next thing I remember is waking up here in the hospital."

Hannah stood up and momentarily turned her back to Carley while she inhaled a long, deep breath. After exhaling, she turned to face her again and asked, "Carley, do you mind if I talk to these gentlemen out in the hall for a minute?"

Carley shook her head. "I'm kind of tired right now anyway. I could use a break."

With a nod and a smile, the three of them made their way out into the hallway, pulling the door closed behind them. As they did, Carley called out to her. "Hannah?"

Hannah opened the door again, stuck her head in and asked, "What is it, Carley? Everything okay?"

"Boots!" she shouted.

Hannah looked puzzled. "Did you say 'boots?'"

"Yes! I remember at one point when he had me tied to the table and was moving around the room, I somehow caught a glimpse of him in the shadow of the bright lights. It's the only time I was able to make out anything at all. And it wasn't even all of him. It was just from the knees down. He was wearing tall green rubber boots. I just thought I should mention that, in case it was important."

"Thanks, kiddo. Now get some rest."

Returning to the hallway, the three determined officers stood huddled in the corner by the maintenance room while Hannah told them about Carley's memory of the rubber boots. She also took that moment to fill them in on a hunch she had.

"I want a second officer posted by her door asap," Hannah announced. "I don't want any screw ups if someone has to leave to take a leak. She's to be guarded around the clock until this bastard is caught. Understood?"

With everyone in agreement, Richard opened his phone and made the necessary arrangements. After he finished, he noted the concern on Hannah's face and prompted, "Tell us what's on your mind, Hannah. What's running through that overactive brain of yours?"

Hannah shuddered, completely revolted by what she was about to say. "This psycho wasn't trying to disembowel these girls—I have a feeling he was just doing a piss poor job at what his real objective was."

Richard and Jake were noticeably apprehensive as they waited to hear the rest of Hannah's theory.

Hannah, her eyes now fully glossed over, slowly and deliberately repeated the words Carley had spoken only moments earlier.

"'*No more bad seeds…no more bad seeds...seeds…seeds*.' Sweet Jesus," she whispered. "He wasn't trying to disembowel them. He was trying to take their uteruses."

Chapter Thirty-One

HANNAH WALKED THROUGH THE door of her apartment, both mentally and physically exhausted, a little after ten p.m. It had been a long day with a lot of new information coming to light—so much to absorb. She placed her briefcase on the kitchen table, knowing full well there were some things she wanted to go over before calling it a night. As she popped another pitiful frozen dinner into the microwave, she glanced at her technologically-challenged answering machine. The red message light was flashing. Pressing the play button, she heard her lawyer's voice on the tape.

Shit, she thought, *I forgot to call him back this morning. What does he want now? More money?* Rolling her eyes, Hannah punched in four minutes on the microwave as she listened in disbelief to what came next.

"Hannah, it's Mark Holden. Listen, I just wanted to let you know I got a call from Kent's lawyer just now and, I have to admit, I was a little surprised to hear that the two of you are going to give the marriage another shot. Apparently, a lot has happened in the last two days—maybe it's good you're working together again. Anyway, I sincerely hope that everything works out for the two of you. Call me if you need anything else. Take care, Hannah."

Hannah stood there completely in shock. Motionless and flabbergasted, she couldn't take her eyes off the answering machine that now echoed a dial tone. *Did I just hallucinate?* she wondered. *Did he just say he was glad we were working things out?* Hannah reflexively hit play on the machine—she needed to hear it again. *This can't be happening,* she thought. As the message ended for the second time, she realized she wasn't hallucinating at all.

"Is he shitting me?" she yelled, "What the hell is that asshole up to now?" Hannah stormed out of the kitchen and grabbed the phone that had been laying on the couch. She was livid as she dialed Kent's number, pacing the floor as she waited impatiently for him to pick up. She couldn't contain herself. She was totally fired up and poised to rip him a new one.

Kent picked up on the second ring. "Hello?"

"What in the actual fuck, Kent? What the Hell are you trying to pull?" Hannah screamed into the phone.

"Hannah, it's so nice to hear from you."

She could hear the arrogance dripping from his tone and could just tell he was now sporting the same smug look on his face she wanted to punch off earlier that day.

"I'm serious, Kent. What the Hell are you trying to pull?"

"What are you talking about, Hannah? I'm not trying to pull anything."

"Is that so? Well why don't you tell me why I just got a message from my lawyer congratulating us on 'working things out?'" As she paced back and forth across the parquet flooring in her living room, Hannah made air quotes with her fingers to emphasize the *working things out* point.

Kent was silent for a moment before speaking. "Listen, Hannah, don't be mad. Maybe I did say something to my lawyer about being happy I was working with you again; happy you were back in my life. So, sue me. Can I help it if I'm still in love with you?"

There was total silence on the other end of the phone.

"Hannah, are you still there?"

The silence was long and deafening.

"Hannah," Kent snickered, "breathe for Christ's sake."

"What do you mean, you still love me? Are you delusional?"

"No, Hannah. As a matter of fact, I'm not. So, I'll say it again. I'm still in love with you."

Standing there in total disbelief, Hannah yelled, "Kent, you cheated on me! You broke my heart, ruined our marriage, took me for everything I had, and now you're telling me you still love me? It's ludicrous—you've obviously lost your mind thinking you'd ever have a second chance. Are you on crack?"

"I know I screwed up, Hannah. I admit that. But I never stopped loving you."

Hannah was at an utter loss. Kent had completely blind-sided her, and she wasn't even armed with an intelligent rebuttal. For once in her life, all words escaped her.

Stammering to vocalize her thoughts, and failing miserably, she just sighed into the receiver. *What am I supposed to say to that?* she wondered. *How am I supposed to react?* She wanted to be pissed off. She wanted to yell and scream and call him a fucking asshole. She wanted to reach through the phone and strangle him—but something stopped her.

"Hannah?" Kent's voice had softened.

It was the voice she knew from so long ago. The voice of the man she had fallen in love with. The voice of the man she had married. The voice of the man she was still married to. Hannah was infuriated with herself. When it came to her job, she was fierce. As a matter of fact, she was tough as nails in every aspect of her life. Why did she struggle now? She knew it wasn't love. So, what was it? Was it fear of giving up on her marriage too easily? Was it fear of being alone or feeling like a failure? Did Kent actually deserve her forgiveness? Or was it finally time to stand up to him and demand the divorce she rightfully deserved? She was mentally drained as she tried to analyze her thoughts.

"Hannah? Are you still there?" Kent's tone was relaxed.

"Listen, I'm exhausted and I can't deal with this right now."

"This isn't finished, Hannah. We'll talk later?" he asked.

She was silent.

"Good night, Hannah."

Not even responding, she hung up the phone, slowly lowering herself on to the leather sofa behind her. *Why is this so difficult?* she wondered. *Why can't I finally just let myself be happy?*

Chapter Thirty-Two

HANNAH ARRIVED AT HER desk, coffee in hand, just before seven a.m. She had a death grip on her cup as she leafed through her stack of unread phone messages. Most of them could wait. However, there was one she remembered seeing yesterday.

Bobby Ross.

She had totally forgotten to call him back. Hannah recalled being interrupted yesterday before getting the chance to leave him a message. She knew it was a little early in the morning to call, but this might be the only chance she would get all day.

She dialed the number and got his voice mail. After the beep, she left a detailed message, including her cell phone number if he needed to reach her. The name still sounded familiar to her. *Why can't I place it?* Probably because she was still half asleep. She had tossed and turned all night thinking about her conversation with Kent.

Still sifting through her messages, she also found one from Mrs. Griggs, the mother of the latest missing girl, Kelly. Before returning her call, Hannah walked down the hall and turned into the Conference Room. She studied the display of photos, descriptions, and details of all five young girls on the wall. Standing in front of Kelly's picture, she examined her face, the brightness and innocence in her young eyes, her body structure, and the description written below.

Hannah's heart leapt. She read it again. Then she moved back and re-read Sydney Ashton's description. When finished reading that one, she stepped back and re-read Carley Wilson's description. Hannah spun around and was in a full jog as she headed back to her office.

Why did nobody notice this before now? she wondered. *How had they possibly missed this?*

Hannah was eagerly punching numbers on her cell phone as she rounded the corner and headed into her office. "Jake," she said sharply. "It's me. Where are you right now?"

"I'm just leaving my house, why?"

"Listen, there's something I've got to ask you—but in person. How quickly can you get here?"

"I'll be there inside of fifteen minutes."

"Great, see you soon." Hannah placed the phone on her desk, slowly sat down in her chair, and attempted to sort through the countless frenzied thoughts now racing through her mind. Moments later, she picked up her phone and called Mrs. Griggs. After a brief conversation with her, she closed her phone and found herself talking out loud just as Richard walked into her office. She was eager to share this new information with him.

"I can't believe we missed this, Richard. Listen up," she commanded, excitement apparent in her voice.

"Well good morning to you, too," Richard teased as he pulled another chair up to Hannah's desk.

Hannah dismissed his comment and started right into her theory. "Our fourth victim," she said, "Sydney Ashton, worked in a library right here in Oshawa. Our third victim, Carley Wilson, works for a plastic surgeon who has a couple different offices: one here in Oshawa and one downtown Toronto. Last, but not least, we have Kelly Griggs, victim number five. She's a nursing student at UOIT right here in Oshawa—missing."

She could tell by the confused look on Richard's face that he wasn't quite following where she was going. "Okay, Hannah, we know this already, so what's the connection? What are we missing?"

Her smile widened as if she was about to pull back the curtain to reveal the wizard. "None of us saw it right away, Richard, but this is it. This is the link to our killer!"

Hannah repositioned herself and was now standing in front of the whiteboard hanging on the wall in her office. She was jotting things down all over the place, attempting a flowchart to help demonstrate her explanation. As she quickly scribbled down her thought process, her scattered internal dialogue was voiced aloud. "Kelly…nursing student…medical training. Carley…works in a doctor's office…medical training. Sydney… works in a library…" Hannah didn't finish her sentence, leaving Richard totally hanging.

"Okay," he said pausing. "I'll give you the first two, but how does working in a library have anything to do with medical training?" He still looked perplexed, and even a little concerned, with Hannah's behaviour.

"I was waiting for you to ask," she smirked. "It has everything to do with it when this particular library is located right next door to a certain plastic surgeon's office. And I just got off the phone with Mrs. Griggs, who confirmed it's the same library where Kelly goes to study after class. Coincidence? I think not." Hannah proudly sat back down in her chair, propped her feet up on her desk, and took a long sip of her coffee. "Now we just have to figure out the connections with our first two victims, Ana Stonehouse and Jessica Wright."

"Great work, D.S. Phillips," Richard announced, nodding his approval. "How about a visit to the doctor's office?"

"You read my mind. We just need to wait for Jake—he'll be here in five."

"Why?" Richard cocked his head to the side as he looked at Hannah.

"Remember I told you he thinks there's a connection between this case and his sister's death?"

He nodded as she continued. "We need to run this by him to see if he notices any similarities."

Richard agreed. As they waited for Jake, Hannah couldn't help but notice Richard was staring at her with a strange look on his face.

"What's up Richard? Why are you looking at me like that?"

"I was just wondering how you were doing. You look a little tired, and to be honest, I worry about you."

"Thanks, but I'm fine. I've just got a lot on my mind, that's all." Her answer was short, to hopefully deter any further questions.

"Anything you want to talk about? Anything I can help with?" he offered.

Hannah didn't respond. She just stared at the photocopier in the corner of the office. She was avoiding his question, and she knew he realized that.

Richard didn't accept the brush off. "Hannah, what's going on with you? No offence, but you look like Hell. What's eating you?"

She decided she had to tell him. She needed to get this off her chest, and Richard was her rock. She trusted him to be a good sounding board for her. "Alright, but promise you'll hear me out before you say anything."

He nodded his agreement.

She proceeded to tell him everything that happened the night before, from the message the lawyer left to the conversation she had with Kent proclaiming his love for her. Richard kept his promise to not say anything until she was finished. As a matter of fact, even then he didn't say a single word. He was just staring at her while she quietly awaited his remarks—or judgements. But surprisingly, he had none to offer. She knew all too well how Richard felt about Kent Phillips, so why would he bother saying anything at all? But what Hannah had absolutely no way of knowing was, in those sixty short seconds, she had broken Richard's heart.

It was during that awkward silence that Jake came through her office door. The tension in the air was palpable, and they both welcomed the distraction.

Jake glanced at each of them. "What's up?" he asked. "You sounded urgent on the phone. What did you need to ask me?"

Hannah looked solemn as she said, "It's about your sister, Jake."

"Okay?" he nodded, pensively.

"At the time she was killed, was she in school or was she employed somewhere?"

Jake's facial expression quickly changed to that of concern. "As a matter of fact, she had just graduated from Fanshawe College as an X-ray Technician."

Hannah immediately shot an uneasy look across to Richard before she asked the next question. "Do you know if she'd secured a job after she graduated?"

"She went for an interview, got the job, but died before she actually started working there. Why?"

"Where was the job, Jake?" Hannah held her breath while she waited for her colleague to answer.

"I don't remember the guy's name off the top of my head, but I know it was some hoity-toity plastic surgeon in Toronto."

Hannah and Richard jumped up simultaneously, grabbed Jake by the arm, and said, "You're coming with us."

CHAPTER THIRTY-THREE

MATT DAVIDSON WAS ANXIOUS even thinking about his impending court date. You'd think he would be prepared for such an occasion, having already been through it twice before, but he wasn't. After everything he'd been through, he still maintained his innocence, whether people believed him or not. Matt knew his father didn't believe him and probably wouldn't care if he rotted away in some prison cell. *But what about this GQ guy?* he thought. *This reporter, Bobby Ross? What's his story?*

Matt replayed his unusual encounter with Bobby the other night at the bar over and over in his head. It did seem a little peculiar, but Matt had absolutely nothing to lose. At this point, it seemed like Bobby was the only person in the world who believed in him. They had talked at great length about what happened, going right back to his first arrest nearly three years earlier. It seemed kind of odd that Bobby knew so much about Matt—his life, his family, even his childhood. Not to mention, he had compiled a huge dossier containing everything he'd been collecting over the past three years—some of it probably obtained using exceptionally *creative* tactics. Matt didn't care in the least what methods Bobby used to obtain all this data, not if it was going to help prove his innocence. The dossier included copies of sworn affidavits, depositions, arrest reports, warrants, news clippings—you name it. Using his charisma and resourceful ideas, Bobby was easily able to smooth talk copies of everything right into the palm of his hand. Matt desperately wanted to believe Bobby was being genuine and truthful, but even with all this information laid out in front of him, doubt about his intentions crept into his mind.

When Bobby had first introduced himself at the bar that night, he had told Matt, "*I'm here to help you.*" He had then spent the next two hours in the smoke-filled dive, yelling over the loud music and infantile male banter, to prove this. He had maintained that Matt's alleged guilt was, in fact, followed by a large question mark, and he wanted to be the one to get to the bottom of it.

Matt couldn't help but question this stranger's integrity to a certain extent. *Is he doing this to play the hero? Is he doing it for the scoop on a doctor's rebellious son? Or is he truly here to help me?*

Bobby's answer to that question had been direct and honest. Matt appreciated his candor. He had stared straight into Matt's eyes and, without blinking, said, "*Matt, I've got too many facts here that just keep getting swept under the carpet. They all seem to point in the same direction—your innocence. Maybe the people doing the sweeping can live with what they are doing to you, but I can't sit back and let it happen.*" He had smiled and followed that with, "*And yes, I want the exclusive interview.*"

Matt vividly recalled leaning back in his chair, taking a long swig of his Corona, and just smiling when Bobby suggested he come down to his office within the next couple of days to start preparing a strategy for his upcoming court date.

Now, on this bright autumn morning, Matt lay smiling in his bed. Half of a pale blue cotton sheet covered the lower part of his body while the other half laid on the floor beside him. The blanket was nowhere to be found—most likely crumpled on the floor at the foot of the bed. He didn't care though. He wasn't the least bit cold. In fact, he was nice and warm. He had been laying there vividly replaying the mind-blowing night he'd spent with a beautiful blonde he'd picked up at his favourite bar a while back. He'd brought her back to his place, ferocity and excitement devouring them, and they'd spent the rest of the night hungrily exploring each other over and over—and then over one more time.

It had been quite some time since he'd gotten laid, so that hot flashback was still very fresh in his mind and was working wonders at keeping him warm. *What was her name again?* he pondered. Smiling now as he remembered, he rolled onto his side and said it aloud. "Sydney."

Setting those warm thoughts off to the side for the time being, Matt knew he needed to get his butt in gear if he was going to make it into Bobby's downtown office before noon. As he got out of bed and headed towards the bathroom to take a shower, he couldn't help but wonder if he'd ever see this mystery girl again. *Would she want to see me again?* he wondered. Uncertain of either answer, his thoughts were interrupted by the noise of loud sirens outside his apartment window. Not thinking much of it as he closed the bathroom door behind him, he thought to himself, *I wonder what poor schmuck they're after this time?*

Chapter Thirty-Four

HANNAH, RICHARD, AND JAKE arrived at the Front Street office building of Dr. William Davidson a little after nine a.m. Richard had already reached out to Toronto Police Service Chief of Police, Ted Donnelly, to inform him of their presence in his jurisdiction. Chief Donnelly was more than obliging, having a good grasp on the on-going investigation, and offering any assistance they may need. Richard knew the protocol. Even though they were not planning an arrest, it's always important to get the appropriate approval before poking around where they don't belong.

Standing before the enormous skyscraper that overlooked Lake Ontario, the officers knew business hours were just getting under way as they entered through the revolving glass door. They immediately spotted a security guard in the elaborate lobby, and while holding their badges up for the six-foot two-inch African American man to verify, they inquired as to the location of Dr. Davidson's office. The guard complied immediately, informing them that, not only was his office located on the 17th floor, his office *was* the 17th floor.

Not impressed by this fact in the least, they piled into the first available elevator and ascended the floors without interruption. About sixty seconds later, the doors opened directly into Dr. Davidson's high-class, luxury office.

"Pretty swanky," Richard remarked, emphasizing this with a two-tone whistle typically associated with a pretty girl passing a construction site. They departed the elevator and were all rendered speechless at the prestigious decor, a blatantly obvious display of wealth. Taking it all in, Hannah had to admit it was indisputably magnificent—although not her taste in design.

"This guy's office probably cost more to decorate than I've made in my entire career." Jake's observant remark vocalized their collective opinions.

With that sad thought aside, Hannah approached the reception desk while the other two officers held back a bit. The young, bubbly receptionist greeted Hannah immediately, her eyes not leaving the two serious-looking men in the long trench coats.

"Can I help you, Ma'am?"

Ma'am? she thought. *Who the hell is she calling Ma'am? Jesus, I'm not that old!* Hannah thought. Instead of saying what was really on her mind, Hannah smiled politely and held up her badge for the young woman to see. "Yes, you can," she continued. "My name is Detective Sergeant Phillips and I'm with the Durham Regional Police Service. My colleagues and I are here to speak with Dr. Davidson. Is he in?" Hannah folded her badge closed and replaced it in her jacket pocket.

It was evident the red-haired receptionist was taken by surprise. Her eyes darted back and forth between the three officers, and then she finally uttered some words. "If you'll just have a seat for a moment, I'll go get Dr. Davidson."

Sliding her chair back out of the way, she turned and headed down the hall to a room near the back of the office. It was only a matter of moments before she returned, followed quite closely by a tall man who looked to be in his late fifties. He was statuesque, with salt and pepper hair, chiseled features, and a prominent chin dimple. Hannah knew that, as a woman, she wouldn't be alone in thinking this man was attractive. His sophisticated stride as he moved down the hall radiated his confidence, power, and obvious wealth.

"Can I help you with something?" The doctor was looking directly at Hannah when he spoke, but she knew his peripheral vision was monitoring the two gentlemen standing nearby.

Hannah held out her badge for the man to see. "Dr. Davidson, I'm Detective Sergeant Phillips and I'm with Durham Regional Police Service." Gesturing behind her as the two officers moved closer to her, she continued with, "And these are my colleagues, Detective Young and Detective Constable Connors." She pointed to each man respectively. "We'd like to ask you a few questions if you don't mind?"

"Why don't we talk in my office?" Extending his arm out behind him, he gestured down the hall toward the room he had emerged from moments earlier.

Hannah observed many treatment rooms along the way. Most of them looked like an ordinary exam room that you'd see in any clinic. However, a couple of the rooms had some pretty high-tech, scary looking contraptions in them. Not having any sort of clue what cosmetic purpose the machines would serve, she let the thought go. Upon entering Dr. Davidson's office, the officers each took seats in the visitor's chairs in front of his organized desk, while the doctor made his way behind it to the comfortable leather chair by the window. Adjusting his long white lab coat, while at the same time clearing his throat, he looked at Hannah and asked, "What exactly can I do for you, Detectives?"

Richard and Hannah both knew that Jake wanted to take the lead on this one. He wanted to feel him out, ask his own questions, and see if the doctor started to squirm. He was also well aware of the fact that he needed to keep his emotions in check because, if this guy was somehow involved in his sister's death, he certainly didn't want to be the one to spoil the punchline.

"Dr. Davidson," Jake started, "I'd just like to caution you that I'll be recording this informal interview. Not to worry though, it's just a formality."

Before the doctor could even respond, Jake dove right into his first question. "Dr. Davidson, does the name Carley Wilson mean anything to you?"

The doctor repeated this name out loud, "Carley Wilson?" He was nonchalantly stroking his chin with his thumb and index finger while he pondered the name for a moment. "Yes, it does actually. Isn't she the young girl who's been in the news recently? The one who was kidnapped by—oh what was his name? Oh yeah—The Pallbearer?"

Not one of them liked that answer. It was way too smooth and too quick. "Yes, that's her," Jake nodded.

The doctor drizzled more syrup on his previous comment, adding, "Poor girl, I hope she's okay. There are some pretty sick people in this world." With that said, he shook his head.

Hannah and Richard were biting their tongues as Jake stiffened in his chair. This guy stunk and they all knew it. As Jake continued with his questions, Hannah's eyes scanned the room. It was a nice office that held a personal feel. There were two large Ficus trees in one corner of the room, expensive looking artwork on the largest wall, and a retro-looking oak and black metal shelf in another corner holding a variety of framed pictures. *Friends and family?* she wondered. She glanced quickly at each of the pictures, curious to see if any were of his famous patients. She highly doubted it, but was feeling a little nosy, so she searched the faces regardless.

When Hannah's attention came back to the conversation, she heard Jake ask, "Dr. Davidson, isn't it true that Carley Wilson worked for you part-time as one of your receptionists?"

Dr. Davidson shook his head. "No, not that I'm aware of. I've got quite a large staff, most of whom I don't pay much attention to. A lot of these part-time girls are just here to answer phones and schedule my appointments." He paused for a moment and then repeated his original answer. "No, I don't remember her, but I'm not the one who takes care of the hiring and firing. That would be Denise's job. She's my office manager and, trust me when I tell you, I don't know where I'd be if I didn't have someone like her to keep my practices running smoothly." Arrogantly, he added, "I have another practice in Oshawa, you know. Between the two offices, I am kept extremely busy." He sat back in his oversized leather chair as if to say, *God, I'm good.*

Richard had a sudden urge to reach across the doctor's desk and bitch slap him. He hated his *"I'm a doctor holier than thou"* attitude, especially coming from a man who had a few too many suspicious ties to this investigation.

"Interesting, Dr. Davidson," Jake remarked. "I say this because Carley Wilson was, in fact, in your employ at the time she was abducted." Jake let him ponder that for a moment before continuing. "I also find it quite fascinating, Doctor, that she was working at your Oshawa location, with you, on the day she disappeared."

It was evident to the detectives that the doctor had been caught off guard, as his body language suddenly shifted. They watched the rapid stroking of his chin, his wandering eyes uncertain of where to look, followed by the instinctive scratching of the back of his head. He resembled a cornered animal searching for an escape, and his three guests were savouring every moment.

Picking up a pen in his right hand, he proceeded to slowly click it repeatedly. It was never his intention to write with it—the fidgeting merely provided security to keep his hands occupied and try to calm his nerves. Unsuccessful in his attempts to conceal his nervousness, the three officers waited for him to start backtracking.

First looking down at the pen in his hand, and then directly at Jake, he said, "Now that you mention it, I think I do remember Carley working at my Oshawa office. Yes, nice girl, very professional and efficient, too." The doctor apologized for his memory, blaming his little lapse on the need for a long overdue vacation.

"Isn't it funny how things can come back to you just like that?" Jake said, simultaneously snapping his fingers.

Richard and Hannah watched the doctor's face as he cleared his throat and adjusted awkwardly in his seat. "I'm not exactly sure what you're implying, detective, but I assure you, it's not what you're thinking."

They were all anxious to hear what would come out of his mouth next. *And what exactly does he assume we're all thinking,* Jake wondered?

"You see," Dr. Davidson explained, "the reason I remembered her just now is because of an incident that happened shortly before she disappeared. And to be honest, I'd totally forgotten it even happened until you just brought her up."

"Okay, what incident might you be referring to?" Jake was indignant.

"Well, my son had stopped by the office to see me. He usually just came by when he needed or wanted something from me, but when I came out of the exam room, he was leaning on the counter talking to her—to Carley."

Jake looked puzzled. "What's wrong with that?"

"It just really bothered me. I pay these girls good money to work for me, and I don't like them fraternizing with anyone, especially my son, when they have work to do."

"It sounds like you run a pretty tight ship around here, Dr. Davidson." Jake couldn't believe the power trip this guy was on.

The doctor didn't stop there. "You just don't get it. My son has a serious problem. He will sleep with anything that moves."

Jake noted the sudden contorted looks on Richard and Hannah's faces and remarked accordingly. "Dr. Davidson, you think your son has a *problem* because he's flirtatious? I'd say it's actually quite normal—healthy even, and to be expected from a young man, wouldn't you?"

Flustered, the doctor continued. "You don't get it. He's just a player—always in trouble and expecting me to keep bailing him out. When he broke this girl's heart, which he would most certainly do, I'd be the one to deal with all the drama and fallout here at the office. That's precisely why I never mix business with pleasure. It's totally unacceptable behaviour in my books and, quite frankly, I'm sick and tired of his antics. Everything my son does reflects directly on me and my practice, and I refuse to let him ruin my good reputation."

They were all wide-eyed at the doctor's very angry and unprovoked rant about his son. *This guy certainly won't be winning the father of the year award,* Jake thought. *What a loser.*

"Dr. Davidson, are you aware if your son ever pursued anything with Carley outside of your office?"

"I have no idea. I told him to stay away from her, but he never listens to me anyway, so who knows? He's a lot to handle with all the other crap he gets himself into."

"What kind of stuff are you referring to?"

"You name it, he's been in trouble for it. Mostly mischief—teenage boy stuff over the years. I guess he was bored and needed some excitement. But lately, it's been more serious."

"Serious like what?" Jake questioned.

"Drugs. He's been arrested three times in the last few years."

"Any convictions?"

"No. The charges were dropped for some reason or another. The first two times, against my better judgement, I caved and bailed him out. But the charges being dropped didn't matter to the reporters. They were still slamming my name all over the front page thanks to my idiot son's stupidity." They watched on in silence as he followed with, "What a waste. I should have let him stay there. If I'd done that, then maybe he would have grown up and made something of his life instead of being a little punk. And just maybe he wouldn't have ended up in the same situation again."

"What do you mean, 'same situation?'"

"What I mean, Detective, is that he was just arrested for the third time last week—drugs again. But this time, he got no help from me. He's got another court date coming up, so maybe this time he'll finally get what he deserves and learn his lesson once and for all." Dr. Davidson sat back in his chair and stared out the window at the massive blue waters of Lake Ontario.

Jake interrupted the doctor's thoughts of his son with a totally different question. "Dr. Davidson, does the name Stephanie Connors mean anything to you?" Jake was waiting for the right moment to mention his sister's name.

He watched as the doctor hung his head towards his chest and let out a long sigh. "Yes, it does. Why do you ask?"

"It's just routine. How do you know Stephanie?" Jake asked, extremely anxious to hear his response.

"I never met her; I just remember hearing her name a few times."

"Where did you hear her name?" he asked curiously.

"From my son. I think he used to date her."

Jake's stomach tightened and he could feel the bile rising in the back of his throat. He sat motionless, just staring at Dr. Davidson, terrified of losing his composure. Richard and Hannah could feel his anger and abruptly finished off the interview, thanking the doctor very much for his time. As they headed out of his office, Hannah turned to him and asked, "One last question, Dr. Davidson?"

He nodded.

"What is your son's name?"

Turning his attention back to the window as if ashamed to say it aloud, he said, "Matt. His name is Matt Davidson."

Chapter Thirty-Five

MATT CAME RUNNING OUT of the bathroom as he heard his front door crashing open. His feet suddenly anchored in place as he stood in the middle of his apartment, nothing but a dark grey towel secured around his waist. A half-dozen men clad in dark tactical uniforms, armed with M4 automatic rifles or Glock 22s, now surrounded the stunned young man. Before he could register what was happening, the men had him face down on the floor of his bedroom, yelling his name and pulling his arms behind his back. As the handcuffs tightened around his wrists, the officers pulled Matt to his feet and sat him down on the bed. A large man, one of the few not in an official police uniform, approached the bedroom door. As he entered the room, the other officers spread out to allow him to get to Matt.

His voice was gruff—almost gravelly—when he questioned, "Are you Matthew William Davidson?"

Matt just nodded, terrified and panicked at the unexpected arrival of all these cops, most of whom had some type of firearm pointed directly at him.

"I'm Detective Joe Robertson," he continued. "Matthew Davidson, you are under arrest for the murder of Sydney Ashton."

Matt's mind started racing, his heart pounding heavily in his chest. *Sydney Ashton? The girl from the other night?* he thought. *What are they talking about?* This time he spoke aloud, mainly out of fear and total confusion. "Sydney Ashton? Murder? Listen man, there's been some kind of mistake here."

"There's no mistake, son. And you *are* under arrest."

"But wait a minute—Sydney's not dead! She was just here..."

The cops stared blankly at him with the sights from their weapons—one even being a C8 shotgun—boldly targeting the centre mass of Matt's upper torso.

Matt was panic-stricken. His head was spinning a mile a minute when his eyes met those of Detective Robertson, and his pleading was now redirected towards him.

"Listen Detective. Are you telling me that Sydney is dead? That she's been murdered?"

"We'll talk at the station," he promised. "Right now, I am going to read you your rights."

"No. Listen to me. I didn't do this. I didn't kill anyone. You've got to believe me."

Matt's pleas went totally ignored as two members of the Tactical Support Unit led him out of his apartment and down to a squad car that was waiting to transport him to Central East Division. As they passed him off to the two uniformed constables, he was clearly in shock—and total disbelief. He couldn't even begin to grasp what was happening to him. He refused to accept that the beautiful blonde girl who had just recently come into his life was now dead. He just couldn't wrap his head around it; it was unspeakable. He was truly terrified by everything that was happening right now, but what frightened Matt the most wasn't the fact that he was being arrested. It wasn't going to jail again. It wasn't anything to do with what might happen to him next. What frightened him the most was wondering, *what will my father think?*

As the patrol car pulled out onto the street and into traffic, Matt sat quietly in the backseat, divided from the officers by a metal cage. He stared out the window motionless—almost catatonic—just watching as they drove past some of his nosey neighbours, the market where he bought most of his groceries, his favourite deli, and the bodega where he grabbed his coffee every morning. He even watched as a black SUV pulled out onto the street and followed a few cars behind them.

Chapter Thirty-Six

RICHARD, JAKE, AND HANNAH piled back into the elevator following their insightful meeting with Dr. Davidson. They stood in silence, hearing only the subtle chiming of the elevator as it descended past many floors on its journey to the lobby. No words were spoken until Jake broke the silence nine floors later.

Having had some time to digest what the doctor had just told them, he shook his head and punched his right fist powerfully into the palm of his left hand. "Goddammit," he yelled. "Who the hell is this Matt asshole? We need to find him now. I believe he and I are about to have a little chat."

The elevator doors opened. The three heated detectives stepped into the lobby and weaved their way through the scads of bystanders and out onto the street. It was nine forty-five a.m. as they climbed back into their cruiser and headed for the Gardiner Expressway. Hannah was lost in thought as her eyes followed the many luxury yachts she saw departing the marina. She envied those fortunate enough to afford that kind of lifestyle. It was shaping up to be a beautiful day and there was no place she'd rather be right now than on the water—and not in the middle of this nightmare case.

"What's on your mind, Hannah?" Richard asked. Between his two passengers, he sensed there was a lot of contemplating going on. Jake was on his cell phone in the back seat, trying to locate an address for Matt

Davidson, while Hannah stared out the window looking completely lost in thought.

"I was just thinking about the connection between Carley, Sydney, and Kelly."

She verbalized her train of thought hoping Richard could help her make sense of it all. "Those three girls are clearly connected—that we know for sure. But what I don't know is this. If it turns out there is a connection that goes back to Jake's sister, then that would mean the two victims after Stephanie—Ana Stonehouse and Jessica Wright—would have to be connected in some way as well. Do you follow me?"

Richard nodded. "Yeah, I'm with you. What do you want to do?"

Hannah stopped to consider this for a moment. Finally, she said, "I think when we get back to the station, we should go back over the timelines again. We'll start with Jake's sister from three years ago and work forward from there. We've potentially got six girls now, yet we've only linked four of them together, and that bothers me."

She took a moment to think before she came back with, "We were so sure this was all the work of one monster, but now I'm starting to wonder if there are actually two of them out there that just have similar M.O.s. Or maybe our monster has a partner?" Hannah's head was full of so many scattered thoughts at the moment that trying to concentrate on only one, would be like trying to catch a fart in a mitt: impossible.

Richard knew how Hannah's mind worked, and he certainly understood her frustration. However, it didn't change the fact that his gut was still telling him all of this was the work of one man.

"Hey guys, sorry to interrupt." Jake was smiling from the back seat as Hannah turned to face him. "I just got the DNA results back on the samples taken from Sydney Ashton. The vaginal swabs were inconclusive but there were enough similar genetic markers to match the scrapings taken from under her fingernails to get a hit."

"And?" she prompted.

"They got a match," Jake happily announced. "They're bringing him in as we speak."

Richard and Hannah were elated. Finally, they were getting somewhere.

"Does this guy have a name?" Hannah's curiosity was getting the best of her as they waited for Jake to spill it.

He smiled. "Oh yeah, he's got a name alright. His name is Matt Davidson."

Hannah was speechless.

Chapter Thirty-Seven

BOBBY LOOKED AT HIS watch again. It was eleven o'clock. He'd been in his office for three hours working on Matt's file. Matt said he would meet him here before noon but there was still no sign of him. *Maybe he slept in?* Bobby wondered. *Or maybe, even after all that I'm trying to do to help him, Matt decided to blow me off. No. Why would Matt blow off the only person who believed he was innocent? That would be crazy.*

Bobby decided to take a break from his work, stretch his legs, and grab another cup of coffee. When he returned to his office, he turned on the small Panasonic TV that sat perched on a glass shelf in the corner of his office. He thought that, while he waited for Matt to arrive, he could catch the morning's headlines. He'd had his nose buried so deep in those files for hours and hadn't even heard a whisper of any of the morning news circulating through his own office.

As he shuffled papers on his desk, hunting for a specific phone message, he heard the shocking news. The mug he was holding slipped from his grasp and bounced off his desk, splattering coffee everywhere.

"What the…?" Bobby quickly moved towards the window and stood directly in front of the TV. He stood there in shock, arms crossed, listening closely to the anchorman's exceptionally deep voice as he continued his announcement.

"And making headlines once again is none other than Matthew Davidson, only child of Toronto's own prominent plastic surgeon, Dr. William Davidson. Matthew Davidson, who has repeatedly made headlines in recent years for drug-related offenses, has now been arrested for a fourth time. This time, he is charged with first degree murder in the stabbing death of 19-year-old Sydney Ashton, whose body was found two days ago in a large, wooded area just north of Oshawa. This is the first arrest made in the grisly ongoing investigation, as police work diligently to locate the person who has been dubbed 'The Pallbearer.' Now, let's head over to Collin to get a check on the weather forecast."

Bobby couldn't believe his ears. *What the hell did Matt get himself into now?* he wondered. Quickly moving back to his desk, he reached for his phone as he searched through the mound of messages in front of him. When he found the piece of paper he was looking for, he quickly punched in the numbers and waited patiently for a response. The voice on the other end finally answered.

"Detective Sergeant Phillips."

Bobby felt relieved. He had been playing phone tag with this woman for days now and was thrilled to finally get the chance to speak to her in person. "Detective Sergeant Phillips. My name is Bobby Ross. I've been trying to reach you for some time now."

"Oh yes, Mr. Ross. I got your messages. Sorry about the phone tag but I've been extremely busy with work. What can I do for you?"

"Actually, I'd really rather discuss this in person, if you don't mind. It's complicated."

"Isn't everything?" Hannah remarked. "Mr. Ross, have we met before? I'm sorry, your name sounds very familiar to me but I can't quite place you."

"No, actually, we've never met. My name is probably familiar because of my work. I'm a reporter with the Toronto Star."

That explains it, she thought to herself. Hannah had read some of his work. He was pretty good. She liked his style. His work always seemed fair and unbiased; not overplayed or sensationalized. It was authentic and factual which made for a solid reporter.

"Mr. Ross, can I ask what this is regarding? I'm in the middle of a very important case right now. Can it wait?"

"Oh, I don't think you'll want to wait, Detective Sergeant. It's about someone I think you'll have a huge interest in."

"And who might that be?" Hannah was intrigued and waited for him to drop the bomb.

"Matt Davidson," he replied. "I believe you're familiar with him?"

Hannah had been waiting for the bomb to drop all right, but she just didn't expect there'd be quite the explosion when it hit. "That seems to be a pretty popular name around here, Mr. Ross. Meet me at the station in an hour. I'm on my way."

Chapter Thirty-Eight

HAVING ARRIVED AT THE station quicker than expected, Hannah slipped into her office to make a quick phone call before heading downstairs to meet Bobby Ross. Something had been eating away at her since they left Nancy Ashton's house yesterday afternoon. She needed to clear something up—something that wasn't sitting right with her. As she dialed the phone, Hannah moved some files off her chair so she could sit down.

Picking up on the fourth ring, Hannah heard the voice of Mrs. Ashton. "Hello?"

"Mrs. Ashton, it's Detective Sergeant Phillips calling. Did I catch you at a bad time?"

"No, of course not. What can I do for you?"

"There's something I need to clear up that's been on my mind since we spoke yesterday."

"Certainly, what is it?"

Hannah smiled. Even after everything this woman had been through, she was still so eager to help. Most people would have thrown in the towel by now, been pissed off at the world. Not Mrs. Ashton. Her attitude was to be admired.

"Mrs. Ashton, you said that you had reported your daughter missing more than once. Is that correct?"

"Yes, that's correct," she explained. "When I spoke with the officer, I explained that I was in a wheelchair, and it was difficult to get around having no family or friends nearby to help me get to the police station in person—other than Sydney of course. I explained that all my friends were back home in Vancouver. I thought he understood my circumstances, but I guess I was wrong. The officer had me convinced I was completely overreacting anyway. He also said that, because Sydney had run away before, the police wouldn't look into it or even take it seriously. He told me not to bother trying to find a way to come into the station and make a report—that it would be a waste of time.

Mrs. Ashton paused to take a few breaths. It seemed as though she was getting quite worked up. Hannah sensed her urgency and overwhelming feeling of helplessness.

"Did he actually say that the police wouldn't look into it?" Hannah asked, mortified. She hoped like Hell that Mrs. Ashton was mistaken. Even if it was just a misunderstanding, it was a grave one, and grossly incompetent.

"Yes, he said it. That's why I was so frustrated. I begged the officer for help, and instead of helping, my little girl shows up dead." Mrs. Ashton was sobbing now. It crushed Hannah. "You see, Detective Sergeant, it was out of my hands. All I could do was pray she'd come home safely. When the officer told me that the department itself wouldn't take it seriously, he assured me he would still *personally* look into it for me—as if he was doing me a favour."

Hannah was silent. If what Mrs. Ashton was saying was in fact true, she was utterly and completely embarrassed to be on the same department as that cop. That officer was way out of line and should be fired on the spot for negligence. How dare he not take a missing person's report seriously?

Mrs. Ashton added, "I think he said he'd look into it just to shut me up because I had called so many times. I never should have trusted him or assumed that the police were actually looking for her. I'll have to live with that for the rest of my life."

Hannah again heard laboured sobs through the phone and felt completely helpless. "Mrs. Ashton, I don't suppose you thought to get the name of the officer you spoke with about your daughter?"

"I certainly did," she replied. "Actually, it's very easy to remember."

"Why's that?" Hannah asked curiously.

"Because it's the same as yours, Detective Sergeant. His name was Phillips. Detective Kent Phillips."

Hannah felt like she was going to throw up.

Chapter Thirty-Nine

HANNAH LEANED OVER THE sink in the bathroom to splash cold water on her face and fix herself up before she met Bobby Ross downstairs. She didn't want it to be obvious that she'd just been sick to her stomach.

She was mortified. What the Hell was Kent thinking? This was a major screw up and he hadn't even been there two weeks yet. She was so mad she could spit nails, but she didn't know what to do first. What she really wanted to do was punch on his face for a while. *Should I give him some warning first?* she wondered. *Or just walk up and sucker punch him?* It didn't matter. All she knew was she had to confront him immediately. Glancing once more at her reflection in the mirror, Hannah found herself on the receiving end of her own little pep talk.

"Not this time, Kent. I don't love you, I don't even like you, and I don't want you in my life anymore. You only ever hurt me and caused heartache. I deserve to be happy now."

As she desperately tried to reaffirm that she was doing the right thing, her cell phone intruded on her quiet thoughts. Answering it promptly, she heard Richard's voice on the other end. He informed her that Bobby Ross hadn't shown up yet, and suggested that while she waited, she stop by the interrogation room to see Matt Davidson. They had just brought him in and Jake was about to question him.

"Thanks, Richard. I'll be right down."

Hannah took one last quick glance at herself in the mirror as she popped a breath mint in her mouth. Richard was right. She did look tired. The olive suit jacket she was wearing brought out the intensity of her eyes, but it also brought out the dark bags underneath them. She quickly ran her fingers through her chestnut hair, which she had worn down for a change.

"It'll have to do," she said as she walked out of the bathroom. As her eyes scanned the long corridor, they landed on a very unwelcome sight. *Great,* she thought to herself. *Perfect timing as always.* As Hannah realized what was in store for her, she took a long, deep breath. It was Kent, waiting for the elevator at the end of the hall. Trying to muster up every ounce of strength left in her, she took another deep breath on approach as she reluctantly moved towards him.

Turning around as her footsteps grew closer, he said, "Hannah, what a pleasant surprise. How are you?"

The elevator doors opened and they stepped in. Once the doors were securely closed, she turned to Kent and said, "What the Hell's the matter with you, Kent?"

He stood there looking clueless. It was a face he wore well. "What do you mean, Hannah? Is this about the other night—about me telling you that I still loved you? Because if it is, I have only one thing to say about that."

In an instant, Kent had scooped Hannah up into his arms without warning. Before she had time to react, his mouth was on hers. It was a soft, passionate kiss. Something Hannah hadn't experienced in a long time. It was nice to feel that closeness with somebody again. She missed that tenderness, that personal contact. She didn't even have time to process the fact that she had absolutely no desire to be kissing Kent. She wanted no part of it at all. Her mind was screaming to stop him, but her body wasn't responding fast enough. Kent's unprovoked actions finally registered in her brain seconds later, but before her arms had the chance to push him away, the elevator doors had opened. A half dozen officers were walking by the elevator at that precise moment, but when she was finally able to pull away, she saw only one face in that crowd of people. And it wasn't a happy face. It was the face of Richard Young.

Chapter Forty

HANNAH CHOSE TO STAY in the elevator with Kent. Not because she wanted to kiss him again, or even be near him, but because she felt the strong urge to tear him a new one. First, she needed to make it clear that she had absolutely no feelings for him. And second, she needed to confront him about Nancy Ashton's allegations. Loudly and firmly, she yelled, "First of all, you son of a bitch. Don't ever kiss me again, you got that?"

"Come on, Hannah. Admit it. You enjoyed that as much as I did."

"Kent, I'm serious. We're done. Do you understand what I'm saying? Because I'm not going to say it again."

"I get it, Hannah."

Kent was pouting now like a spoiled child who didn't get their way. It always amazed her how he could switch from being a grown man to a toddler in only seconds. She didn't care anymore. He was no longer her concern and hadn't been for a long time.

The elevators opened into the parking garage, and they stepped out. Hannah grabbed Kent firmly by the arm to prevent him walking away. "Kent, there's something more important we need to discuss right now. Something that needs to be dealt with immediately."

"What's that?" Kent seemed completely uninterested in what she had to say.

"It's about Nancy Ashton."

Kent just stared at her with a blank look on his face. "Who?"

"Nancy Ashton. She's the woman you spoke to quite a few times on the phone—the one who called to file a missing person's report on her daughter, Sydney." Hannah paused, waiting for some hint of recognition to cross Kent's face. Seeing no sign at all, she continued. "You remember her, don't you? She's the girl who turned up dead and is now lying on a slab in the morgue because of your huge error in judgement and lack of action." Hannah's tongue was sharp as she attempted to tweak his memory. Kent nodded, his response flippant. "Oh yeah, her. What about her?"

Hannah was irate and could feel her face flushing. "'What about her?' Are you kidding me? What in the actual fuck, Kent?"

"What's the big deal?" he asked. "Why are you getting so upset?"

Hannah could not believe her ears. *Is this guy for real? Is he actually being serious? Please, tell me he's joking,* she thought.

"Kent!" Hannah was yelling now. "Nancy Ashton called the police for help, and you turned her away. No, better yet: you lied to her, told her you'd look into it, and then did nothing about it. You didn't even fill out a god-damned report. What the Hell is the matter with you?" She paused only long enough to take another breath before the yelling started again. "Jesus Christ, Kent. I know there's an adjustment period with a transfer but give me a break. What you did was grossly incompetent. You're supposed to be a cop for Christ's sake!"

Kent didn't respond. Instead, he just stared off towards the noisy car wash and watched as a white cruiser emerged shiny and clean.

Louder this time and totally pissed off, she yelled, "Kent. What the fuck? Don't you have anything to say at all?"

Once Hannah had concluded her outburst and the chastising was finished, Kent took a moment to reflect before he looked directly at her and said, "I fucked up. What can I say? I thought she was some nut job. If your kid goes missing, you'd think the least she could do is get off her ass and come down to the station in person. Come on, Hannah. What kind of mother does that?"

Hannah felt nauseous again as she tried to reason with Kent. "Mrs. Ashton explained to you her reasons for not coming down in person. She said she'd come in and give a statement, but you told her not to. She was counting on you, Kent. And you let her down."

Kent scoffed and rolled his eyes. "Oh, that's right, she's in a wheelchair. Nice excuse."

Hannah couldn't believe how cold-hearted this bastard was being, not only with respect to Mrs. Ashton's situation, but with respect to his duties as a police officer. *Who the Hell does he think he is?*

With very little emotion and even less remorse, Kent admitted, "Like I said, Hannah, I screwed up. I thought it was just a case of a teenager running away from a mother who didn't care. I guess I was wrong."

Hannah didn't feel reassured in the least by his pathetic attempt at an apology. "You 'guess' you were wrong?" she repeated, now thoroughly disgusted. Shaking her head, she calmly said, "Listen, Kent. I'm going to be lodging a formal complaint with Professional Standards—we'll let Internal Affairs figure this mess out. It's protocol and you've left me no other option."

Kent, having nothing else to say, sighed as he walked away. She knew he was pissed off but, as a Detective Sergeant, she had a duty to report him for professional misconduct and negligence. He would probably be fired over this colossal fuck up, but he had no one to blame but himself. Hannah stepped back into the elevator and rode up to where Richard had been standing only a few minutes earlier. She had a lot of explaining to do.

Chapter Forty-One

HANNAH ARRIVED MOMENTS LATER and peered through the one-way glass into the interrogation room. She saw a young man in his early twenties seated across from Jake and Richard. Matt Davidson had a look of sheer panic on his face as his head bounced back and forth between the two detectives as if watching a tennis match. It was obvious that the officers were firing questions at him in rapid succession.

Matt's shaggy black hair was messy, with one lock tucked behind his ear. He had the whole grunge look going on, with his left ear pierced and the bottom of a tattoo showing just below the left sleeve of his black t-shirt. His cuffed hands rested comfortably on the table in front of him while also secured to a steel ring fastened directly to the table itself. Appearances aside, he seemed to be complying with the officers. Hannah had trouble believing that this kid was the son of a rich doctor; he certainly didn't mesh with the stereotype. She was anxious to speak to Matt and to ask him some questions of her own, but that would have to wait. Out of the corner of her eye, she saw a man approaching her. He was carrying a tray of coffee in one hand and a large briefcase in the other.

As she turned to face the man, he cocked his head to the right, gave a huge smile, and politely inquired, "Detective Sergeant Phillips?"

Returning the smile, she knew right away it was Bobby Ross. Meeting him in person, she remembered seeing him from a distance at an awards ceremony about a year ago. Nodding, she responded, "Yes, Mr. Ross. It's so nice to finally meet you." She extended her arm and motioned towards her office down the hall.

Making small talk as they walked to her office, Bobby held up the tray of coffee and announced, "I don't like to show up anywhere empty-handed. I took a chance that you'd like one. Is black okay?"

Hannah smiled, very appreciative of his kind gesture. "Yes, thank you. That was very thoughtful of you, Mr. Ross."

Holding a hand up, he quickly interjected. "Please, call me Bobby."

Hannah smiled at his remark. They sat down and Bobby proceeded to retrieve a stack of file folders from his briefcase and neatly arrange them on Hannah's desk. It didn't take long before he jumped right into explaining his reason for meeting with her.

Hesitantly, but with confidence, Bobby looked at Hannah and announced, "I know this sounds crazy, but I have a very strong feeling about something that I was hoping I could share with you. It's a theory I have about our mutual acquaintance, Matt Davidson."

"What about Matt Davidson?" She wanted to see where this was leading.

"I know he was arrested for the murder of Sydney Ashton and, to be honest, I'm not buying it for a second.

"Why's that, Bobby?" Hannah's head tilted slightly, curious to hear his response.

He didn't hesitate for a second before he quickly divulged, "Because I don't think he did it. I believe that Matt Davidson is innocent—of all of his alleged crimes."

Interesting, Hannah thought, as she decided to explore this statement more closely. "Why do you say that?"

"Well, for a number of reasons, actually. The first one being that I have followed Matt Davidson's story since his first arrest nearly three years ago. It was kind of a pet project for me really. As an investigative reporter, I'm used to digging a little deeper than most reporters. Something about his arrests didn't sit well with me, so I continued to follow his case—follow his life really. I had a hunch after his first mysterious acquittal that we would be seeing more of this young man, and I was right. It's been one arrest after another, but no convictions. The charges have always been mysteriously dropped." He paused for a moment, flipping through some documents in his file. "That's why I was trying to help him. I met with him the other night, proved to him that I believe he's innocent, and finally established enough trust for him to agree to let me help. Detective, he's a good kid with a shitty backstory, a father who doesn't care, and nobody in the world who believes in him. And now this whole murder charge? Something stinks. Drugs are one thing. But murder, that's a whole new ball game."

Hannah absorbed everything this bright young man was saying, but she still needed more. *Why me*? she wondered. *What does he want from me? What does he need?*

After a lengthy silence, he looked at her, his palms held high, and asked, "So? What do you think?"

His smile is contagious, Hannah thought.

"I think…" she pondered his words again, "First of all, call me Hannah. And second, I think I need to know more. It's great that you have this hunch, Bobby, but I'm a cop. We like facts, not hunches." Even saying the words aloud, Hannah felt like a hypocrite. She trusted her hunches plenty in her line of work. Yes, it was always substantiated with fact, but she'd rely on her gut as well.

"Touché," Bobby grinned.

"You said he didn't have anyone who believed in him. What about his father?" Hannah already had her opinion of Dr. Davidson, but she wanted to hear what Bobby's thoughts of the man were. Her question was swiftly answered by his reaction.

Bobby scoffed. "His father? The man doesn't even deserve that title. Trust me. He's been no father to this kid."

She was surprised. She knew she didn't think much of the doctor, but she figured other people would be taken in by his powerful persona and stature that goes hand in hand with being a world-renowned surgeon. She was impressed Bobby hadn't fallen for that—he wasn't one of those people who believed that, just because you were wearing a long white lab coat and had the letters DR. in front of your name, you were automatically heroic and invincible. There was more to it than that. "You don't seem to think much of Dr. Davidson, or his parenting skills for that matter. Why's that?"

"Because I've watched him, I've spoken with him on numerous occasions over the last few years, and I've witnessed firsthand how he's treated Matt—or should I say mistreated. He constantly degrades and belittles him, and always treats him like a screwed-up child who can't do anything right. He is so high on himself and his image. The only thing that man worries about is his reputation and the viability of his practices, not his son. He emotionally abandoned Matt years ago." Bobby shook his head in disgust as Hannah took another sip of her coffee. "It's quite clear to me, Hannah, that this man takes more pride in his career, and has more love and passion for his patients and his precious reputation than he does for his own goddamned son. What does that tell you about 'Dad?'"

Hannah leaned back in her chair, causally glancing at her watch. She wanted to make sure she left some time to meet the infamous Matt Davidson. That is, if Richard and Jake hadn't chewed him up too badly. "Okay, so this guy's a bad father, I'll give you that. That still doesn't help me understand why you feel so strongly about Matt's innocence. Besides that, I had a little chat with Dr. Davidson, and he informed me that he had been the one to bail his son out each time he got arrested. What do you make of that?"

Bobby backtracked, grabbed a different file folder from his collection of case info, and flipped through its contents. Finding what he was looking for, he continued. "I was in the courtroom the first time Matt appeared after being charged with possession for the purpose of trafficking. News of his arrest blew through my office like a tornado, and I wanted the story. This was the son of a famous doctor, and it would make a great headline. I rushed over to the courthouse for the bail hearing and when I got there, I saw he'd been assigned a court-appointed lawyer. Wouldn't you think that, if his father really wanted to help him, he'd have sent along a high-priced suit to take care of his little boy? But he didn't. Instead, he gets stuck with a slime ball has-been who I wouldn't let defend my dog. I know this guy, Charlie Gibson, and I wouldn't trust him as far as I could throw him. The guy's an underhanded weasel who doesn't know his ass from a hole in the ground."

Hannah smiled at his candor and teased, "Don't hold anything back, Bobby. Tell me how you really feel."

His flawless white teeth emerged from his former scowl, showcasing a pretty incredible smile that made Hannah feel weirdly like a schoolgirl again. Taking a drink from her now tepid coffee was a good distraction as Bobby continued.

"Three times Matt gets stuck with this loser to defend him. Don't you think that's rather unlikely? So, this last time I was sitting directly behind the defendant's table. When Gibson asked for a few minutes to speak with his client and the officer brought Matt over, I seized the opportunity. During their brief huddle, I could see Matt getting upset with his lawyer about something, but I couldn't quite make out what they were saying." Bobby paused for a moment, almost hesitant to continue. "I know this isn't the most principled way to hear their conversation, but sometimes I have to get a little creative if I want to get to the bottom of something. So, I pulled out my cell, pretended to be texting, hit voice record, and just casually leaned in a bit. Voila."

Hannah raised her eyebrows as she watched Bobby shift uneasily in his seat. She appreciated the fact that he was uncomfortable revealing that little tidbit, suspecting it might seem a tad unethical, but he obviously had his reasons and trusted her discretion. She could tell by his body language that he was suddenly feeling a bit ill at ease as he cleared his throat and proceeded slowly with the rest of his story.

"Anyway, when I got back to my office and listened to the recording, I was surprised by how much it actually picked up, including the reason Matt was so upset with his lawyer." Grinning, Bobby pulled out his cell phone, held it up in front of Hannah, and with a shrug asked, "Interested?"

No more words were needed. "I'm intrigued, what can I say?"

She smiled as the voices on the recording revealed the truth of what Bobby was trying to explain. There was some background noise—mostly shuffling of papers and movement in the chairs—but most of the dialogue between the two men was clear enough to make out. The majority of the conversation was spoken in hushed tones, almost whispering, so nobody would hear them.

"What do you mean?"

"I mean, just sit there and shut up."

"No! I won't shut up. Why aren't you saying anything? You're my lawyer—you're supposed to be helping me! Why are you letting them do this?"

"I'm not letting anyone do this, Matt. You did this. You brought this on all by yourself."

"But that's my point. I didn't do anything. I've told you that a million times. Why can't you believe I was set up? They did a blood test. That should prove it right there."

"Matt, I want you to drop this act now, or find yourself another lawyer."

"Jesus Christ, Charlie, I'm telling you the truth. I don't do drugs and I sure as shit don't sell them. For the last time, check the fucking test results!"

Hannah stopped the recording and could tell by the look on Bobby's face that he was very pleased with himself. "Now you believe me, don't you?"

"This Charlie Gibson sounds like a real prize," she sneered as she opened the file on Matt. What she'd heard on that recording triggered something she recalled seeing in his police file. Scanning the pages quickly, she smiled when she found it. "Aha," she said curiously. "Isn't that interesting? How do you think that went overlooked?"

"What is it?" Bobby curiously leaned over to see what she was looking at.

"Well, I find it pretty interesting that Matt Davidson was arrested and charged with drug-related offences, and yet somehow, there are no blood tests or results to back it up. On the recording, Matt sounded very confident when he told his lawyer they had done blood tests. If he was guilty, he certainly wouldn't be offering up any suggestions that would ensure a conviction."

"So, they never did any blood tests? Wouldn't that be mandatory?" he questioned curiously.

"Well, that's what's so fascinating. The police file has a record of the dates and times his blood was taken, but nowhere does it show any results."

Bobby watched Hannah as she searched through each piece of paper in Matt's police file, then he asked, "Isn't it kind of important to keep those records, especially when you're facing charges and would need them for court?"

She sat silent for a moment, just nodding her head, then replied curiously, "Absolutely. But guess what? Somebody has taken them out."

Hannah abruptly wrapped up her meeting with Bobby, explaining the urgency to question Matt. She was still contemplating his theory. A theory that now appeared to have the potential to disrupt this whole investigation and completely change the trajectory of its outcome. Her mind was whirling as she attempted to wrap her brain around all of it. Bobby had made copies of everything he'd collected on Matt and left it all with Hannah. There would be a lot of information in there that wouldn't be in Matt's police file. There was a substantial amount to go through. It would be a great deal of work, but much like Bobby's, her gut was telling her it would be worth it. They were meeting again tomorrow morning to brainstorm with Richard. Now more than ever, she wanted to talk to Matt Davidson. She had so many questions that needed answers, some of which she was certain Jake and Richard would have already obtained from him.

She reached for her phone to call Richard. He would definitely need a detailed update before she stepped in to question Matt. He answered after only two rings.

"Richard, it's me. How's it going down there? Is he talking?"

"Yeah, he's talking, but he's denying everything. You know the drill—says he met her in a bar, took her home, had sex with her, and never saw her after that." Frustrated, he scratched the back of his head as he watched Matt through the one-way glass, shifting anxiously on the metal chair. "He just doesn't get it. We told him we found his DNA all over her and the stubborn little shit still maintains he's innocent."

Hannah calmly responded with, "Go easy on the kid, Richard, I'm heading down now and I'll explain everything. There's stuff you don't know."

"Go easy on him?" he barked. "Why? Sydney Ashton is dead, and this guy's DNA is all over her."

"Why?" she snapped back. "Because I think he's telling you the truth, Richard. This kid might very well be innocent. I'm on my way down."

Richard pulled the phone away from his ear, held it out in front of his face, and just stared at it for a minute. After hanging up and placing it back in his pocket, he looked back at Matt through the one-way glass and all he could say was, "Innocent my ass."

Chapter Forty-Two

HE SAT QUIETLY IN the dark, silent room, hearing only the sounds of the crackling fire. He was planning his next move and it had to be perfect. He had come so far already; it would be a shame to get caught now.

He was looking for something in the stack of papers in front of him, and when he found it, he smiled. He knew what the next step would be. It had to be. It was the only answer.

Slowly and purposefully, he picked up the phone and dialed a number.

"It's me," he said. "You're up."

That was all he had to say.

He hung up the phone and returned his attention to the fire. He walked over to the fireplace and threw the piece of paper into the flames. He didn't need it anymore. Why keep it around for someone else to find? Clutched in his hand was something he would keep though. A manilla envelope containing the pictures of six young women.

Such pretty girls, all of them. It was a shame they had to die. Well, except Carley, she was lucky. For now. A temporary reprieve, if you will.

But Kelly.

Poor Kelly didn't have a clue what she was in for. He gently stroked the pictures by the light of the fire as a single tear rolled down his cheek. This tear wasn't from remorse. No, this tear was from sheer excitement. He was so thrilled with himself and of all his accomplishments.

He was almost there.

It was almost over.

Finally.

Chapter Forty-Three

RICHARD WAS THOROUGHLY PISSED, his blood now boiling, as Hannah recapped what she'd learned during her phone conversation with Nancy Aston. His overwhelming disgust with Kent's actions and complete disregard for following protocol had him unconsciously clenching his fists as she spoke. Hannah gave him a minute to process before proceeding to fill him in on her meeting with Bobby Ross. After explaining everything to him, it did make sense and pieces were starting to fall into place. Maybe she and Bobby were really on to something. He listened as Hannah shared another peculiar account from Bobby.

"Richard, Bobby described to me, in detail, the huge uproar that Matt instigated in the middle of his bail hearing the other day—accusing his lawyer of being totally incompetent while still declaring his innocence. Bobby even showed me the story he'd done on it for the paper, including a picture of Matt being tackled by the bail court officer during his outburst." She passed the article to Richard as they spoke.

Examining the article, Richard responded, "It does seem odd, and he's right about the court-appointed lawyer. If his father was sincerely interested in helping and protecting him, why not send a high-priced lawyer? Why this ground slug?"

He watched Hannah shake her head, appearing frustrated and exhausted, and it was only seven p.m. They were going to have a long night ahead of them, sifting and filtering through all this material, but he trusted Hannah and believed they were on the right track.

It was clear to Richard that Hannah was looking for an excuse to change the subject when she suddenly looked up at him and blurted out, "*He* kissed *me*."

Richard's eyes didn't leave the stack of papers laying in front of him. He pretended he hadn't heard her, but suspected Hannah knew this wasn't the case. The last thing Richard wanted to talk about was her intimacy issues with Kent Phillips. Even thinking about it made his blood boil.

"Richard?" Hannah pushed for a response.

Trying to change the subject, Richard curtly responded, "Listen, Hannah. What you do with Kent is your business, not mine. Now can we drop it and focus please?"

"No," she insisted. "We can't drop it. I need to get something straight with you."

Richard pushed the papers aside and turned to face the woman who was not only his partner, his friend, and his confidant, but the woman he now realized he was completely in love with. It was tearing him apart knowing he'd never have the chance to tell her. His eyes never left hers as she continued.

"I told you that Kent confessed he still loved me and wanted another chance, but what you don't know is far more important. What you don't know, Richard, is that I don't love him, and I certainly don't want him back."

Richard could feel his heart flutter and his eyes soften as he explored every fleck in her bright, emerald eyes. Slowly, he moved his hand, resting it gently on hers.

It was electric.

It was exciting.

His eyes held her gaze, watching as she took a slow deep breath and prepared to finish expressing what she had started to reveal.

"Richard, today in the elevator, Kent kissed *me*. Not the other way around. I didn't ask for it, I didn't want it, and I made it very clear to him that we are finished. I don't want Kent."

His eyes followed hers as they slowly explored his face and hesitated on his lips, the desire now manifesting in her actions. A sultry smile emerged on his face as he glanced quickly over his shoulder, making sure they were alone. He needed to kiss her right then and there, the urge overwhelming him. Not caring where they were, he slowly ran his hand up the side of her face as his thumb gently caressed her cheek. Her head moved softly into his palm as he watched her eyes close slowly. He knew in his heart they had both craved this for a long time, making the moment perfectly surreal. He could feel her warmth and desire as her eyes opened, tracking his mouth as he leaned in, searching for hers. As his lips were about to meet hers, an unexpected loud howl echoed through the room.

Startled, they quickly spun around, only to discover Kent standing in the doorway looking smug and very proud of himself for ruining their intimate moment. Richard was pissed off, and from the look on Hannah's face, he was certain she was going to throw something at him. Something sharp. Frustrated, Richard sat back in his chair, searching for the appropriate thing to do at this moment, his eyes not finding any answers on the floor beneath him. His hands balled into fists as he thought about how much he hated this bastard.

As Kent moved towards them, he let out another raunchy howl. Smiling, he said, "I'm sorry boys and girls. Did I interrupt something?"

The words had barely left his lips when Richard stood up and landed a powerful right hook to Kent's jaw, knocking him backwards onto Hannah's desk and spilling papers to the floor as he hit the ground. He laid there stunned for a moment, a curious look on his face as his hand massaged his jaw.

Hannah just watched and smiled.

After finally completing his long overdue mission, a grinning Richard stood beside Hannah shaking his hand and repeatedly flexing his fingers.

"You asshole, Richard. You didn't have to punch me," Kent snapped, still looking a little stunned.

A very satisfied Richard simply responded with, "Oh, yes I did."

As Kent collected himself off the floor, Richard concluded their little encounter by strongly suggesting, "And a piece of advice dick swab, reporting me after how badly you fucked up with Mrs. Ashton wouldn't be the smartest thing you've ever done. *This*," he said, pointing his finger back and forth between them, "*never* happened. You got me?"

No more words were spoken. As Kent left the room, a peculiar smile crossing his face, neither Hannah nor Richard had any clue what was running through his mind. It was probably good that they didn't. They only knew two things for sure: Kent now despised Richard even more than he had ten minutes ago, and they'd both be grinning about that punch for a very long time. What they didn't know was that Kent was smiling about something completely different.

Chapter Forty-Four

KELLY WAS HUDDLED IN the corner of the room, clutching her knees for security. From the moment she'd heard his eerie voice from within the darkness, she had given up on any attempt to open the door. It wouldn't budge. Instead, she had fumbled her way through the darkness, finding the corner in which she now sat shaking uncontrollably.

The silence was broken once again as she heard his soft, sinister laugh.

It chilled her blood not knowing where he was.

Is he in front of me? she wondered.

Beside me?

She had no way of knowing.

Am I suddenly going to feel his unwanted touch?

Her thoughts and fear of the unknown saturated her mind, completely overwhelming her. Terrified and trembling, she began waving her arms in front of her, trying to find him, trying to feel something.

Anything.

Suddenly, through the darkness, he grabbed her arm. A shrill, terrorized scream escaped her dry throat. She tried desperately to pull away, but he was too strong. Her heart was racing as she struggled to free herself from his cold, firm grip. Struggling wildly to hit him, she fought for her life. Her screams turned into sobs as she felt her bare feet sliding across the dirt and closer to his voice. He pulled her in close, holding her tight to his body.

Kelly froze.

She could smell him. His breath. His sweat. His insanity. The mere thought of being this close to him was more than she could endure.

Through the darkness, he navigated his way towards the door.

How? she wondered. *How can he see? Where is he taking me?* With her head now feeling suddenly woozy, she was certain she was going to faint. But she couldn't let that happen.

Her bruised and battered body still ached from his repeated beatings, but her mind was swiftly becoming clearer. Her mind was bombarded with sudden flashes, mental images, and thoughts of escape. Adrenaline was starting to kick in.

Maybe this is it? she thought. *My chance to escape.*

Or maybe I'm going to die here, alone in the dark. Or worse yet, strapped to a cold table in that sadistic room with the bright lights!

No! her head screamed. *You can't think like that! You're not going to die here! You are a fighter, and you will get out of here!* she kept reassuring herself.

He had her wrists pinned together behind her back, holding them securely in place while his hands momentarily fumbled at his side.

Keys? she wondered. *Is that what I heard amidst the fumbling? Is he unlocking the door?*

Her heart came alive with the sudden surge of adrenaline. She knew what she had to do, but she wasn't going to make her move until she was certain the door was unlocked. Instead, she chose to stop resisting his brute force and just waited until the timing was right.

As the heavy wooden door scraped across the dirt floor, his throaty voice whispered in her ear, "And in case you're thinking of trying something stupid…"

His fist came out of the darkness like a hammer and struck Kelly across her right temple.

She crumpled to the floor like a rag doll, but she was still conscious. Even though her head felt like there was a jackhammer inside it, she didn't move a muscle. She just laid there, limp and motionless. She tried to slow down her breathing, but it was difficult to do with her heart pounding so rapidly. She knew her life depended on it. If she was able to convince him that she was unconscious, she might have a chance to get away.

He grabbed her by her left arm and dragged her out into the hall. Her arm was killing her, yet she kept it as relaxed as possible. She tried not to wince as her head bumped and bounced repeatedly off the uneven ground. Carefully, she cracked her right eye open just a sliver and attempted to see her surroundings.

The hallway seemed bright, making it difficult for her eyes to adjust after the darkness. Squinting through one eye, she observed everything and made mental notes as he dragged her haphazardly down the hall.

Unexpectedly, her head smashed off a wall as she was pulled around a corner. She bit her tongue to avoid crying out while simultaneously ensuring she kept her arm relaxed.

She now knew for sure she was in some type of house. It wasn't a barn or warehouse or any of the other places she had pictured. It was a house of some sort—a very primitive one.

But where? she wondered.

Her thoughts came to an abrupt halt as he released her arm. She let it fall limp to the floor. She couldn't let him realize she was actually conscious. If he did, he'd kill her for sure. Her arm hit the ground with a hard thud. She lay there motionless, her eyes closed, as she listened to the movements all around her. Panic filled her. Her eyes didn't even have to be open to feel the sheer intensity of the glaring light she remembered so well from before.

Her inner voice was screaming, *Oh my God! I'm back in that room!*

Again, her heart pounded wildly while unmistakable images of death engulfed her mind. She needed to calm down. She needed to regain the clarity she had found only moments before.

Then she heard him.

The whistling.

It was the same as before. She knew what was coming next.

In her heart, Kelly knew that if she was going to make her move, it would have to be now. As she endeavored to mentally pull herself together and muster up the courage and the strength needed to survive this nightmare, he started talking. He was speaking as if certain she was unaware of what he was saying, morbidly explaining the reason why he was about to kill her.

Sick, twisted bastard, she thought, as the cold voice spoke.

"Poor Kelly. You never had a chance, did you? Why did you have to go and get involved with him? Don't you realize he's trash? He was just using you, Kelly. He's a bad seed. And now he's passed it on to you. Now, my sweet thing, it's out of our hands. Because of him, The Pallbearer has to free you of the evil. You brought this on yourself, Kelly. It must stop here. It must stop now. There can't be any more bad seeds."

Unable to resist, Kelly cracked her eye open, just enough to see his feet coming towards her. He was wearing tall green rubber boots and some kind of green smock. As his heavy footsteps drew closer, she summoned up every ounce of strength she had and sprang to her feet. She quickly glanced at his face.

I have to see it.

But I can't.

What she did see was his fierce green eyes peering furiously at her from above a blue disposable surgical mask. Panic escalated and her eyes swelled with tears as the reality of her situation hit her without warning. Recognizing that she was now standing in the middle of a crude, improvised operating room, she knew she had no time to think about what was going to happen to her.

I have to run.

Now!

As she sprang for the door, she saw it. *The hatchet!* It was still hanging on the wall right where she remembered seeing it. Her heart leapt into her throat as she lunged forward, narrowly missing his grasp, and ripped the hatchet from the wall. Without hesitation, she drew her arm back and started swinging with every ounce of strength she had. He was too quick for her though, dodging all her swings. She couldn't make contact.

With each laboured swing, her arm tired more—her energy completely depleted from hunger and dehydration.

He was charging her now.

This is it.

She knew in her heart this would be her last chance. She raised the hatchet over her head, then swiftly came down with every ounce of strength that still lingered in her weak, battered body.

I hit him! She didn't know where or how badly, and she didn't care. She scrambled through the door, not looking back once. She knew every second counted. She had to put some distance between them, and she had to do it fast. She tore down the dimly-lit dirt hallway, looking in every direction for a door, a window, a staircase—anything that would lead her out of this hellhole to freedom.

There they are!

Just a few feet in front of me!

Stairs!

She scrambled and clawed her way up the crude wooden steps until she reached the top. Glancing left, then right, her eyes landed on it. *Straight ahead!* A large window, covered with bits of tattered newspaper partially obscuring her line of sight to the outside world. She couldn't hear him behind her, but she wasn't about to take any chances. In a full run now, and without missing a step, she headed straight towards the window. She gave it a quick nudge up, but it wouldn't budge.

Locked!

Frantically, she ran her palms along the surface of the dirty glass, tearing bits of faded, discoloured newspaper as she went. Her fingers found their way around the splintered edges of the window frame, hoping to stumble upon a lock. Now covered with thick cobwebs, her filthy fingers located the latch to unlock it. As she slid it open, she immediately glanced back over her shoulder, searching for him, but all was silent. She thrust her belly up onto the ledge of the open window and teeter-tottered her way through the opening until she was face down with her palms touching the soggy ground. Shifting her weight slightly, her legs quickly followed, making a soft thud as they too hit the ground. Squinting against the sudden glare of the sun, she quickly repositioned onto her right side and attempted to get her bearings. With a panicked glance, first up towards the open window and then out towards the forest about a hundred feet in front of her, she quickly sprang to her feet. Swinging her head from side to side, she searched all directions expecting to see him—but there wasn't anyone in sight.

There wasn't much of anything around except for the small, beautiful lake to her right. Other than that, she was surrounded by nothing but rocks and trees. She could see no houses—no buildings—and she was all alone again.

But I'm free.

She would find help. *I have to*! Within seconds she was headed for the trees, rocks and branches cutting sharply into the bottoms of her bare feet. She didn't feel the pain. All she felt was the exhilaration of being alive, and the fear that he was going to find her. As she ran, zigzagging between the dense trees, she periodically glanced over her shoulder, praying she wouldn't see him behind her. But she was smart. She wasn't going to let him find her.

Not this time.

Chapter Forty-Five

IT WAS AFTER TEN p.m. and Richard was still flipping through some of the files from Bobby Ross. He was physically exhausted and had to get up to walk around before his legs started to cramp. Rubbing his neck as he moved awkwardly around the table, he smiled at Hannah and said, "I think my ass is asleep."

Rubbing her own neck as she leaned back in her chair, she smiled when Richard came around behind her and gently began massaging her shoulders. A soft moan escaped her throat as she felt the tension start to melt away, worry by worry, beneath his strong hands. He continued to caress her shoulders until she bolted upright in her seat without warning. She gasped, her eyes not believing what she saw. It was an old newspaper clipping, one of many from Bobby's collection of documents. The article was written many years ago about Dr. Davidson and his family, and it totally threw her for a loop.

His curiosity rising, Richard asked, "What's wrong? Did you find something?"

Hannah's mouth hung open. Her eyes were wide as saucers as he came around and sat down in the chair to her right. He looked down at the article, but nothing immediately jumped out at him. Hannah's finger pointed to a name listed in the old article. He thought about it for a moment, then it hit him.

"Well holy shit," he said, in disbelief. "Do you think it's the same guy, or just a coincidence?"

From the bewildered look on her face, he could tell Hannah wasn't sure what to think, but there was only one way to find out. "I think we need to make another house call," she said.

Their discussion was interrupted when Hannah's phone began to ring. While she answered the call, Richard stood staring at the name listed in the article. He was dumbfounded.

Paul Ashton.

Interesting, he thought. *I wonder what Nancy Ashton has to say about all of this.*

Hannah's voice sounded tired as she answered with her usual, "Phillips," swiftly followed by, "Hey Jake, what's up?"

There was a long silence before Hannah's head spun quickly around, searching for Richard, her eyes teeming with emotion. Her gaze then turned up towards the ceiling, making it obvious that she was trying to hold back tears.

Richard mouthed the words, *what's going on,* but all she could do was shake her head. He knew that whatever it was she'd just been told, it wasn't good.

"When?" she asked solemnly. After another short pause, she said, "Okay, thanks Jake. We're on our way now."

Hannah closed her phone and slowly, almost methodically, lowered herself back down in her chair, her face coming to rest in her hands. After a few quiet moments, enough time to regain her composure, she looked across to Richard and said, "You're not going to believe this."

Richard's eyes revealed nothing but genuine concern now as he anticipated only bad news.

Softly, Hannah whispered, "Bobby Ross is dead."

Chapter Forty-Six

When Hannah and Richard arrived on the scene, they were greeted by Jake, who proceeded to brief them in full as they walked towards the accident site.

"I can't even fathom how this is possible," Hannah said, shaking her head. "I was just with him. He was sharing a theory he had that Matt Davidson was being framed, and now this..." Hannah couldn't find the words to finish her thought.

Jake started nodding his head as he put two and two together. "Well, now that all makes sense," he said. "During the interview today, Matt alluded to the fact that *someone* was going to help him more than his own lawyer had. It must have been Bobby he was referring to."

As the three detectives approached Bobby's mangled car, Hannah cringed. What used to be a 2015 Hyundai Tucson was now nothing more than a crumpled heap of metal crushed against a broken telephone pole. The impact had carried such force, the pole had snapped in half and fallen back onto the car. If the impact from the collision didn't kill Bobby, the falling pole most certainly would have.

"Was it an accident?" Hannah needed to know.

Jake shook his head. "No. We have witnesses that say they saw a black, late model SUV travelling at a high rate of speed, forcing the Tucson off the road. Kershaw is taking their statements."

Hannah was devastated. *Poor Bobby,* she thought. He was on to something big, and they all knew it. Something so big, in fact, he was killed to stop it from surfacing. She stared at the car for a minute and then remembered something from the other day. When she was leaving her lawyer's office, she had seen a black SUV parked beside her. She knew at the time that something wasn't right about it, but her mind was preoccupied so she had just let it go. *Damnit,* she thought. *I should have trusted my gut—I should have done more.*

Even though it was late, Hannah pulled out her phone and dialed the number for Nancy Ashton. She needed to talk to her.

Now.

When the woman answered the phone, Hannah said, "Mrs. Ashton, it's Detective Sergeant Phillips. I'm so sorry to bother you at this hour but it's urgent that I speak to you about your late husband." Hannah moved away from the scene as she proceeded to question Nancy Ashton.

Jake and Richard compared notes on Bobby Ross and Matt Davidson. When Richard brought up Matt's mother, Jake looked strangely at him out of the corner of his eye.

Curiously, Richard asked, "Why are you looking at me like that?"

Jake shook his head, replying, "You were there. Don't you remember?"

Frustrated, Richard scrubbed his hands quickly over his face as if washing away the day. "No. I don't remember so would you please fill me in?"

"Matt's mother was found dead by her husband, Dr. Davidson, in their swimming pool when Matt was just a couple of weeks old."

Richard was dumbfounded. "Really?" He paused for a minute before continuing. "Christ, Jake, I wouldn't forget something like that. Matt must have told you that when I stepped out of the room to talk to Hannah. What happened?" Richard asked. "Did she drown?"

Clearly exhausted, Jake replied, "All Matt said was that his father 'never really talked about her. He said people shouldn't dwell on the past; that they should only focus on the future.'"

Richard shook his head. "Once again, nice parenting skills from daddy. What's your take on it, Jake?"

"I'm not entirely sure. It seems strange to me that a father wouldn't talk about his kid's mother. If the mother of your child died when they were a baby, wouldn't you raise that child to know who their mother was?"

Richard thought about it for a minute and agreed. "Jake, why don't you follow up on that—see what you can dig up on Mrs. Davidson's death?"

"Sure, but it will take a while to get the records."

"Why's that?"

"Because we don't have access to those records from here. They're out of our jurisdiction."

"What do you mean, 'out of our jurisdiction?'"

"I mean, it happened in Vancouver."

"Vancouver? Dr. Davidson is from Vancouver?"

"Yep, he and his wife lived out there for years. That's where they met. They were high school sweethearts."

Richard's mind was racing as he looked over at Hannah. Recalling something from their conversation the other day, he jogged over and asked her a question he was pretty sure he already knew the answer to, and it was true. Nancy and Paul Ashton were originally from Vancouver. And even better than that, Nancy Ashton remembered William Davidson from way before he became a famous plastic surgeon.

Waiting for Hannah to finish up on the phone, Richard walked over to Jake, who was now back at Bobby's car. "Hey Jake, what did Matt say about your sister?"

"Nothing much. He said they hooked up at a bar once or twice but that it didn't last long."

"And you believe him?"

As much as Jake wanted to find his sister's killer, he was man enough to admit this kid had nothing to do with it. Nodding, he said, "Yeah, I believe him."

Richard gave him a friendly pat on the back as he walked away. Hannah was now off the phone and waving him over. When he got there, all she said was, "We've got work to do."

Chapter Forty-Seven

HANNAH AND RICHARD MET back at the office at seven-thirty the next morning. Although it was hard to stop thinking about Bobby, when she finally did drift off to sleep, Hannah was out like a light. This morning, her alarm woke her up in the same position she'd fallen asleep. She felt rested and rejuvenated, more than she had in a long time. All she needed now was her morning fix.

"Can I interest anyone in an extra-large, black coffee?" Richard was smiling as he watched Hannah practically drool at the sight of the cup he carried towards her. Handing over her caffeinated fuel, he smiled and said, "You look rested."

Hannah took that as a compliment as she tried to take a sip without burning her mouth. Once settled, they went over their game plan. First things first, Hannah needed to talk to Matt Davidson. She still had a lot of questions that needed answers. Second, she wanted to pay Dr. Davidson another visit at his office. He had some explaining to do about his wife's mysterious death. Hannah was curious to hear his account of what happened, while they waited for Jake to receive the police records from the RCMP in Vancouver.

Time was running out and they knew it. Hannah decided it only made sense for them to split up. Richard would head out and talk to Dr. Davidson again while she questioned his son. She called down to the holding cells and had them place Matt in the interrogation room. As she made her way there, she had a last-minute thought. She and Richard had gone through all the files Bobby had brought over yesterday because it was all information that wouldn't have been in his official police file. But when this all started, she had only skimmed through Matt's records, specifically searching for the drug and blood test results—which turned out to be missing. She didn't think for a second that anything else in his file would be amiss. *What if anything else was missing?* she wondered. She needed to go back and have a closer look.

Finding Matt's police file buried amidst a stack of papers on her desk, she flipped through it slowly, page by page, reading everything more carefully this time. Something still wasn't right. Again, information was missing. The file contained almost everything it was supposed to, including Matt's personal information, mugshots, fingerprints, CPIC reports, the Crown Brief containing all the criminal information and charge sheets, copies of the search warrants, the certificate of analysis for the drugs found in his apartment—everything was in there. Except for his arrest reports. They should have been in with the Crown Brief, but they weren't.

Now she was pissed off. Neither she nor Bobby even noticed them missing yesterday. They were so focused on the missing drug and blood test results. Now she was going to have to go back three years to Matt's original arrest and filter through everything until she found what she needed. *Thank God for computers,* she thought. She had spent enough time sifting through paper files over the last few days. As she headed back down the hall, her phone rang. After answering it, she learned from Jake that the hospital had just called him.

"What happened?" she asked, not wanting any more bad news.

"Somebody got past the officers on protection detail at Carley's door." He sounded deflated.

"Is she alright?" Hannah held her breath awaiting his response, praying he'd say yes.

"She's fine, just a little shaken up. Something was injected into her IV. One of the officers heard her choking, so luckily the nurses were able to flush whatever it was out of her system straight away."

Hannah exhaled and her shoulders dropped. “That’s fantastic, but what the Hell happened? There were two cops posted outside her room. Where the Hell were they?”

“One was in the restroom, but the other was there. Hannah, he’s insisting nobody entered Carley’s room that wasn’t supposed to be there. He claims that other than law enforcement, the only people who went into her room during the night were doctors or nurses, all providing the proper identification. He’s positive about that.”

Hannah was silent for a minute before she said, “Doctors, eh? What time did this happen?”

“Around two a.m.” he replied. “Why?”

She didn’t answer. All she said was, “Thanks Jake. Keep me posted on how she’s doing.” Hannah didn’t close her phone. Instead, she immediately punched in another number. When Richard answered, she said, “Find out where our doctor friend was this morning between one and three a.m.”

“Why? What happened?”

“Somebody tried to kill Carley Wilson again, and both officers on duty said that other than law enforcement, only doctors and nurses with the proper ID were in that room with her.”

A little shocked, he responded, “I’ll take care of it.”

Placing the phone in her back pocket while she walked, she reached the interrogation room in minutes. She found Matt waiting inside, hands cuffed directly to the table in front of him, looking somewhat defeated.

“Matt, I’m Detective Sergeant Phillips. I need to ask you a few questions.”

He nodded.

Hannah truly believed Matt was no murderer, especially after what happened to Bobby. Somebody was definitely trying to frame him, and now it was her job to carry out Bobby’s objective of finding the real person responsible for these murders.

“Matt, how did you know Sydney Ashton?”

“Like I told the other officers, I met her at this club that I go to. She came in one night, we hooked up and I haven’t seen her since.”

“Did you have sex with her?”

Matt nodded. “They told me they found my DNA on her, and I get that. But I didn’t kill her. I liked Sydney.”

"Does the name Paul Ashton ring any bells?"

Matt thought about it and shook his head, so Hannah continued with her next question. "What about—"

Matt interrupted before she could finish, "Actually, now that I think about it, I do know it. Paul Ashton. God, I haven't heard that name in years, but I remember now. My father used to talk about him all the time. They were best friends. They used to go fishing together all the time before he died."

Hannah took a deep breath before asking, "Do you know how he died, Matt?"

"I was little when it happened so I don't remember that much. I do know it happened when we lived in Vancouver. I think he was a cop—killed in the line of duty."

"What about the name Carley Wilson? Do you know her?"

"Yeah, she's the hot chick that works in my dad's office." Matt was nodding his approval, obviously picturing her in his mind.

Hannah looked pensive. He didn't seem to have any idea at all about Carley's disappearance. "Matt, I'm curious. Do you listen to the news at all?"

Matt scoffed out loud. "No friggin' way. I hate those bastards. They basically ruined my life. After how badly they've treated me over the years, I quit the news. Literally. I don't read the newspaper and I don't watch the news or even listen to it—ever. Just ask my father why; he'll tell you." Matt almost looked defensive as he quickly amended his previous comment. "Although there is this one guy I do like. He's cool—really nice. He says he's going to help prove I've been set up. He's the one and only reporter I trust."

Matt didn't have to say his name. Hannah knew he was referring to Bobby, and now she had to be the one to tell him the bad news.

"Matt, listen, there's something I have to tell you." Hannah continued, explaining her involvement with Bobby and how he had persuaded her to help him look into Matt's case more thoroughly. She also made it clear to Matt that Bobby was the one and only person who believed in him so completely, he was willing to stick his neck out and put everything on the line just to prove his innocence.

Matt was nodding as she spoke, seemingly thrilled to have such a stand-up guy like Bobby in his corner.

After finishing her explanation, she looked him in the eyes and said, "Matt, I'm so sorry to have to tell you this, but Bobby Ross was killed last night."

Matt sat motionless in his chair, staring intently into Hannah's eyes. The look of sorrow and defeat that washed over his face tugged at Hannah's heartstrings. It looked like he had just lost his best friend, which was probably pretty accurate considering the circumstances. She ached for this poor kid, and she was going to do everything in her power to help him.

Chapter Forty-Eight

HANNAH WASN'T EXPECTING RICHARD at the station for another hour. This gave her time to start filtering through Matt's police records she was trying to pull up on the computer—*trying* being the key word. She needed the files dating right back to Matt's first arrest so she could hopefully dig up copies of the missing drug and blood test results, but more importantly, the missing arrest reports. She needed to see those asap.

As she sat working away at her computer, Kent casually strolled in to her office. Hannah didn't want to deal with him right now. He was probably going to make a big scene about what he witnessed between her and Richard last night, and she wasn't in the mood for it.

"What are you working on?" Kent asked, glancing over her shoulder at the screen.

Hannah was relieved his question wasn't about Richard. "I'm just trying to get Matt Davidson's arrest records off the system. It would appear they aren't in his file."

"Hmm? Interesting. Why do you need those? The son of a bitch is a murderer, isn't that good enough for you?"

Before she had a chance to respond to his biased and less than judicial remark, her cell phone interrupted them. It was Richard. "Hey, Richard, what did you find out?"

"Dr. Davidson wasn't the one in Carley's room last night. He has an airtight alibi, and it checks out."

"Really?" She was both surprised and disappointed at the same time. *If the doctor wasn't at the hospital, who was there?* She knew the other obvious suspect would be Matt, but he was still in custody—safe and accounted for downstairs in a holding cell all night.

"I asked him about his wife," Richard said. "He told me she drowned in their swimming pool, but it still sounded a little fishy to me. He got pretty flustered when I brought it up. Jake's going to let me know when he gets the records from Vancouver. I'll look into it more then."

"What about Paul Ashton? Did Dr. Davidson's story match Nancy Ashton's?"

"Yeah, he confirmed everything Nancy told us last night. Best friends growing up, cop killed in the line of duty, old fishing buddy." Richard rhymed off the many bullet points and concluded with, "Their stories mesh."

Hannah repeated his comment out loud, "Fishing buddies?" She remembered seeing a picture in Dr. Davidson's office yesterday that now piqued her interest. "Hey Richard, have a look around his office. I saw a framed picture on one of the shelves when we were there; the one with the two guys holding up their fishing rods and their catch. Grab that and bring it back with you. I think we should have a closer look at it, okay?"

At that moment, Kent gave her a quick wave as he turned to leave. *Good,* she thought, extremely glad to see him leave. *Go do some work for a change.* Hannah watched as he limped out the door and headed towards the elevator. A wide smile crossed her face as she said to Richard, "By the way, nice right hook last night. Kent was just here and he's actually limping."

She knew Richard would be smiling, too.

CHAPTER FORTY-NINE

RICHARD ARRIVED CARRYING A tray of coffee in his right hand, while a framed picture of Dr. Davidson with the late Paul Ashton was held tightly in his left. They had already seen the picture Nancy Ashton had so proudly displayed on her mantle, but they wanted to have a closer look at Dr. Davidson's. *Why we're obsessing about a dead man, I have no idea.* But somehow, his name kept creeping up, and that bothered Hannah.

Jake came into the office, announcing that the documents they'd been waiting for from the RCMP in Vancouver had just been dropped off by FedEx. Dividing the contents of the shipping box equally, Jake took everything pertaining to the late Mrs. Davidson and Richard took any information on the late Paul Ashton. Meanwhile, Hannah impatiently waited for Matt's arrest records to upload into her computer system. She needed to talk to Matt's arresting officer, and she couldn't do that until the damn records showed up in her system. This put Hannah in a holding pattern until she got those files.

After thumbing through the RCMP file on the late Mrs. Davidson, Jake said, "Hey guys, you're not going to believe this."

They both stopped what they were working on to listen as he continued. "It says here that Mrs. Lynn Marie Davidson's death was originally ruled as suspicious, but the official cause of death was later ruled as an accidental drowning, based on the investigating officer's statement and report."

"That's strange," Hannah questioned as she anxiously fiddled with her hair. "Why wasn't there an autopsy performed?"

"An autopsy wouldn't be indicated if it was considered an accident."

Hannah looked pensive. "So, what next?"

Jake continued scanning the file. "Hey, get this. Guess who the investigating officer was?"

Both Richard and Hannah, making the connection at the exact same moment, stared straight at Jake when they announced in unison, "Paul Ashton."

Jake's wide grin was accompanied by the proud words, "You got it."

"So, Paul Ashton was a dirty cop?" Richard hated to hear about any crooked cop. It pissed him off, and the story only got worse. The more he read through the file on Paul Ashton, the more he hated the guy. His record was a joke. He'd had more reprimands in three years than ten cops combined. These reprimands included conduct unbecoming an officer, assault and battery of a suspect, assaulting another police officer, and the list went on. The guy was out of control, and from the looks of it his fellow officers knew this. He was even forced to take mandatory psych leave shortly before his death—for beating a female suspect unconscious after it was revealed she had cheated on her husband.

Richard was appalled. "This guy was a psychopath. I hate to say it, but the RCMP was way better off without him."

That left Hannah searching for what she needed, and she found it only moments later. All she needed to do now was be patient while it uploaded to her screen, but that was interrupted by another phone call.

Richard and Jake listened in on the quick conversation.

"Phillips." The pause was followed by a delighted, "Oh my God, are you serious? We're on our way." Hannah slipped her phone back into her pocket while she reached for her jacket. Heading for the door, Jake and Richard eagerly followed suit, not even certain of what was happening or where they were headed.

"You guys aren't going to believe this," she announced happily. "They just found Kelly Griggs, and she's alive."

They were already out the door before Hannah had the chance to see the documents that had finally uploaded to her system. Boldly displayed on her computer screen was the name of Matt Davidson's arresting officer. Ironically, it was the same name for all three arrests.

Detective Kent Phillips.

Chapter Fifty

THE THREE DETECTIVES ARRIVED at Sunnybrook Hospital forty-five minutes later. Kelly had been flown in on the air ambulance Ornge, the oversized helicopter that transported critically injured patients to whichever hospital they needed to get to in the absolute quickest and most direct way possible.

Kelly had flagged down a passing motorist just outside of Cowan's Bay near Reaboro. The elderly woman who stopped to help, recognized Kelly from the many news stories circulating, so she picked her up and drove her straight to the local hospital. The hospital staff were able to get her stabilized, and immediately called the police before having Ornge transfer her to Sunnybrook Hospital in Toronto for treatment and observation.

As the detectives approached the entrance to the hospital, they were swarmed by several media crews jamming microphones in their faces, all in the hopes of getting a comment about Kelly Griggs. One local journalist called out, "Can you tell us if Kelly Griggs is alive? What's her condition? Is this the work of the Pallbearer?"

Hannah, Richard, and Jake just pushed by, holding their hands up and replying, "We have no comment at this time."

After being escorted directly to Kelly's room, they entered to find her quietly sitting up in the bed with her mother at her side. She looked exhausted. Her face was a mess of cuts and bruises, some concealed beneath layers of white gauze. One eye was a deep shade of purple and partially swollen shut. Other than that, she appeared to be uninjured, which her doctor had confirmed. She had a mild concussion, but even with that trauma, Kelly was a lot more fortunate than the other victims.

After smiling and introducing herself to the two women, Hannah turned to Kelly and asked, "How are you feeling, Kelly?"

Kelly responded with a weak smile, saying, "I'm alive! I'm safe and I'm going home soon."

Hannah could feel the relief oozing from Kelly. "We have some questions we'd like to ask you, if that's alright?"

She nodded her approval as she adjusted the lumpy hospital pillow behind her back.

"Do you remember anything at all about the man who did this to you?" Hannah asked.

Again, she nodded. "I tried to remember everything I could, just in case I got out of there. I knew the more I was able to tell the police, the better the chances you'd have of finding him."

Hannah was impressed with the girl. She was smart. She was a survivor.

"Plus," Kelly continued with a slightly warped, almost embarrassed look, "I watch a lot of crime shows and had a pretty good idea of the things you'd ask me if I actually made it out of there alive. Is that morbid, or what?"

Hannah truly appreciated all her efforts—not only to stay alive, but to try to recall each and every detail she could to help find this psycho.

Kelly continued, "I never saw his whole face, just his eyes…" She paused for a moment, then followed with, "but I'll never forget them."

"Can you describe him for me?"

"He was about six feet tall, give or take, big build—like muscular, not fat. He had dark hair and intense green eyes."

Hannah was taking notes as Kelly shared every detail she recalled. Kelly's surprising attention to detail made it obvious to Hannah that she wanted the police to catch this maniac no matter what—even if it meant reliving the most horrific and traumatic time of her life.

"I remember he was wearing tall green rubber boots and a green smock."

Hannah glanced at her colleagues' reactions as they all remembered Carley Wilson giving that same description. Their eyes grew wide as Kelly finished her description, "I know this may sound weird, but he almost reminded me of a guy you'd see on one of those fishing shows on tv."

The silence was deafening as they looked at one another, processing what Kelly had just said. *Fishing gear—of course.* Hannah shot Richard a look and he knew immediately what she was thinking.

"I'm on it," was all he said as he opened his phone, stepped out into the hallway, and called the station. He was almost certainly overheard by passing nurses telling someone on the other end, "I want you to get your asses over to Dr. Davidson's office now and pick him up. But be careful. He may be armed and dangerous." He nodded and closed his phone as it was taken care of.

Kelly continued, step by step, describing the rooms she had been held captive in, including the dark cellar and the crude, improvised operating room. But when she revealed to them what he had said to her, it sent chills through each and every one of them.

"He said that I shouldn't have gotten involved with him—whoever *him* is. He said that he was a 'bad seed' and it was 'out of our hands now.'"

The part that Hannah recognized from Carley's original recount was the bad seed portion, but what they hadn't realized until just that second was that there was definitely more than one person involved.

"'*Our* hands?'" Hannah questioned, feeling anxious about the answer. They knew Dr. Davidson was involved, but it was clear he had an accomplice—*but who?*

How were they doing this? she wondered. Wherever these girls were being held had to be private, but accessible.

Was he the mastermind behind this?

Or the killer?

Or both?

Who was he sharing time with?

Hannah's mind was in chaos as she tried to piece it all together. She needed to understand. *Who is The Pallbearer?*

Kelly continued recounting as much detail as she could possibly remember about the cabin where she was held. She was certain she'd be able to take them to it, but for now, time was of the essence. She described the location of the cabin the best she could, based on the location where she was found.

"It was the only cabin I could see on the lake," Kelly said. "There was nothing else around, just trees and rocks."

The uniformed OPP constable stationed out of the Omemee detachment who had accompanied Kelly in the Ornge helicopter was waiting patiently in the hall in case his services were further required. Hannah quickly summoned him into the room. After describing the location of the cabin in detail, he nodded his head. Having lived in the area his entire life, Constable Martin knew the area quite well and said, "The place you're describing, I know exactly where it is. It's on Cowan's Bay—Nancy Ashton's old cabin."

The three detectives' jaws dropped as Constable Martin continued. "It's been abandoned for years though. She hasn't been up there since her accident; it's not exactly wheelchair accessible. She kept it though, paid the taxes, had someone doing some minor annual maintenance. She said she wanted to keep it in the family and pass it on to her daughter when she was old enough." After hearing the words that had unintentionally escaped his lips, he paused for a moment before finishing his sentence. "I guess that won't be happening now that Sydney's gone."

Jake was up and out the door before Constable Martin had even finished talking. He had to have a chat with Nancy Ashton.

Being from the same small town, Constable Martin seemed to know a lot about the Ashtons. None of them wanted to stop the wealth of knowledge he was turning out to be as he shared every little detail he knew.

"Mrs. Ashton said she just couldn't bring herself to sell the old cabin after he died, said it had too many memories. Her husband used to go fishing there all the time with his buddy."

They collectively recognized the fact that this "buddy" he was referring to was Dr. William Davidson.

A strange look crossed Kelly's face, and as the officers stood to leave, she added one more significant detail. "I guess I should tell you that I'm pretty sure I hit him with a hatchet."

They all stopped as Kelly continued. "I don't know where I hit him, but he's definitely wounded. That's the only way I was able to escape. I found a hatchet and the first chance I had, I grabbed it and just started swinging."

As Kelly's sad eyes drifted over to her mother's, Hannah got the sense that she felt remorse for her actions, and that wasn't fair to her. Patting her leg as she was leaving the room, Hannah paused to reassure her. "Kelly, if you hadn't done what you did, I guarantee that he would have killed you. You did the only thing you could do to get out of there alive, and it was the right thing to do. Don't ever doubt that for one second."

Kelly attempted a smile.

Thanking Kelly for all her help, they departed for the cabin in Cowan's Bay, following closely behind the lights and siren of Constable Martin's police escort.

Meanwhile, about forty kilometers away, Dr. Davidson was being arrested on multiple charges at his Oshawa office, in front of many frightened patients.

So much for the good doctor's reputation.

CHAPTER FIFTY-ONE

DURING THEIR HIGH-SPEED DRIVE to Cowan's Bay, Hannah received a call from Jake. "Nancy hasn't been to the cabin since Paul's death—says it's too hard. She also swears she had absolutely no idea anyone was using it, and I believe her. She's absolutely mortified to think her own daughter was killed there. She's a complete mess right now."

"Thanks, Jake."

"One more thing you should know, Hannah."

"What's that?"

"Nancy Ashton broke down crying when I asked why she held on to the cabin if she never even went there. She said she kept it out of guilt. Paul loved that place so much, she felt she owed it to him to keep it."

"Guilt about what?" Hannah asked.

"It took a bit to get it out of her, but it turns out Mrs. Ashton had an affair. She's not proud of her actions in the least, but she's pretty sure Paul figured it out. And to make it worse, Hannah, she got pregnant by her lover. So, it turns out Sydney was not his biological daughter—and Paul knew this."

Again, Hannah was baffled. Her only response was, "Thanks, Jake." As she closed her phone, Hannah shared this new information with Richard.

Glancing over at her, Richard asked, "Do you remember what it said in his file? It said he was forced to take psych leave when he beat a female suspect unconscious after discovering the woman had cheated on her husband."

Hannah shuddered just thinking about how sick this guy was. The rage and hatred he carried for women, especially unfaithful women, was absolutely revolting and unfathomable.

They turned off the main highway and were closing in on the cabin, which meant they were hopefully that much closer to learning the identity of The Pallbearer. Richard's phone rang and he reached for it immediately. As he answered, he heard the incredibly anxious voice of Detective Joe Robertson.

"Hey, Joe. We're almost at the cabin. What do you have for us?"

Joe had to talk quickly. He needed them to hear what he had to say before they reached the cabin. "Turns out, we arrested the wrong guy—Matt didn't do it. We just cracked Dr. Davidson," he blurted out. "He folded like a house of cards."

Richard was thrilled. "Well, that's gotta be some kind of a record—guess he was tired of all the secrets and lies. What's his story?"

"Well, it would seem that almost two decades ago, the good doctor was being blackmailed."

"Blackmailed? By who? And why?"

There was a pause before he finished. "By the person he hired to kill his wife."

"What? Are you serious?" Richard looked at Hannah, totally dumbfounded. This case was throwing them some serious curveballs, and he was doing his best to digest and process everything.

Joe continued, "It turns out Mrs. Davidson was having an affair and the doctor found out about it. The real twist is that she was pregnant at the time he found out about it. And guess what? It wasn't the doctor's kid."

This was sounding way too familiar. Richard was speechless as he listened to Joe finish his story. "Dr. Davidson admitted that after the kid was born, he hired someone to kill his wife. It was supposed to look like an accidental drowning while he was at work. The baby was supposed to die, too. Sick bastard. As it turns out, the killer finished off Mrs. Davidson, but before he could get to the kid, the housekeeper showed up totally unannounced. It would have raised huge flags if the kid mysteriously died soon after, so the doctor had no other choice but to raise the kid as his own. Although, not without its price for poor Matt."

"So," Richard concluded, "that explains his lack of paternal love. Matt's not his biological son. That's why it was so easy for the doctor to frame him now." Richard stopped speaking for a minute while he was thinking. He couldn't wrap his head around it when he asked, "But why? Why would he have to frame Matt? What about the man who killed Mrs. Davidson? The housekeeper caught him in the act. Why wasn't he a suspect?"

"When the housekeeper came in," Joe explained, "the guy pretended he had just arrived there and found her like that. He just started yelling at her to call for help."

"Still, why wasn't he ever investigated?" Richard asked, trying so hard to understand and make sense of this twisted story.

"Who would think to question the investigating officer?" Joe remarked.

Richard's mind was in a whirlwind as he quickly processed everything, and then simply came back with, "Sweet Jesus—the investigating officer was Paul Ashton."

Hannah sat in silence, staring at Richard as she listened to his end of the conversation. She couldn't believe what she was hearing, but everything was making sense to her now.

"Okay," Richard continued, trying to piece it all together. "We know that Dr. Davidson hired his loyal buddy, Paul Ashton, to kill his wife and then cover it up. But what was Ashton blackmailing him with? Nothing unusual showed up when we checked his financials; no large withdrawals were ever made. No money was ever..." Richard didn't get a chance to finish his sentence before Joe cut him off, overly eager to drop the bomb.

"Are you ready for this?" Joe asked.

Richard was silent with a combination of anticipation and utter confusion as he waited for Joe's response.

"Plastic surgery," Joe declared proudly. "He wasn't after money. He was after plastic surgery."

Richard was stunned and completely speechless as Joe continued. "It would seem our Paul Ashton, the dirty cop, had some secrets of his own.

He found out about his own wife's affair and the fact that she was pregnant with another man's child. And just like he helped his doctor friend, he too was making sure there were no more bad seeds. He staged a phony home invasion with the full intention of killing both Nancy and Sydney, but it all went wrong. When his plan failed, he couldn't bear being Paul Ashton anymore. He had already lost his marbles by this point—was completely off his rocker, so he just took it one step further. He faked his own death in the warehouse explosion and then blackmailed his pal, Dr. Davidson, forcing him to give him a whole new identity—a whole new appearance."

That was a lot of information for Richard to digest in thirty seconds. As he was trying to process everything Joe had just told him, his mouth instantly dried up and his palms started to sweat. Hesitantly, he asked, "Joe, are you telling me that...?"

Joe jumped in to answer his question without hesitation. "That's right. Paul Ashton is alive and well, living under a new name with a completely different appearance."

Richard swallowed hard. He couldn't believe what he'd just heard. As he replayed Joe's words slowly in his head, it all clicked together, and as he emphasized his words carefully, something else now made sense as well.

His name.

He repeated it out loud, over and over until he actually heard it himself.

"Paul Ashton couldn't bear to be Paul Ashton anymore. Paul Ashton couldn't bear to be Paul Ashton anymore. Paul couldn't bear it. Paul couldn't bear it. Paul bear it...Paul bear it..."

He completed his horrific realization by saying it slowly out loud, "Nice name, asshole. Paul Ashton is The Pallbearer."

Chapter Fifty-Two

AS HANNAH AND RICHARD approached the isolated cabin, they were now fully aware that Paul Ashton, aka The Pallbearer, would be inside. What they still didn't know was his new identity. Who had he been for the last two decades?

Pulling up the long gravel driveway, they saw a black SUV parked off to the side, half in the bushes. There was damage to the front quarter panel. They knew this had to be the same vehicle that ran Bobby Ross off the road, killing him instantly. It was also the same car Hannah had seen when she left her lawyer's office the other day, as well as the one she had seen in the underground parking garage at the police station.

Could that be right? she wondered. *How would The Pallbearer get inside the underground parking lot at the station? He must have been following me. This meant he had been right under my nose, and I missed it.*

Before they got out of their cars, Hannah's phone rang. When she answered it, she heard Jake's voice. He was almost hysterical.

"Calm down, Jake," Hannah said. "You're talking too fast. Slow down, take a deep breath, and tell me what's wrong."

She listened intently, not taking her eyes off the cabin. Suddenly, her jaw dropped. She was in total denial. Jake had uncovered a lot more in the last hour as everything was coming to a head. This news was almost impossible for Hannah to swallow. He ended the call by saying, "Watch your back, Hannah. He's crazy."

Hannah may have been in shock at the moment, but she knew what Jake had just told her was the truth. It was all making sense to her now, and she felt like she was going to throw up. *I want this bastard dead. And I want to be the one to pull the trigger.* Slowly and haphazardly, she fumbled to close her phone. She double checked her gun and removed the safety before turning to face Richard.

She looked at him, her eyes filled with a combination of fear, rage, and sadness. She said, "That was Jake. He just got an update on the car Mark Goslin reported seeing the night he found Carley Wilson." She paused before finishing, not wanting to say the words out loud. "It was registered to Matt Davidson." Knowing full well that Matt was being framed, she continued slowly with, "But all the insurance information was registered to Kent Phillips."

Richard froze, obviously as blindsided as she was.

Hannah slowly added, "And guess who Matt's arresting officer was all three times?"

Richard saw it all now and responded without hesitation. "Sweet Jesus. Kent Phillips is The Pallbearer."

His eyes never left the cabin as it all came crashing into reality, finally registering with Hannah. She ended with, "And Kent Phillips is the *late* Paul Ashton."

The silence was deafening as they stared at the isolated cabin that had brought so much terror to those undeserving young women.

"But how?" Richard asked, trying to put it all together.

Hannah, still feeling nauseated, attempted to weave it all together. Bit by bit, they began to see the whole picture as it slowly unraveled.

Hannah spoke first when she started connecting Kent to Matt. "Kent must have had it planned from the start," she explained. "He knew deep down his inner Paul Ashton was starting to resurface, and he needed a fall guy for when the killings resumed. So, he started laying the groundwork—that's where Matt came in. Kent knew that Dr. Davidson didn't care what happened to his bastard son. He had already wanted him dead, so they used him as their fall guy. Kent planted drugs on him, staged phony arrests, and removed the drug and blood test results from his police file so it couldn't be disputed, therefore successfully launching Matt's phony criminal record. He had access to Service Ontario to submit the phony paperwork on the car—which explains why the insurance and registration information didn't match. Then he made absolute certain Matt could be personally linked to each and every one of the victims in some way or another. The first two victims, Ana Stonehouse and Jessica Wright, had been patrons at the club he frequented. He met Carley while she was working at his father's office in Oshawa, and Sydney was a recent sexual encounter who also just happened to work at the library beside his father's office. He'd met Kelly one day as she was coming out of that same library—right beside dad's office. They went on a couple of dates, but that was it. This linked Matt to every one of our victims. They stacked so much phony evidence against him, including indisputable DNA on Sydney, then gave him a shitty lawyer who was most likely being paid to sink Matt's case instead of help him. Combine that with a totally bogus rap sheet that included a murder he didn't actually commit and, in a jury's eyes, the case would appear to be open and shut. They would find Matt guilty and convict in a heartbeat—end of story."

They were both appalled as they continued to piece it all together.

"That also explains," Hannah continued, "why Kent deliberately mishandled Nancy Ashton's missing person's report on Sydney. He was actually talking to his own goddamned widow on the phone and was probably scared shitless she'd recognize him in some way. And when Kent was following Matt, he must have seen Sydney with him in the bar and figured out she was actually his illegitimate daughter. Jesus, not so lucky for her." Inhaling deeply as she digested all the facts, she looked at Richard and said, "Fuck, this is so friggin' twisted."

Hannah truly felt like she was going to throw up, so she stopped for a moment to take a couple of deep breaths. Once the nausea had passed, she turned to Richard and said, "Remember when I told you Kent was limping out of my office."

Richard nodded, "Yeah, what about it?"

"I bet it wasn't from you knocking him on his ass," she wagered. "I'll bet you it was courtesy of Kelly Griggs—with the help of a hatchet."

Richard was shaking his head, still eyeing the cabin, and anxiously waiting for their backup to arrive.

Hannah was still replaying things in her head, trying to make sense of it all. Turning again to Richard, she added, "That would also explain why Kent suddenly left my office when he overheard us on the phone talking about Dr. Davidson's old fishing buddy. He knew it was only a matter of time before we put everything together. He's been living under the guise and security of being a cop for far too long. It's almost as if he wanted to get caught—taking all those risks right under our noses."

Hannah collected her thoughts before she listed them off one by one. "Transferring here in the middle of the investigation, driving his victims back into his own jurisdiction when he killed them, driving a vehicle similar to one used in a vehicular manslaughter, risking a second attempt on Carley's life, not taking or filing a missing person's report, framing an innocent man because he was the byproduct of an affair..."

She paused as she thought longer about the last point. *The byproduct of an affair?* she thought. Hannah's memory replayed Richard's voice as he read out a particular sentence from Paul Ashton's police file. *"He beat a female suspect unconscious because she had cheated on her husband."*

She was still nauseous, and her mind was in turmoil. These two men were complete psychopaths, and all because their wives had cheated on them. The betrayal they felt created a whole new world of hatred against all women. They must have felt completely emasculated, like all their power had been stripped from them, their manhood stolen, and their trust forever broken. These two cheating women had given birth to "bad seeds." As a result, all women would pay the ultimate price. The only way to make that happen was to take away their true source of power, their womanhood, their potential to create more bad seeds.

Their uterus.

Chapter Fifty-Three

Constable Martin, Richard and Hannah now sat huddled at the rear of Martin's police cruiser, shielded from the potential threat of Kent Phillips—The Pallbearer. Their standard issue Glock 22s were drawn, the sights pointing directly at the front door of the cabin. What seemed like hours since the identity of The Pallbearer had been established was really only minutes. Their police backup, including the Tactical Response Unit, was en route, but the anticipation and uncertainty of what was yet to come was weighing heavily on them.

It was a little after seven p.m. The brilliant, orange glow of the setting sun was vibrantly mirrored in the windows of the cabin, leaving the officers partially blinded by the reflection. They realized they would need to reposition themselves to ensure their safety. If they remained in their current position, it would almost certainly be suicide. Should an armed Kent suddenly emerge from the cabin, he would have the advantage since the glare would compromise their sightline. Because of that disadvantage, one or more of them could end up dead. Richard motioned his head towards the south side of the cabin. Hannah and Constable Martin's eyes did a quick survey of the location. It seemed suitable, with lots of cover nearby and no signs of a vantage point from inside the cabin. One at a time, under the cover of the other two officers, they crouched low to the ground and ran to the south side of the cabin. With their Glocks locked, loaded, and clutched tightly in their grasps, their extended arms panned the entire area, completely prepared for any hint of movement. With their backs now pressed flush against the cabin, Hannah's eyes were drawn to a reflection bouncing off some shards of broken glass to her right. She glanced up quickly and noted that the window directly above had been broken—not completely, but more than a third of it was smashed, and its remnants were now lying on the ground.

Hannah was still trying to comprehend the reality of the twisted situation that faced her. As she eyed the large pieces of glass lying in the dirt, she was even more aware of why she was hunched beside this isolated cabin in the middle of nowhere—why the three of them were now in danger, waiting for their backup to arrive. They were there because of her husband.

Her husband.

The thought still horrified her and filled her with an overwhelming desire to hit something. She started to doubt every single thing she ever knew to be real. This was a man who she had loved, trusted, and believed in more than any other person in the world.

How the Hell did I not see this?

How did I not see that he was a sociopath?

Was I really that blind—that oblivious?

She was a Detective Sergeant for Christ's sake. She spent her career analyzing people every day, yet she didn't have a clue that she was married to a psychotic killer. She felt so humiliated, so dirty—so betrayed.

The sound of glass crunching emanated from the broken window above her. Richard heard it too. Immediately, her body swung around, gun raised and aimed in the direction from which the noise had come. Richard covered her from the left.

Kent was laughing from the window. They couldn't see him; they could only hear his deranged laughter tormenting them from the sanctity of his hideaway. Glancing quickly at Richard and then at Constable Martin, Hannah slowly started backing away from the window. She needed to reposition herself for better cover—for more protection than what she had now. She was feeling vulnerable and exposed as a shiver of goosebumps tickled the back of her neck. She had a sick feeling in the pit of her stomach that something bad was about to happen. It had only been six minutes since they called for backup, but it seemed like an eternity. Knowing that before long, this cabin was going to be swarming with cops should have appeased her, but it wasn't alleviating her concerns in the least. Coming into this scenario, not one of them had any intentions of trying to move in and apprehend this maniac until their backup arrived, but Hannah was now doubtful it would actually play out that way. Her gut instinct rarely failed her, and right now it was telling her to watch her back.

They heard the glass crunching again as Kent moved around inside the cabin. Up until this point, he had made no attempt to escape or even retaliate. This scared Hannah. This man, like most sociopaths, was a genius. He had a keen, diabolical mind that was always plotting ten steps ahead of everyone else. He had to be brilliant to keep up with his many tangled lies, plans, and deceptions. *But what is he planning now?* she wondered. *Why hasn't he tried to do anything yet?* Hannah had expected a very panicked and cornered Kent to come out guns blazing, or even attempt an elaborate escape now that he'd been caught.

Something.

Anything.

But he didn't.

She desperately wanted Kent to try something stupid so she could be the one to take him down. She wanted him to know that he'd been beaten—that she had won. But not another sound was made.

And that left Hannah pissed off—and scared to death.

Chapter Fifty-Four

As Hannah squatted low with her back snug to the wall under the broken window, she heard a sudden movement coming from inside the cabin. Startled, she reflexively tightened her grip around the pistol. This time it wasn't just subtle movement she heard, this time he was running. The fading sound of heavy footsteps was receding from where he had been standing only moments ago. Hannah's heart was pumping harder and faster as images flashed through her mind at lightning speed.

Yes. He's definitely running now.

This was it—he was trying to make his escape. With the three officers huddled at one end of the cabin and no reinforcements to assist them, he was choosing now to make a run for it. If he could safely make it to his SUV parked at the other side of the cabin, away from where the officers were currently positioned, he might just have a chance. Knowing he'd be completely surrounded by a very well-armed Tactical Response Unit and countless other uniformed officers in a matter of minutes, Kent would be desperate enough to try anything. This would include diving through the window at the opposite end of the cabin and making a run for his SUV roughly thirty feet away.

Hannah didn't have time to think. She only had a split second to assess the situation and make her decision. Before she had even a moment to second-guess it, she was up on her feet. She swiftly popped her head up in front of the broken window in an attempt to target her suspect. But at first glance, she couldn't see him—and she could no longer hear his heavy footsteps retreating.

Why? Where is he?

Crouching back down and re-checking her gun, a wave of panic swept through her. The blood was coursing through her veins as swiftly as raging rapids, her palms damp with sweat. Her eyes found Richard's and they contained a look that screamed *Where did he go? I can't see him!*

Hannah couldn't answer that question, nor could Constable Martin. None of them could see or hear Kent anymore, and that worried them. Anything was possible with this lunatic, and not knowing what to expect was pure and simple torture for each of them.

A sudden, thunderous crash had all three of their heads spinning towards the direction of the chaos, the loud noise reverberating for kilometres over the silent lake.

He had jumped!

The bastard had jumped through the far window and was attempting to make it to his SUV before they'd have time to get to him. But they were damned if they were going to let that happen. All three were on their feet, sprinting around the side of the cabin. Richard and Hannah were running in standard two-by-two cover formation towards the front of the cabin, while Constable Martin headed around the back. If Kent decided to change his mind and attempt to escape on foot through the woods, he would have to run into one of them, and then it would be game over. As they carefully rounded the opposite side of the cabin, Hannah realized she had not yet heard the SUV's engine start up—which should have happened by now.

What is he doing now? she wondered anxiously. *Where did he go?*

The three officers converged at the side of the cabin. Skillfully panning the area with his gun, Constable Martin approached Richard and Hannah from the rear. Leaning with their backs pressed tight against the cabin, they spotted it. An old fishing tackle box. Its contents were strewn all over the gravel, laying on the ground fifteen feet away amidst an array of shattered glass. Hannah and Richard now realized that if Kent was out there, they were completely exposed. They were vulnerable. With no immediate place to seek cover, they made a run for the SUV. Martin chose to reposition and carefully made his way back through the broken glass, perching himself up beneath the broken window.

Hannah was mystified as she looked at Richard and whispered, "Where the Hell did he go?"

Richard was shaking his head, his eyes constantly darting from one place to another, ensuring Kent was nowhere in the vicinity. Hannah knew Kent was playing with them now, trying to screw with their heads.

Did he actually jump through the window? she thought.

Or did he only want us to think he did? Was the tackle box just a decoy? Christ, she hated fucking mind games.

With his left hand pointing from his eyes to his ear, Richard signaled across to Martin about twenty feet away, gesturing, *did you see him? Can you hear anything?*

Martin shook his head, indicating he had no clue where Kent was hiding. As he looked from side to side and readied himself to steal a peek through the window, Richard rethought his positioning. If Martin was able to target Kent through the window, Richard needed to be ready to back him up at all costs. This meant repositioning his line of sight. After crawling on all fours around the back of the SUV, the gravel digging into his forearms and knees, he returned to a squatting position. He maintained a firm grip on his weapon, now with a much clearer view of the shattered window.

Hannah knew Richard's actions meant he was feeling very uneasy about this. It didn't happen often, but this entire situation was so unpredictable it was hard not to feel unnerved.

Where the hell is our backup? she wondered anxiously. She watched as Richard gave Martin the go-ahead nod, his stance reflecting his readiness to shoot if necessary. Martin slowly and cautiously raised his body up towards the broken window, Richard's eyes never leaving him for one second. It was then that they heard the scream.

Richard's heart stopped.

It was Hannah.

Before he had time to see what was happening on the other side of the SUV that now obscured his view, Richard watched Constable Martin drop to one knee with his gun aimed in the direction of where he'd just left her. Martin didn't even have time to fire off one round before the sheer force of a bullet sent him catapulting backwards. It spun him around like a top before he landed hard on his back, his left leg folded awkwardly beneath him. There was no hint of movement from him at all. He lay there as if rooted to the ground, so silent—so still.

Hannah was screaming at the top of her lungs, "You fucking bastard, let go of me! Martin! Martin! Talk to me, Martin!" The motionless officer didn't respond.

Within seconds, Richard was on his feet and standing face-to-face with Kent Phillips—The Pallbearer. He was holding Hannah from behind with his left arm, struggling to keep her still, while his right hand held a large fishing knife to her throat. On the ground beside him was the DRPS Glock 22 standard issue sidearm he'd just used to shoot Constable Martin. Tears welled up in Hannah's eyes as fresh blood trickled from a cut on her neck where the knife had slipped. Hannah was furious with herself for not realizing the bastard had been outside with them, hiding in the bushes and waiting for the perfect opportunity—which he got. She now realized the tackle box was just a decoy to get to her.

She knew this situation would leave Richard feeling helpless. Their eyes locked, and she was certain he could sense her fear and outrage. And from the infuriated look in his eyes, Hannah suspected that all Richard wanted to do now was kill him. She watched helplessly as he tried to talk to Kent. She knew he was stalling, hoping to bide time until their backup arrived.

Shifting his eyes from Hannah to Kent, Richard flinched as the knife Kent was holding pressed down harder against her vulnerable throat. She was at his mercy, and she knew it. At any given moment, he could slice her throat wide open, and Richard wouldn't be able to do a damn thing about it. *This must be devasting for him,* she thought.

Richard's tone was soft as he tried to reason with him. "Why, Kent?"

Kent was laughing now—a deranged laugh that told them both that he didn't give a shit anymore. Still clutching Hannah securely in his arms, he said, "'Why?' Why not?"

For Hannah's sake, Richard didn't want to piss this guy off, so he had to be very cautious with how he worded his questions.

"When I thought Hannah was doing Jake on the side, I decided I'd go after his sister as payback. I never liked the guy anyway, so it was easy. One night, I just followed her to some random bar and offered to buy her a drink. It was that simple. Three drinks later, the slut wanted to take me home. Can you believe that?"

Richard and Hannah had no choice but to listen to this lunatic as he ranted on. It was obvious to them that he was getting more and more agitated as he relived this.

Almost sounding excited, he continued, "And guess what? She used to date young Matty; ain't that a coincidence? That guy banged anything with a pulse, so I had to take her power away. It was just a bonus that I got to hurt Jake at the same time. I was so excited to dump her cold, lifeless body in the trunk of that car near his house. I bet he still wakes up screaming in the middle of the night."

Hannah couldn't listen to him anymore. She was certain she was going to pass out. Her knees were weak and felt like they would buckle beneath her at any moment.

"What do you mean by 'take away her power?'" Richard needed to understand how this killer's warped mind operated.

"Ah, their power." Kent was nodding now, smiling at his reminiscence. "The doc and I—sorry—I mean Dr. Davidson and I, had been trying to figure it out for years, and then one day, we finally understood."

Hannah and Richard were equally scared and eager to hear this nut-job's epiphany.

"It's so simple." Kent tightened his grip around Hannah's upper body as he continued to explain. "Women have a secret source of power that men just don't have. It's the only explanation as to why they are the way they are. It's the reason why they are nothing but whores; why they fuck any man they want, why they get knocked up with the offspring of other men's bad seeds. It's so fucking simple. The source of all evil is rooted inside every woman. It's their uterus. And that's why I remove them. Once their uterus is gone, they can finally be free. They won't feel the need to be better than a man, or have a better job, or have to sleep with someone other than their own man. You see, by killing these women, I have saved the world from being burdened with more bad seeds—more evil spawn. These women all had sex with Matt, and the doc and I couldn't bear the thought of him impregnating one of them with his bad seed. If he did, the evil would never stop. They had to die. It had to stop once and for all."

Silence fell over them as Hannah and Richard listened in total disbelief, watching the ludicrous display of pure insanity that unraveled before them like a twisted psycho's manifesto.

Hannah watched as sweat trickled down Richard's brow while she prayed for the sound of screaming sirens in the distance. This had to end now. She knew how volatile Kent was and it was only going to be a matter of seconds before he actually followed through and killed her. She needed Richard to make his move—they were out of time. Kent was escalating and they both knew he was going to kill her while he still had the chance to escape. Richard made direct eye contact with Hannah, signaling his intentions. She needed to be prepared to fight back when this all went down. As their eyes met, Hannah knew what she had to do. Mentally, she psyched herself up, gathering every ounce of strength she had to fight off Kent. He was a strong man, but she needed to be stronger.

Richard started slowly edging towards the two of them. Kent's eyes grew wider as he dragged Hannah backwards, towards the broken window where Constable Martin lay motionless and bleeding on the ground. He was becoming more agitated and was shouting at the top of his lungs. "Stay back Richard! You don't want to fuck with me! I'll slice your girlfriend's neck wide open! Do you hear me?"

Hannah watched as Richard slowly dropped his right arm to his side, the Glock 22 still clutched tightly in his grasp but ready to go if needed. He held his left arm out in front of him, trying to reassure Kent and keep him as calm as possible. As the three of them were retreating towards the cabin, they finally heard the welcoming sound of screaming sirens approaching. It had been the longest eight minutes of their lives, and those sirens were the most majestic music to their ears.

"You have nowhere to go, Kent. Now drop the knife. It's all over," Richard ordered.

Kent looked panic-stricken. His eyes were darting all over the place, not landing on any one specific thing. He was visibly flustered and looked completely unsure of what to do next. This scared Hannah.

Will he panic and kill me? she thought. *Will he make a run for it? What is he going to do next?*

"Kent," Richard repeated. "Let her go. It's all over. You know you don't want to hurt Hannah. You love her. You don't want to hurt her so just let her go."

She watched as Richard understandably held his breath while Kent contemplated his options. She could hear gravel crunching beneath tires as the cars turned up the driveway. All she could think was *twenty more seconds*, just hold on twenty more seconds.

But before Richard could even raise his gun, Kent did the unimaginable. Richard watched in horror as Kent's knife moved swiftly from Hannah's neck, out to his side, and then plunged hungrily into Hannah's abdomen. Her eyes never left his as her hands clutched her stomach, her knees buckled, and she dropped to the ground like a paperweight. Still conscious, she was rolling around the gravel, her hands covered with the thick red blood that seeped from the gaping wound in her side. Without hesitation, Richard had his sidearm raised and pointed directly at Kent's forehead. He wanted this guy dead. The police cruisers screeched to a halt as more than a dozen uniformed officers scrambled out, taking immediate cover behind their patrol cars.

Kent had no escape now. His time was over, and Richard knew he had absolutely no intention of leaving in handcuffs. He wasn't going to go down without a fight. Surrounded now by sixteen police officers—armed with C8 shotguns, M4 automatic rifles, and Glock 22s—he dropped to his knees behind Hannah, who was still conscious but struggling to hang on. He grabbed her by the hair, pulled her head off the ground, and positioned the knife back at her vulnerable throat. The officers were ordering him to drop his weapon, but he was just cocky enough to think he'd be quicker than them. Judging by the look on his face, he knew he wouldn't make it out of there alive, but he'd have the satisfaction of taking Hannah with him.

There were no more words. He smiled arrogantly and yanked her head back, totally prepared to slit her throat in one swift motion. Richard watched it happen—and Kent didn't even feel it go in.

Constable Martin was now standing behind him, his own hand bleeding thanks to the large shard of glass he had plunged mercilessly yet precisely into Kent's upper torso. Kent's hold on Hannah released as he fell forward over Hannah and onto the driveway. In an instant, Richard and several other officers ran to Kent with their sights pointed directly at his head. Kicking the knife clear of his reach, Richard holstered his weapon as he dropped to Hannah's side.

"Get an ambulance in here now!" Richard demanded, as he placed his hand over Hannah's abdomen in an attempt to compress the bleeding. His eyes were filled with tears as he stared into her helpless, green eyes and thought of what might happen next. "Hannah! Hannah! Stay with me, Hannah! Open your eyes!" Richard pleaded frantically.

I can't lose her.

Not now.

Not this way.

He was cradling her in his arms and talking to her, begging her to hold on. "Hannah! Fight! Stay with me! Don't you do this to me! You have to fight, goddammit. Fight!"

He heard more sirens approaching as the first two ambulances came up the driveway, but he didn't let go of her. He couldn't let go. He wouldn't leave her. As he held her in his arms, he watched three members of the tactical unit confirm that Kent was dead and then move out of the way to allow the ambulance teams a clear path to get to Hannah. Equipped with a stretcher and medical bags, four paramedics came running towards them.

Richard looked down into Hannah's eyes and said, "It's alright now, baby, they're here. They're going to take care of you now." But as the words escaped his lips, he watched Hannah's eyes close one last time. More tears emerged as he watched the paramedics working desperately to revive her. Medications were being injected, IVs were being inserted, mobile monitors were being hooked up, and life saving measures were being implemented. The CPR continued. One paramedic rhythmically maintained chest compressions while another alternately squeezed the Ambu bag directly over her nose and mouth, supplying ventilation to her lungs. All this continued as the other two paramedics loaded the stretcher into the back of ambulance. Desperate attempts to revive her were still happening, even as the rear doors of the ambulance slammed shut, completely stealing his view. Richard watched painfully as the ambulance pulled out the driveway—lights flashing and sirens screaming—and vanished from sight.

All he could do now was pray.

Chapter Fifty-Five

RICHARD AND MATT STOOD solemnly among the gravestones, their heads bowed while the crisp winter air nipped at their cheeks. It had been thirteen months since The Pallbearer case had been solved, but sometimes it still felt like yesterday. As they stood looking down at the granite headstone, they were reflecting on how determined and inspiring their friend had been. A single tear ran down Matt's cheek as he read the epitaph aloud.

"In loving memory of Robert Andrew Ross

Beloved son, brother, and friend

April 27,1990-October 19,2019

'Be brave to stand for what you believe in even if you stand alone'"

The air was crisp on Hannah's neck as she tightened the belt on her jacket. Richard lovingly placed his arm around her side and drew her closer. They stood in silence, each with their own thoughts and memories of the courageous young man who had not only saved Matt from a terrible injustice but had shown Hannah the importance of trusting her intuition. Bobby had gone above and beyond his obligations as a reporter to be true to himself, and in turn sacrificed his life so that someone else could regain theirs.

He was a true hero, and they all knew it.

Matt stepped towards the gravestone and knelt down in front of it. He was eternally grateful to this unsung hero who had believed in him when nobody else in the world had. He reached over and gently laid a single white rose on the grave. After saying a silent prayer for his friend, he ended by saying aloud, "Thank you, Bobby."

After crossing himself, he rose to his feet and turned to face Hannah and Richard.

Hannah walked over, put her arms around Matt and gave him a warm hug. Whispering in his ear, she said, "He would be so proud right now."

Matt seemed touched by her kind words, then gratefully announced, "I'm just glad it's finally over."

He tried to follow that with a smile, but Hannah could tell he was still too emotional for small talk. His father, William Davidson, had just been sentenced to three consecutive life sentences as the co-conspirator in The Pallbearer murders, and Matt seemed both happy and relieved.

Hannah, now thinking out loud, said, "It's just so hard to believe. You think you know someone, and then look at what happens." She looked sombre thinking about what these two monsters had put everyone through during their twisted lives. It still gave her chills.

Richard grabbed Hannah's hand and held it tightly in his as he said, "They were sick—both of them. But it's over now. Kent is dead and the good doctor is locked up so tight, he'll never see the light of day again. Neither of them can hurt anyone anymore. Let's just be thankful that something good came out of this and that Constable Martin pulled through."

As the three of them turned and headed back towards their cars, Matt noticed something shiny reflecting off Hannah's hand. "Whoa, what are you trying to do, blind me?" He teased.

Hannah brought her left hand up and held it out to admire her ring again. "It's pretty great, isn't it?" She was gazing down at her three-quarter carat diamond engagement ring that Richard had placed on her finger just three months earlier.

"Yeah, you can't even see where the Titanic hit it," Matt teased.

Following a romantic dinner, Richard had proposed to Hannah while enjoying a moonlit stroll around the upper deck of the CN Tower. The sun had just started to set, leaving a spectacular orange glow over Lake

Ontario, while the first stars emerged in the clear night sky. It was, without a doubt, the most romantic setting she could have ever imagined.

As they approached their cars, Hannah stopped, remembering something Bobby had once told her. He had said, "*always trust your intuition.*" And that is exactly what she had done—for him. At one time, Hannah had truly believed she would never be able to love again, but she was wrong. She loved Richard, wholly and completely, finally allowing herself to be happy and to trust in someone again.

As she caressed her protruding abdomen, her own source of power was growing inside of her with each passing day. She trusted her intuition, trusted her strong love for Richard, and was now going to pass that love onto their baby boy.

A boy who was to be named Bobby.

About the Author

Christa Loughlin has always had a passion for crime fiction. She attributes that to having six police officers in her family and listening to their many stories over the years. As a result, she became familiar with the various aspects of policework including procedures and terminology. Christa's love for murder mysteries grew even more through reading, watching, and listening to anything that left her trying to figure out the who's and why's of the story.

Christa lives in Peterborough, Ontario with her husband, Paul, and dog, Dexter. For more information, please visit www.christaloughlin.com.

CPSIA information can be obtained
at www.ICGtesting.com
Printed in the USA
LVHW101913220122
709124LV00017B/528

9 781039 12966